WHEN A *Heartless* THUG HOLDS ME CLOSE 4

A NOVEL BY

TYA MARIE

Royalty Publishing House is now accepting manuscripts from aspiring or experienced urban romance authors!

WHAT MAY PLACE YOU ABOVE THE REST:

Heroes who are the ultimate book bae: strong-willed, maybe a little rough around the edges but willing to risk it all for the woman he loves.

Heroines who are the ultimate match: the girl next door type, not perfect - has her faults but is still a decent person. One who is willing to risk it all for the man she loves.

The rest is up to you! Just be creative, think out of the box, keep it sexy and intriguing!

If you'd like to join the Royal family, send us the first 15K words (60 pages) of your completed manuscript to submissions@royaltypublishinghouse.com

SYNOPSIS

Zeus Townsend has always held it together for his brothers. Being the oldest of four, Zeus was not only their older brother, but a father figure after the jailhouse murder of their father nearly fifteen years ago. However, with the Assan Brothers gone for good, Zeus is able to start building the life he sacrificed for the sake of holding his family down. Three years later, he has done exactly that: his position as connect has brought him wealth, he has the woman of his dreams by his side, and for the first time since he was younger, he's happy. Unfortunately for the eldest Townsend Brother, happiness can only be short lived. In a twist of events, Zeus' blissful existence is ruined by a secret that was supposed to be taken to the grave. Forced to move on without the love of his life, Zeus is convinced that he'll never love again until he meets the mysterious Quincy Burton. She's the best thing he never knew he needed, yet their connection goes deeper than between the sheets. She's an Assan Sister and while her intentions are pure, her bloodline isn't.

While Zeus focuses on starting over, his brother, Hasani, and sister-in-law, Gia, are newlyweds maneuvering marital problems made for veteran unions. When it comes to remaining faithful to his fiancée, Hasani Townsend has come a long way from the remorseless adulterer he once was. Too bad for him, his history is known to someone who threatens to not only take down his family, but ruin his marriage before it even begins. One drunken night at his bachelor party is the first nail in the coffin of their dying marriage. Two fatal gunshots change the trajectory of their entire relationship, placing a deep crack in an already shaky foundation. Three years of relationship building is destroyed at a discovery made by Hasani, causing him to wonder if he wasn't the only one sneaking and creeping. However, for all of their marital lows, Hasani and Gia remain connected through their ability to push aside their issues and be the rock each other needs when life gets tough. But with all of their secrets and lies coming out, Hasani has to decide whether he's going to tough it out and remain with the woman he loves, or if it's best to walk away.

Born into the Luchesi Crime Family, Gianna Luchesi was raised with access to guns, money, and power. Instead of relying on her family name to create her legacy, Gia goes to medical school and uses her position as a front for her real job, which is running a lucrative arms business from New York City. While her position as an arms dealer brings her joy, Gia is constantly at odds with Hasani when it comes to her future. Hasani is supportive in every way possible, but aside from his past transgressions, he wants her to play it safe when the life she has chosen for herself is anything but. However, when an enemy targeting the Townsend Brothers places a bullseye on her back, Gia has no choice but to insert herself and everyone bearing her notorious last name into a war for the ages. Gia remains strong on the business side despite her personal life suffering. Her marriage to Hasani has taken several blows over a short amount of time due to enemies who wish to see her suffer, but when Gia discovers that the fatal blow was delivered by someone who was supposed to have her back, Gia has to save her marriage before Hasani throws in the towel.

When a Heartless Thug Holds Me Close 4, a true love story, is filled with earth shattering secrets, volatile lies, and a reminder that like ghosts, real grudges never die.

ACKNOWLEDGMENTS

First off, I'd like to thank God for the gift of pen as I like to call it. Twenty-something books later and you're still blessing me with an abundance of ideas, all of which I'm grateful for.

I would also like to thank my family, who has done nothing but support me from book one. Mommy, Daddy, Crystal, I appreciate the kind words and motivation you've provided me. I love you. Muah.

Derrick, thanks for being my human drawing board and helping me flesh this book out. The struggle was real, but I did it.

To my pen sisters, Bianca and Asia. Thank you for being there for me when I was ready to do nothing but throw the whole book away (literally, lol). Together we're the Dream Team and I can't wait for us to embark on another literary journey together.

To the Royalty Publishing House Team. A special thank you to Porscha Sterling, the best publisher in the world. Your kind words and motivation have not only given me a platform to write my books, but you've helped me come a long way from the girl with a notebook and a dream. Michelle Davis, thank you for your positive spirit, encouragement, and feedback! Whether it's as a test reader or simply helping with solid marketing advice, I appreciate you taking the time out to help me. To the rest of the Royal family, love you lots and let's keep grinding and dropping dope books!

ZEUS

"Uncle Zeus, do you believe in heaven?"

I looked up from the business section of the *Wall Street Journal* and peered at my nephew, whose bright eyes shined with innocence. He was always asking me a loaded question early in the morning, and I had grown quite used to them. Baby Quade, who was more affectionately known as Little Quade, was all grown up now, and I'll be damned if he didn't remind me of his father. Except without the mild homicidal tendencies.

"Yes, Li'l Q, I believe in heaven," I replied, placing the newspaper to the side and giving all of my attention to my only nephew.

Little Quade scrunched up his face. "Is that where my brother is?"

"That's exactly where your brother is."

"If I'm good will I see him again? 'Cause you gotta be good if you wanna get into heaven," Little Quade replied matter-of-factly. He picked up the spoon in his now soggy bowl of Fruity Pebbles and went back to snacking. "Uncle Zeus, do you have anyone in heaven?"

"My mother, father, and grandparents are there."

Little Quade nodded his head understandably. "If you're good you'll get to see them too."

The conversation developed into a peaceful silence after that, with Little Quade joyfully munching on his cereal as I picked up my fork and finished off the western omelette in front of me. I had taken my last bite when I heard what had to be an angel singing. The joyful humming grew closer, sweetening my ears like sugar. Lauren appeared in the kitchen with a bright smile on her face. She was wearing her signature jeans with a white tee and leather jacket. I swear for every suit I owned she had to have at least two leather jackets, and even more shoes. Today was a pair of Saint Laurent combat boots.

"Good morning everyone," she chirped, kissing Little Quade on the forehead.

She came around the table and leaned in to kiss me on mine, but I grabbed her before she could react, and pulled her onto my lap, peppering her neck with kisses with the final one reaching her lips.

"Eww," Little Quade noted between slurps from the last bit of milk in his bowl.

Lauren stuck her tongue out at him. "There's nothing nasty about love. I'm sure you see your mom and dad kiss all the time."

"No, they don't kiss anymore. They don't dance anymore either," Little Quade said nonchalantly.

"Aww, I didn't know Yara and Quade danced," Lauren said, looking at me for confirmation.

I shrugged my shoulders. "I didn't know either."

"They danced in bed with each other. There was a lot of moving and singing. I tried to dance with them one time and they started screaming."

Little Quade lifted the bowl to his face to finish off the last of his milk, which was enough time for Lauren and me to stare at each other in openmouthed shock. I swear having this little boy never gets old. If he was catching his parents having sex, I could only imagine what he may or may not have caught us doing in the middle of the night. Lauren was adamant we weren't going to have any kids until we were married, but some days, like today, with Little Quade sitting here, I would marry her at the justice of the peace if it meant starting a family tomorrow.

"Are you ready to go home?" I asked Little Quade as he wiped his mouth on his sleeve.

He nodded vehemently, sending those hazel eyes of his rolling around his head. "Yup, I can't wait to see my mom. I miss her and my dad. I know they miss me too."

"Alright, grab your jacket and so we can head over there." I waited for his light footsteps on the stairs to speak with Lauren. "Do you think it's too soon for me to take him home? I mean, they asked for him to come home, but I don't think he needs to be in that environment just yet. Maybe in another month or so?"

Lauren cocked her head to the side. "A month or so? Zeus, you can't take their son away from them for another month. He needs his mother and father—"

"Who are still mourning the loss of a child, Lauren. Have you seen the way Yara looks? Because I have. She looks like a shell of herself. And Quade—"

"I'm surprised you mentioned Quade this time around," Lauren replied hotly, her smile dropping at the mention of Yara. "Usually you're quick to point out how your sister-in-law is when your main focus should be on your brother."

"Don't start that shit again, Lauren. If Yara isn't good, then Quade isn't good. That's where my concern stems from. I have to make sure they're both good before leaving my nephew in their care, or are you focusing too much on something that doesn't matter to see what does: my family."

Lauren rolled her eyes. "If you say so..."

She tried rising out of my lap, but I wasn't letting her get away that easy. "How many times do I have to tell you that you're the only woman for me, Lauren? I love the fuck outta you. I want you to bear my children...all five of them."

The grimace on Lauren's face slipped at the mention of having five kids. "You must have me confused with someone else, Zeus

Townsend, because there ain't no way in hell five kids are coming out of this here body. Nuh-uh."

"How about three?"

"How about three times zero?"

"Lauren, don't be like that," I groaned, kissing her up her neck until I reached her ear, giving it a gentle nibble. "All the practicing we've been doing and I ain't getting my Zeus the third?"

I felt her melt into my lap at the feeling of my tongue trailing the tip of her earlobe. Lauren rolled her head to the side, her eyes meeting mine. "You will get your little Zeus when I get my big diamond ring. I already told you: Grammy is not going for me having a child out of wedlock."

"Grammy made that very clear when she told me that no matter how nice my suits and smiles are, I better make an honest woman out of her granddaughter or else she would give me an old school ass whuppin'."

"Don't think because she looks like Mother Winslow that she's the one to mess with. I've been getting hit in the shins with her cane my entire life. Trust me, you don't want those problems..."

I finished her sentence with a kiss. "No amount of pain would ever keep me from you, Lauren. Nothing, or *no one,* can come between us either. You hear me?"

"I hear you, but now I want you to show me."

I had my hand on the waistband of her jeans, ready to slide my hand inside of them when Little Quade appeared. I could see the slight pep in his step at the idea of going home to see his parents after being away from them for so long. Lauren and I could spend as much time alone as we wanted tonight, but right now I had to reunite a family that had been through more than they deserved.

LITTLE QUADE RAN up the stairs to his parents' brownstone in the heart of Bed Stuy. It was still hard to picture the minimalist Quade living in anything other than that small ass apartment he had on the other side of town, but for the past three years this was the place he called home. As I stepped inside and removed my coat, the eerie silence made it feel like a house. Yara seemed just as empty, with her eyes only lighting up at the sight of her son, who wrapped his arms around her waist and smiled up at her. She held on to him tight, rocking him back and forth and bending over to kiss his forehead. Lauren stood next to me, visibly uncomfortable and probably feeling ridiculous for claiming that what I felt for Yara was anything more than a sibling love.

"Mama, I missed you so much," Little Quade exclaimed, kissing Yara on each of her cheeks. "Where's Daddy?"

"Your father went to the store to get something for us to eat. He should be back in a few minutes," Yara replied, giving his hair a little ruffle. "How about we grab something to drink while we wait?"

She turned on her heel and disappeared down the hall, Little Quade following behind her like a nesting doll. I noticed what was once a warm home had become quite cold, like all the love had been sucked out of it. Neither the den or living room looked like they had been used in a long time. Lauren was quick to notice the difference in the house as well; her brows knitted as she ran her hands over picture frames covered in a light film of dust. I knew I had to pick Yara's brain to see where she was mentally because this house had me feeling like she would be our new live in roommate.

"How have you been holding up, Yara? Getting plenty of rest?" I asked as we followed her down the hall to the kitchen.

I stopped short at the sight in front of me. Lauren bumped into my back and opened her mouth to ask me what the problem was when she saw the state of the kitchen. It was a complete mess, with dishes overflowing in the sink, pots and pans littering the stove, and a half-eaten plate of food on the table. Yara ignored the mess almost as if she didn't see it, however Little Quade was quick to address the situation.

"Mama, it's a mess in here. What's going on?"

Yara rummaged through the fridge, emerging with three bottles of water and a Capri Sun. Her eyes went from her son to the mess he was referring to, widening at the sight. "You guys caught me in the middle of cleaning. I've been working on upstairs all day and I'm just now getting around to cleaning down here."

"You want us to help?" he piped up, smiling up at her expectantly. "I can sing the 'Clean Up' song really good too."

Yara bent down to look at Little Quade. "I would love your help, little man, but Mama's gotta clean this mess up herself, okay? Why don't you enjoy a juice and watch some TV while I clean?"

"Are you sure? Because this is a really big mess and it's gonna take you forever if you do it by yourself."

"She's not going to have to do it by herself because I'm going to help," I said, shrugging out of my coat and suit jacket.

"Really, Uncle Zeus?" Little Quade replied with a bright smile. He ran over and gave me a hug, nearly knocking me over. "Thanks for helping my mom. Lauren, you wanna see my room?"

"Sure, I'd love to," Lauren replied, extending her hand to Little Quade and allowing him to lead her out of the kitchen, leaving Yara and me in an awkward silence.

Yara placed all but one water on the cabinet and popped the third one open, chugging it in five gulps. When she was finished, she threw the bottle into the garbage can like it was a basketball.

"That's probably the most action that garbage can has seen in a long time," I said before I could stop myself. I motioned to the filthy kitchen. "Yara, what's going on? I asked if you were ready to have Little Q back at home, and your reply was yes, but this kitchen is saying otherwise."

"Like I said, I was in the middle of cleaning when you guys showed up. Don't stand in my house and accuse me of being an unfit parent, Zeus. You've had my son for a month, and I'm extremely grateful for that, but that's all you've had him for—a month. I've raised him from the day he was born."

"Don't forget I was there for you well before he was born," I shot back with more venom than I intended. In a softer voice, I continued, "Yara, I think you need to consider moving in with us for a few weeks. I'll have a cleaning service come through and take care of everything while you… Yara, what's wrong?"

In the middle of my planning, Yara's lip started quivering. The tears followed shortly after, sliding into her mouth and creating a salty pool I watched her swallow. She motioned to the kitchen as if trying to figure out where to start.

"Quade and I got rid of the clothes. We donated it all to the Goodwill. Next was the crib, which was a fight to take down. We cleared out the entire room of everything that reminded us of him and tried our best to resume our routines. Mine was cooking," Yara explained, wiping at the furious flow of tears falling down her cheeks. "I kept coming down here to make us something, anything to eat, and I would fail each time because there's no going back to normal with him gone. My baby is gone, Zeus."

I reached her as her knees gave out. She clung to me for dear life as she sobbed into my shirt, soaking it with the tears we had been begging her to cry for the past month and a half. Yara insisted on being a rock, but the way she dissolved in my arms let me know it was all a front. No telling how long she was living in this mental prison, putting on a brave face for her family. She didn't have to do that anymore; I wouldn't allow her to.

"I know I'm not a father, Yara," I said into her hair. "However, I've raised my brothers on my own for the past thirteen years, and I know when I thought Hasani was gone a part of me died. For you to carry your baby boy for ten months and have to deliver him…like that…I know it's a pain you'll never stop feeling. But guess what? You have a baby boy upstairs you need to live for. He needs you. He needs Quade too."

"You think I don't know that? I keep trying to pull it together for the sake of Little Quade, but I'll try to do something normal and fall apart."

I gave her a gentle squeeze. "We all have those moments, Yara. Instead of holding it all in, you need to confide in someone. When was the last time you spoke with Cash?"

Silence. "Not since Chenille was born."

"Yara—"

"I told her the best way to be here for me was to keep me in her prayers. After everything I've been through, my heart won't allow me to see a baby when mine is..."

She broke down into another fit of sobs. I rocked her back and forth, patting her back in encouragement for her to let it all out. "You don't have to tell me, Yara. I know. How about this? Why don't you pack yourself a weekend bag and come back to my place? Little Quade doesn't care where he is: all he wants is to be with his mother and father. Speaking of, where's Quade? How far did he go for food?"

"I lied," Yara admitted. "He didn't go get food. I kicked him out a few days ago. It doesn't stop him from coming home though. If I'm not mistaken, he's out handling business."

"Are you okay with Lauren taking you and Little Quade back to my place? I need to find my brother and have a long talk with him."

Yara's eyes met mine, and she shot me a watery smile. "Of course I don't mind. Lauren's a sweetheart. She's so good for you, Zeus. You deserve someone nice considering everything you put up with when dealing with us."

"Yara..."

"No, I'm serious. Your time for happiness is coming."

I hoped Yara was right. After three years of taking it slow, I was ready to take our relationship to the next level. There wasn't another woman in the world I could see myself with. Lauren was my heart, and she would make a perfect Mrs. Townsend.

I SEARCHED all over Brooklyn for Quade, hitting up stash houses and several of our legitimate businesses in search of my hardheaded brother. Ever since the passing of his child, Quade was the exact opposite of Yara—he dealt with it by talking about it with whoever would listen. Everyone except Yara. She buried her pain deep and he wore his on his sleeve. With his history of drug abuse we created an open-door policy for Quade; he knew he could call any one of us at any time, day or night, and we'd listen. It worked for the most part—he was still clean—but I knew he was hiding something else behind his brutal honesty. I planned on finding out once I found him. I hit up one last place, the one place Quade would go to let off any steam he was feeling.

"Give me one good reason why I shouldn't slice you the fuck open and feed you your intestines?" Quade asked calmly as he tapped his blade against the crying man's nose. "I got a call from one of my soldiers telling me that instead of keeping an eye on the wash and fold like you're supposed to, you were found knocked out behind the wheel. We got a lot of enemies out here since we expanded, too many to have niggas sleeping on the job. If you're that tired let me know and I can have some eternal sleeping arrangements made for you."

Rashard stared up at Quade through his swollen eyes and begged, "Please don't do this, Quade. I'm sorry, man. My girl gave birth to our baby last week and he's been keeping her up all night. I let her sleep in the day while I watch him, so I'm pulling in only a couple hours of sleep each night. You ain't gotta explain to me how important my role is; I got a family to look out for and I can't without this job."

Quade stared down at him for a full minute, contemplating whether or not he was buying Rashard's excuse. If my memory served me correctly, there was a mention of a baby shower last month. I opened my mouth to tell Quade to let him go when instead he punched him dead in the face. The sound of breaking bone filled the room. Quade's hand rose in the air to deliver another blow, but I was quick to grab it before he could inflict any more damage.

"Get him out of here," I ordered the soldiers standing around watching the exchange, nudging my head at the door. "Take him to Doc to get his nose fixed. Rashard, take the rest of the weekend off with pay."

The men left the warehouse with haste, nearly knocking each other over to get through the door. Quade stalked over the table filled with torture tools and a first aid kit. He popped it open and began cleaning his bruised hand as if nothing happened. I followed behind him, thinking of the best words to say to my little brother during such a dark time in his life.

"You know Rashard didn't deserve that, right?" I said after a few minutes of silence.

"I know."

"So why did you do it?"

Quade glanced up from his handiwork to say in a strained voice, "Because I don't know how else to handle the fact that he's gone."

"I know, Quade."

"No, you don't," he said, shaking his head as he poured rubbing alcohol into his open wound. "You don't know what it's like to deliver your dead son. You don't know what it's like for your wife to wake up in the middle of the night screaming in agony. We were excited, thinking the baby was coming early. The ambulance wasn't going to make it in time, so the 911 operator helped me with the delivery. I got him out and I knew something was wrong the minute I laid eyes on him. He wouldn't cry no matter what the operator told me to do. Yara's looking at me, waiting for me to say something, and when she sees me staring down at him, she knows. We sat there staring at him. He was gone before we even had a chance to meet him."

I choked up. Once again, I was at a loss for words. Yara and Quade have always had a tumultuous relationship only heightened by their past issues. The loss of their child was something that should've brought them together, except it was tearing them apart. I had no idea how to bridge the gap, but I knew if I could get them in the same room as each other, I could help them heal. Everything they said to me they needed to say to each other.

"I know she keeps pushing you away, but she needs you to be there for her whether she likes it or not," I said, slipping on a pair of gloves and finishing up the bandaging.

Quade gave a sad chuckle. "I watch her sleep at night. I climb right up the side of my own house, through the window, sit at the foot of Little Q's bed, and watch her sleep. She threw away the furniture in our bedroom. Sometimes I walk around the house, I come to that bedroom, and I get stuck. I usually leave after that."

"It's okay not to be made of stone. Some of the best strength comes from being broken. The two of you are going to make it through this, kid," I said, clapping him on the shoulder. "Now let's get you over to my place where Little Quade is waiting to see you."

At the mention of seeing his living child, Quade perked up. I might not have been able to feel much when it came to having kids, but seeing the smile on my brother's face at the mention of seeing his son gave me hope for this entire situation.

LAUREN WAS SITTING in the living room watching Yara and Little Quade play a board game when we arrived at my place. Quade hid himself behind me and jumped out to surprise Little Quade, who leapt up from the game and straight into his father's arms. Yara remained seated, but she smiled at the sight. Lauren slipped by the reunion and followed me into my office where I poured both of us a drink.

"I'm sorry," she said, taking a seat in my lap. "I didn't mean to, but I overheard some of the conversation you had with Yara. She's like a little sister to you."

I shook my head. "She's not like a sister; she is my sister. After everything her and Quade went through, she's more like my daughter if anything. I've raised him since the day he was born; hell, I'm still raising him," I said with a laugh. "I'm my brothers' keeper. Sometimes you're going to have to share me with one of them or all of them, and I want you to understand it doesn't take away the love I have for you."

Lauren shook her head. "It doesn't take anything away. If anything, I feel blessed to have met a man with such a big heart."

"You have no idea how happy that makes me feel," I said, sipping on my drink.

My eyes unintentionally drifted to the top drawer of my desk where the engagement ring was. It was a three-carat, princess cut diamond masterpiece designed by me with the help of a well known celebrity jeweler. We spent months making and remaking this ring because each time it never felt good enough for Lauren. This was my forever love and I wanted everything about her ring to be as perfect for me as she was.

"What are you thinking about?" Lauren cut into my thoughts, and her smile erased any worries I had. "It better be me."

I quelled her worries with a kiss. "Of course. You're always on my mind. Forever and always."

LAUREN

Cash and I stood side by side staring at the hundred bricks of Mexico's finest fish scale cocaine waiting to be delivered to our *primeras* all over the city. It was twice our normal shipment, but our connect in Mexico was putting pressure on Zeus and his brothers to up the ante. They were nervous at the idea of us being able to move this much weight in such a short amount of time, but I was all about results. I was never good at coloring in the lines, but even as I finished, a masterpiece was always the result. And this shipment right here was our Picasso.

"Have you spoken with the Haitians? I told Toussaint to have his men here at the rendezvous point within the hour. Same goes for KD40's," Cash said, staring down at the simple Cartier watch on her wrist.

I picked up a brick and began tossing it up and down. "I spoke with Toussaint. He's still mad as fuck that we're doing business with the KD40's because he's convinced it was them that hit his stash house. I keep telling him that's bullshit, but I did promise to conduct a small investigation."

"Please do. I swear, for some grown ass men whose names are supposed to ring bells, these motherfuckers act like some straight bitches sometimes," Cash replied, posting up against the table and running her hand along the bricks of coke. "And I thought I stayed in my feelings when I first got in the game."

"Cash, you lived in your fucking feelings. I pulled a gun on you one time, and some days I swear I don't think you've gotten over it. Especially if you can't get your way on choosing new storefronts. How many hair salons can Brooklyn take?"

"As many as they need to. And I was hoping eventually you would get the hint and do something about that kitchen of yours," Cash joked, slapping herself on the thighs while I stared at her, deadpanned though shaking with laughter of my own. "Did I laugh too hard?"

"Bitch, for a second I though the Kings of Comedy were performing."

Cash shook with silent laughter. "I still can't believe we went from enemies to business partners."

"Neither can I. After the way Yara handled me that night, I would've thought you'd pick her to be your right hand."

"This game had already fucked me up—I didn't want the same for my best friend. Plus, Yara's all soft and sweet...then there's the fact that you saved my life when you didn't have to. You could've turned me over to the Assan Brothers, had all the glory, but you didn't. You couldn't stand me, I fucked up your money, but you were loyal to me *as a woman*. I couldn't think of a more deserving person."

I gave the brick one last toss and placed it back on the table. "You damn right. There's nothing better in this world than two black women coming together and making those money moves they don't expect us to." I took a steadying breath, contemplating whether or not this was the right time to bring up what was on my mind. Cash had paid me a huge compliment, and now I was going to bring up what had to be a sore spot for her. "Cash...when was the last time you spoke to Yara?"

"She called to congratulate me when Chenille was born. Other than that, she's been MIA. I've stopped by her house everyday since she lost the baby, but she's never home. Or if she is, she's hiding from me. I haven't seen Yara this detached in a long time," Cash replied, staring down at her phone to keep me from seeing the tears pooling in her eyes.

I raked a hand through my hair. "She's not doing great, but she's doing much better than she was after the baby..." I couldn't bear finishing my sentence. "Zeus and I brought her home a few days ago. She's spending a lot of time with Little Quade. The changes are subtle, but she's bouncing back."

"If I show up at your house with Chenille, I might set her back a few days, if not a few weeks. I want my daughter to see her godmother, but not at the expense of her mental health." Cash swiped away the stray tears threatening to smudge her makeup. "I miss her so much, Lauren. We haven't been apart this long since I went on my honeymoon."

Being with Steez didn't leave me with too many opportunities to make female friends, let alone a best friend. I wasn't sure if he knew, but Zeus was my best friend, and I couldn't imagine being apart from him for longer than a few days. Cash had to feel like a piece of her heart was missing at the expense of gaining a new piece. As a first-time mother, she was forced to celebrate the birth of her child while mourning her nephew. If Zeus was a surrogate father to everyone, that made me a surrogate mother.

"Cash, I can't promise you that everything will be great by Gia and Hasani's wedding, but I can try my best to make sure your best friend shows up," I said, giving her a gentle squeeze. "Now dry those tears because I think I just heard these niggas pull up to grab this product."

At the mention of anyone seeing her in bad form, Cash straightened up real quick. Her game face was on as our right hand, Joel, entered the warehouse with furrowed brows. I didn't like that look because it told me either our money or product was fucked up. Joel dapped us up and got straight to it, which was one of the things I loved about him.

"We got a situation. One of Sylvester's stash houses got hit this morning. They didn't get much product, and he already had the money in transit, but he thinks it was Toussaint. From what I heard those two still beefing over territory borders. Sly's been allowing some of his soldiers to snatch blocks, and the niggas took one of Toussaint's."

Cash made a *what the fuck?* motion with her hand. "We dealt with that last month. I told these niggas we're all here to eat, which means there's no reason why they should be fighting each other. How much more I gotta do to make them act right, hold hands, and sing 'Kumbaya'?"

"I don't know, but I've heard from a few soldiers that a war is brewing. Maybe we need to have another parlay, put everything on the table to keep this from blowing up," Joel recommended. "I was able to talk him out of a preemptive strike by reasoning with him, but I don't know how long it's going to last."

"How'd you do that?" I asked, crossing my arms as I got comfortable enough to hear this rationalization.

"I told him there ain't no way in hell Toussaint would send a couple of bitches to handle business for him. He's got too many sons and nephews to outsource," Joel replied with a shrug.

Cash shook her head. "Not if he wanted to make it look like someone else."

"Whether it's true or not, it bought us a few days to set up this meeting. I'm thinking we have it this Friday."

"Monday morning," Cash and I replied at the same time. I continued with, "We have an event to attend this weekend."

"Gia and Hasani's wedding. How could I forget? Aight, I'll make sure to keep everything under control over the weekend while you turn up. You think you can bring me back a party favor and a plate? I heard they gon' have some nice shit, like crystal swans, and the caterer is some famous chef."

I slapped Joel on the arm. "You hold this shit down and I'll even bring you back a party bag *and* a slice of cake."

After a few more minutes of talking business, Cash and I dipped out with complete confidence in Joel. On our way out of the warehouse we gave the surrounding area a thorough once over, making sure that no one other than our security was posted up. With $3,000,000 in coke waiting to be distributed throughout the city, we never played when it came to adequate protection. At the sight of everyone aware and alert, I relaxed in my seat. Cash hooked up her phone to the car and we were surrounded by the sounds of Cardi B's new album. "I Like It" bumped through the speakers, turning what was once a dark moment into a party. We were having so much fun jamming out, I didn't hear or feel my phone vibrating in my jacket pocket. I didn't notice the missed calls from the unknown number until Cash pulled up in front of my place.

"You think maybe I should go in and say hi?" Cash asked, staring up at the Harlem brownstone with longing. "Little Quade called me a few days ago asking when he's going to see Chenille again, and I don't want him thinking I forgot about him. We're taking him this weekend, for the wedding. I think he'd like to hear the news from my mouth."

"He would definitely appreciate that, and seeing some pictures of his baby cousin," I said, trying to lure Cash out of her own car so I could return this call.

It didn't take much more convincing at the mention of showing off pictures of little Chenille, who was the perfect mix of Cash and Savion. She had their brown skin with Cash's eyes and button nose, while she had Savion's lips, hair, and feisty attitude. They had their work cut out for them with that little one. Cash was halfway out the car when she turned and saw me still sitting there.

"I'll be right in. I have to return a call."

"Business?"

"Nope, my mother calling to check in on me. You know how paranoid she can be. Plus, she still doesn't like the idea of me shacking up with a man I'm not married to. This must be her weekly check in to make sure I'm not pregnant," I joked, rolling my eyes for extra effect.

Cash's curiosity disappeared; she knew exactly how my mother got down based on the few conversations she overheard. "See you inside, boo..."

I sat in the silence of the car staring at the number, wondering who it belonged to and how they got it. I had two phones, a burner for business and my private line. Whoever had my private number had to know me personally, or at least know someone well enough to talk them out of it because I wasn't known for handing out my information loosely. I pressed the number and put my phone on speaker. It rang three times before the call connected.

"Lauren, what's good? I thought you were ignoring a nigga or something," a man joked with me like we went way back or something.

I stared at my phone like it had grown a third head. "Who the fuck is this and how do you know my name?"

"That's how you greet family? Shit, a nigga only been gone a few years and you forget about him? What type of sister are you?"

"Sadan?"

Sadan let out a hearty chuckle at the fear in my voice. "The one and only. I got out the pen last week, and I've been relaxing, getting assimilated to life on the outside and shit. What you been up to other than fucking Zeus Townsend? Oh you thought I wouldn't find out that you flipped on my brothers and got with the enemy?"

"It's not that I didn't think you weren't going to find out; I was just banking on that murder charge against you sticking for, oh, I don't know, the rest of your life. How did you get out?" I had to know how this crazy motherfucker beat a murder charge that had him spending the rest of his life in maximum security prison.

"Every once in a blue moon some college students come to the prison to help their professors teach classes and shit. I met this one little bad shorty that was in law school. I told her how I was framed, and she started researching my case. Turns out there was another suspect they ain't even consider. She also managed to find video footage of me at the gas station pistol whipping some nigga at the time of the murder."

"You were innocent?"

"I sure was; that was all Salim acting a fool because somebody was fucking his hoe ass baby mama. I'm glad that bitch is dead," Sadan chuckled. "I don't know which one of them Townsend boys did it, but I owe him a drink right before I put his ass down. That is, unless you accept my offer."

"What's the offer, Sadan?"

"I want a million dollars to leave the Townsend Brothers alone. Both you and I know I'm more than capable of taking all them niggas out. My brothers are good for doing some dramatic one-on-one type shit. I'll just wait for a special occasion, something like that wedding that's supposed to be happening this weekend, and blow everybody the fuck up."

Sadan was crazy enough to do exactly what he described. His disregard was almost as severe as Saaid's except he was willing to go as far as dying for this cause. If I could pay him to disappear, then it would be the best million I ever spent.

"All I have is half a million."

"Don't lie, Lauren. I know you got my brother's old job as distro. That brings in what, $25,000 an hour?"

I banged my head against the headrest. "After I clean my money I don't bring in that much. Plus, I have it tied up in my businesses. All I have on hand is half a million. You can take it and get the fuck away from this bullshit or you can fight a war all by yourself and end up dead because if they even get wind of someone coming for them, hell will reign down."

"If they can catch me, Lauren. Both you and I know this is a courtesy call. I've got my plan made up in my head, all I need is to hear the 'no' pass your lips and it's happening. But before it does, why not ruin what you have with Zeus by telling him the truth. You know, that you're a murderer. So, you running me my money or nah?"

I could move some assets around over the next few days and come up with the million. "Fine. I'll give you the money, but you have to promise me that you will leave Zeus and his brothers alone. And my secret...if I pay up, it dies with the two of us."

"You got three days to have my fucking money, Lauren, or else I'll show you why I'm the last Assan standing."

The call disconnected, leaving me sitting there in disbelief. The life I spent three years building could end at any moment. Sadan loved money, but he loved his brothers more and there was no question in my mind that he could take my money and use it to create a small army to take us down. I was still sitting in Cash's car trying to think of what I could sell when she returned with a small smile on her face.

"What's wrong with you? You look like you saw a ghost or something?" she asked with furrowed brows.

I shook my head. "Nothing's wrong. My mom is just wilding as usual…"

I was halfway out of the car when Cash stopped me with, "Lauren, what's the first rule we established when we became partners?"

"Not to lie to each other," I replied, hanging my head in shame.

"Once upon a time, I was lying to everyone I cared about because I thought I had everything under control. In the end I suffered more than I would have if I would've just came clean. Now I'm going to ask you again: who was that on the phone?"

"I can't tell you right now, but I promise when the time is right I'll come clean."

"You better," Cash huffed. "I have a family to look out for, and I can't do that with unknown variables running around. I'll see you tomorrow, Lauren."

Cash barely waited for me to slam the car door shut before she peeled out. I knew I was asking a lot of her at this moment, but I knew telling her about Sadan meant telling her everything. I wasn't ready to risk everything I had built with Zeus. He was the love of my life, but if he knew my entire relationship with Steez he might not love me for much longer.

HASANI

Savion picked up the red checker piece and jumped over three of my black pieces. "Checkmate, nigga!"

"What the fuck do you mean 'checkmate'?" I said, slapping his hand away before he could snatch up my pieces. "First off: this ain't chess. Second: you can't jump backwards in checkers. Leave my pieces right on that board before I jump on you."

"Man, fuck the rules. We playing street checkers. Like if it was some niggas tryna run up on our block and shit. You really think I'm gon' go for one nigga and not the whole team? Fuck outta here."

"This ain't the streets! It's checkers!" I yelled, pointing at the box sitting on the side of the couch. I snatched it up and started packing the game of checkers away. "We have played everything under the sun tonight, and you've managed to turn it all into some bullshit, Savion. I could've stayed my black ass at home and played COD."

Savion sucked his teeth. "You always were a big ass baby when it comes to playing games. I still ain't forget about that time I got my ass whupped for laughing at you crying when Yoshi died in Super Mario Brothers."

"I remember that, because watching Mom chase your ass around the house with her belt cheered me up. And you know what else will cheer me up? Going home to get some sleep since I'm getting married tomorrow."

Savion slapped another board game on the table. "Not yet, li'l nigga. We ain't play Scrabble yet. Since you're a sore loser, I think I can take it easy on you in this game."

"Fine, while you set up the board, I'll grab another bottle," I said, picking up the empty bottle of Henny on the table and giving it a sad little shake.

Even though Savion was happily married, he still kept his East New York bachelor pad. He didn't use it as much as he used to, but I made sure to pick up the slack by taking refuge here whenever Gia's family got a little too overbearing. My house was supposed to feel like a home, but when you had your fiancée's sister and mother visiting daily to go over wedding plans, it got real tiring real quick. Gia did the best she could to grab us some well deserved alone time, but the Luchesi women weren't having that. After playing all these games with Savion, I was willing to deal with whatever loiterers were at my house. At least right after this second platter of Savion's famous buffalo wings.

"Everything's set up and I made us some more drinks," Savion said, motioning to the perfectly set up board and two glasses of Hennessy with pineapple and cranberry juice. "How about you go first, sore loser."

"Bet," I replied as I sat down and looked at the letters on my tile rack. I placed them on the board going downward. "Hazard. Make sure you take note of that double word tile too."

"Yeah, yeah, whatever," Savion said as he tallied up my points. He looked at his own rack, and after a minute of contemplation, used my 'a' to make a word. "Savage. This game already knows what it is. And I'm taking that triple word score. And I double it because I used all my tiles."

"Savage isn't spelled with a 'u,' Savion."

Savion looked down at the word he spelled—sauvage—and back at me. "That's a word, Hasani. Like I said, it's savage but the 'u' is silent."

"Bruh," I said, throwing my head back and staring up at the ceiling.

"You really not about to fuck up Scrabble too. If you can find that word in the dictionary, you got it, but otherwise take away that 'u.' You know who would check your ass if they were here? Zeus. Speaking of, where is Zeus?"

Savion made a noncommittal hand gesture. "He's out handling some business. He said he would stop by our game night if he had the time."

"And Quade?"

"I'ont even know. I think he said he was taking Little Quade to the movies tonight to see some cartoon movie that came out tonight."

I sighed. "That sounds better than what we got going on right now."

"Deadass?" Savion motioned to the drinks, platters of food, and pile of abandoned board games. "You mean to tell me I went through all this trouble giving you the perfect bachelor party, and you gon' say seeing a movie about a mystical dragon is better than this? Fuck you, nigga."

I rose from my seat. "I been waiting for you to say that for the longest so I can get out of here—"

"Nah, you not going nowhere. Sit back down and let's finish this game. And for your information"—Savion placed his phone inches away from my face, showing me the definition for sauvage—"sauvage means 'wild' or 'natural' in French. So I'm taking my triple double, and you just gon' have to be mad about it."

I was getting ready to explain to him that we live in America not France when I got a 911 text from Zeus. Savion's phone went off seconds later. We were on our feet and out the house seconds later, leaving the party behind. There had been some whisperings in the street about a small war starting in the streets because of the Haitians being hit a few days ago, but as far as I was concerned the women had it under control. Now I wasn't too sure about that. Being that Zeus and Savion acted as the connects for our cartel leaders, I maintained our territory since most of my responsibilities involved the day-to-day operations. This possible war could put a dent in relations, and without the right intervention we could have a war on our hands. I told Savion as much on our way to the warehouse.

"I told Cash to make this meeting sooner than Monday, but she was confident this issue could be held off until then. I'm actually happy it went down like this because I don't even want her in the middle of this shit; Chenille needs her mother more than she needs me."

"Nah, she needs both her parents, and losing either of them ain't in the plans tonight. Ever since I got word of this beef I've put everyone on high alert. They're ready to ride out at a moment's notice. Yo, where the fuck we at?"

I was so caught up in making plays in my head that I didn't even notice that we weren't going to our regular rendezvous spot. We were at a warehouse not too far from Myrtle Promenade. The Manhattan skyline lit up the cloudy sky. Gia loved taking the BQE some nights just to get a good look at this view. At first, I didn't understand her excitement, but after a few drive-bys I understood where the allure came from. Savion snapped me out of my thoughts with mention of the warehouse door being open.

"I hope ain't nothing happen," he whispered as he pulled his strap from the waistband of his pants.

I mimicked him, making sure I had my piece ready as we grew closer to the cracked door. Savion pushed it opened with his shoulder, making sure to stay out of range while I brought up the rear.

"I'mma go in first, and you cover me," he whispered.

"Are you crazy? We can't see shit in there. I'm not letting you go in —Savion!" I hissed as he darted into the dark building.

I ran in after him with my gun drawn, ready to pop at the slightest movement when the lights came on and a group of my closest friends and family shouted, "SURPRISE!"

The warehouse had been transformed into a strip club, with some of the best bodies New York City had to offer posed on poles or sitting on the lap of whatever kingpin they were entertaining for the night, and there were quite a few. Anyone who rang bells on the streets was in attendance, and it was good to see that we could all come together outside of making money. For every man of power there had to be at least three beautiful women, some winking while others waved seductively. Zeus and Quade stood in the middle of the festivities, with my older brother keeping it classy with a bottle of Dom P and Cuban cigars while Quade had some rolled up blunts and a bottle of Hennessy Black in hand.

"You thought we would let you get married without a proper send off?" Zeus questioned, extending the bottle to me. "Nah, we had to make sure you were straight. I wish I could say that I put this together, but for the most part it was Quade who set everything up."

Quade pushed Zeus' bottle back into his chest, and said, "Don't even waste your time with that shit, especially since I'm sure they gon' have a bunch of it at the wedding. Since you liked Savion's Henny fountain at his wedding so much, I had to get you a fountain of your own but this one has—ladies, pull back the curtain."

A seven-tiered Patrón fountain stood in the center of the room with rows of shot glasses right beside it. Two women dressed in silver bikinis stood there with salt shakers in their hands, ready to help out if needed. I dapped up each of my brothers, I grabbed a blunt from Quade, and made my way over to the fountain. The ladies were more than accommodating; one of them seductively licked my hand and shook some salt onto it while the other set up my shot. She had the lime placed between her perfect, white teeth. I accepted the glass from her, took it to the head, licked the salt from shorty number one and took the lime with my teeth, careful to make sure I didn't touch her lips.

"Damn, y'all tryna have a nigga caught up out here," I joked as I readied myself another shot.

The women handed out glasses to my brothers, handed them their limes, and dispersed to entertain some more guests. We toasted to the night and took the tequila to the head. What was once one of the driest bachelor party nights ever was quickly turning into one of the best nights of my life. The DJ had every stripper song known to man playing as dancers twirled on every pole in the place. Just by the looks of them, I knew they had to be from the south or something. I was in the middle of grabbing another shot when I felt the room shift to the left.

"Whoa, you better be careful," a sultry voice whispered in my ear, catching me before I fell completely out of my seat.

I blinked three times, thinking it would make my surroundings stop spinning when it only made them multiply. Right now three beautiful women were standing in front of me with a big smile on their faces. They turned into one for a split second, and she was the baddest one of them all. Shorty helped me from my seat and through the party, which was wild at this point. Savion and Zeus were in the middle of getting lap dances by some thick bitches. I spotted Quade having a conversation with a dancer who looked somewhere between intrigued and frightened. He asked her a question, and she nodded her head, licking her lips in anticipation of something. The look of shock on her face when Quade pulled out a pearl handled Beretta and started showing it to her was enough to nearly knock me off of my feet.

"What are you laughing at?" Shorty asked once we were far enough away from the din.

I looked around. "Where your sisters go?"

"You must be really fucked up," she laughed, tugging me into the private office we used for counting money.

Tonight it was completely cleared out and turned into a VIP section. A black leather sofa took up the wall facing the door. Beside it was a table filled with an assortment of liquors and champagnes. Shorty placed me on the sofa with little trouble, making sure I was set before she sashayed over to the table to make up drinks.

"I ain't seen you around the party," I noted, watching her toss together some vodka and cranberry juice in a couple of cups.

She smiled at me over her shoulder. "I was a little late. Doesn't matter now though because I'm here, right?"

I felt the room spin again, this time longer than usual. The already dim room turned black as my lids drooped. They popped back open at the feeling of some plush lips pressed against mine. I pulled my head away from shorty abruptly and ended up with my back on the seat of the sofa. Shorty thought that shit was funny. She gulped down her entire drink, tossed the plastic cup over her shoulder, and laid on top of me. I heard a giggle from the doorway, and there stood another stripper, smiling at me as she sipped on a drink with one hand and texted on her phone with the other.

"Listen," I slurred, fighting the urge to pass out. "I'm marrying the love of my life tomorrow. Whatever you think is gon' go down isn't, so get the fuck up off of me."

I felt the pressure of her body on mine disappear and was ready to sleep this liquor off when I felt the buckle of my jeans loosen. A slight breeze blew against my stomach, followed by the tips of acrylic nails circling my dick. Warm saliva dripped down the shaft, causing it to jump at the introduction of a warm mouth. My hand flailed around weakly, searching for her head so I could move it.

"Didn't I say get off of me, bitch?" I slurred as I finally gave in to the waves of pleasure coursing through my body. "You got another ten seconds to take my dick out of your mouth before I replace it with my piece."

"Nigga, you ain't gon' do a damn thing," she replied with devilish grin. "At the end of the night, we're going to be connected forever, Hasani. You belong to me."

She swallowed my dick whole, ignoring the weak ass slaps I hit her with. There was that pleasure again, turning me into silly putty. My eyes crossed behind closed lids as I felt my body ready for a nut. I tried moving back but she wasn't letting me go for nothing. Seconds later, I felt myself explode in her mouth and I slipped into a restless sleep, muttering apologies to Gia along the way.

GIANNA

If today was supposed to be the happiest day of my life, why did I feel like I was making such a big mistake? This was the constant thought that had been running through my mind since I woke up this morning. My gut kept me in bed when I should have been up from excitement. My reservations had me on the cold bathroom floor throwing up dinner from last night, and my instincts kept me rooted to the spot in front of this mirror. I was standing in a custom Italian wedding gown hand sewn by my grandmother and great aunts, with the intricate beading taking a year of hard work and dedication. *This dress might last longer than my marriage,* I thought and immediately rebuked the thought. *Stop it, Gia, today's your wedding day.*

"You're a successful doctor getting ready to marry the man of your dreams and you're standing here pouting. What's wrong, Gia? Are you having second thoughts? If so, we can cancel this entire wedding." My little sister, Giada, placed her chin on my shoulder and admired me through the mirror. "There's a difference between cold feet and 'I think I'm making the biggest mistake of my life.' You look like you're regretting the past three years of planning this wedding."

"I'm not regretting it," I said with more force than I intended. In a softer tone, I replied, "I love Hasani with all my heart, Giada. He knows how to make me laugh, he believes in me more than I believe in myself, I can't see myself living without him. When I thought he was gone, it felt like someone snatched a piece of my heart. There's no other man in this world I would choose over him."

"Then why are you standing here looking like the exact opposite? Gia, you don't have to lie to me. I'm your sister: no matter what happens today you'll always have my support," Giada said, nuzzling against my shoulder.

I placed my hand on her cheek, grateful for the show of affection I needed amidst the chaos happening behind us. My bridesmaids were running around getting their hair and makeup done, putting on jewelry, and searching through piles of shoes all while trying not to ruin their dresses. Giada had been my rock for this entire process, and if there was one person I could confide my worries in without it getting back to anyone, it was her.

"From the moment I woke up, I felt like something was wrong. I'm not questioning my love for Hasani, I'm questioning if this wedding should happen. Are we ready to do this? Is he ready to do this? I've planned this entire wedding from beginning to end without asking him how he feels."

The more I talked to Giada, the better I felt. Keeping everything bubbled up and running it through my mind was of no help, but talking it out was leading me to the right conclusion. As it turned out, Giada had the perfect solution to my problem.

"I want you to stand right here in this spot," Giada said, leading me onto the balcony of the castle we had rented for the occasion. "Right here, stay just like this, you hear me? Whatever you do, don't turn around."

The grounds were silent on this beautiful Sunday morning. I watched as last-minute chairs were carried into the backyard. Guests were funneling in, their eyes studying every inch of the brick castle, looking for something to compare to whatever past wedding they attended. I expected no less coming from one of the largest crime families in America. People were looking for something to go wrong, and I feared if I married Hasani and shit went sour I would have to constantly relive the embarrassment at every family function, including weddings like this. As if he were summoned by my thoughts, Hasani's voice joined the noise down below.

"Giada, where am I?" Hasani asked.

"You're on the balcony with Gia. She needs to talk to you, but you can't see her because it's bad luck," Giada explained, which helped me understand how adamant she was that I not turn around. "I'll be right on the other side of the door. When you're ready for me to take you back to your room just give me a little wave."

The door shut, leaving us standing there in an awkward silence. I hadn't seen Hasani since our rehearsal dinner. He kissed me on the lips and said, "I'll see you on our wedding day, Mrs. Townsend." Those words tumbled from his lips with ease and warmed my heart just as easily. So why now did my skin crawl at the thought of being Mrs. Townsend?

"Cold feet?" Hasani asked after a minute.

I shook my head even though he couldn't see me. "I don't know what it is, Hasani. Everything about today feels..."

"Wrong? Scary? Like you're making one of the biggest mistakes of your life? I mean, you're marrying me, so it could honestly go either way," Hasani joked in an effort to lighten the mood.

"You don't feel it?"

"I feel like I'm going to throw up, but that has more to do with this hangover I'm battling right now. But my feelings for marrying you? They haven't changed since I asked, Gia. I loved you from the night I met you at that campus party. You were dancing with some cornball—what is it with you and cornball ass niggas—but anyway, I saw you dancing and you lit up the room. My pops would say that about my mother all the time, and I didn't understand it until I saw you. I knew you would be my wife long before I asked you."

I dabbed at the tears pooling in my eyes. "Are you just saying this so I'll marry you?" I replied thickly. "That was my attempt at making a joke to lighten the situation."

"The fact that you had to explain your joke explains why you always attract cornballs—you're one too."

"I am not!"

"Yes, you are, but I love your corny ass. And I'mma love our corny little kids too. I love you so much that I'm willing to spend the rest of my life living in a house with a wife and kids explaining all their jokes to me," Hasani went on over my laughs. "On a serious note: Gia, it doesn't matter if you get all the way to the altar and change your mind when asked if you want to be my wife. I wouldn't be mad. I want you to be as excited about forever as I am, you hear me? But don't wait until we sign the marriage license and shit; I might have to fight you."

This was what I needed. I had been so caught up in planning this wedding and what was supposed to be a representation of our love that I forgot the foundation it was built on. Jokes. Stolen moments. Unconditional love. That nagging feeling in my stomach disappeared at Hasani's words.

"So...we getting married today, Gianna Luchesi?"

A smile blossomed on my face at the mention of my old name. "Actually, it's Gianna Luchesi-Townsend."

"INTRODUCING MR. AND MRS. TOWNSEND!" the DJ announced as Hasani and I entered the grand ballroom.

Seven hundred of our closest family and friends were on their feet clapping and cheering as we took our place on the grand ballroom floor. Hasani placed a soothing kiss on my lips to quell my nerves. We were supposed to take dance lessons before the wedding, but between him running his territory and me being busy with school, we flaked too many times to count. I was sure it would show in our stilted movements, however, once Tony Bennett's "The Way You Look Tonight" came on, Hasani took the lead, guiding me around the dance floor with ease.

"Where did you learn how to ballroom dance?" I asked with a hint of surprise.

Hasani dipped me. "We got this Columbian connect who used to ballroom dance all over the world. It gave her the cover to travel without being noticed. I was only able to take a few lessons, but it feels like enough to not embarrass you during our first dance."

"Embarrass me? Never. Except for that time you tried to order fried chicken at an Italian restaurant," I recalled on our first date. "I ordered for you and you trusted me. That's when I fell in love with you. I want to smile for the rest of my life, and I know you'll be able to always put a smile on my face."

The music went from sweet and sentimental to upbeat, with Michael Jackson's "Love Never Felt So Good" coming on. Everyone slowly joined us on the dance floor. Hasani got to slipping and sliding, dancing around me in circles as he sung the chorus. I sung along with him, dipping my hips to the infectious beat. To my delight, the song brought together everyone—my black and Italian family mixed with each other while welcoming Hasani's brothers into the mix. Yara and Cash were dancing with each other while Savion shared a dance with his baby girl, Chenille. Little Quade was showing Quade his best dance moves. Zeus and Lauren were falling in love with each other all over again. This was my family, and nothing could ruin this moment.

That is, until I saw him sitting in a far corner of the room watching me.

"Give it up for the bride and groom," the DJ announced at the end of the song.

Hasani and I were showered with a deafening round of applause. Hasani dipped me again in a grandiose fashion. The photographer slid in at the perfect time, capturing him planting a kiss on my lips. What broke my heart more than anything in the world was that when I looked back on these pictures years from now and my grandchildren asked me what I was thinking about, I wouldn't be alone to tell them the truth—that I was thinking of another man. No, I didn't love him, but I gave him more power than he ever deserved. My hands were trembling with anger at his blatant disregard of my feelings.

"I thought I made myself clear last night when I revoked your invitation to my wedding," I said to Carmelo in the privacy of my changing room. "I have nothing more to say to you, Carmelo. We're over, we've been over for a long time, and nothing will change that.

You have two options: you can leave quietly through the front door, or you can leave through the back with the help of my Beretta."

Carmelo gave a noncommittal shrug. "I'm not leaving until you admit the truth, Gianna. You married the wrong man today."

"I married the love of my life."

"That's not what your lips said last night."

There were many reasons I fell for Carmelo, with his arrogance being one of them, except today it was less cute and more audacious. Ever since my wedding announcement was sent to his parents, who were close friends with mine, Carmelo had been trying to wiggle his way back into my heart. We had broken up in college, where he decided that he would rather fuck randoms than be in a committed relationship. Now that I had my piece of happily ever after, he was trying to secure what he had lost a long time ago. I wasn't letting that shit go down, not on the most special day of my life.

"I want you to listen to me loud and clear, Carmelo," I said, placing my foot on a step stool and gathering the mounds of fabric that made up my dress. "Last night I gave you the opportunity to speak what was on your heart, which was rather noble of me because you didn't deserve it. When you were finished, I told you that while your words sounded sincere, they meant nothing to me. You mean nothing to me. What else did I say to you?"

"That if you ever saw me again, you would—Gia!" Carmelo placed his hands in the air at the sight of my Magnum Research Baby Desert Eagle. "Gianna, there's no need to point a gun at me. Are you really going to kill me on your wedding day?"

I placed the barrel of the gun underneath his chin, which would prevent the blowback from hitting my face. "Motherfucker, I'm a mafia princess. I will blow your head off your shoulders and have 700 people alibi me without hesitation. I told you last night that if I ever saw you again I would hit you with a bullet right between the eyes. You must've thought a lifelong friendship with my family was enough to disregard those words."

"Gia—"

"Don't interrupt me while I'm talking," I barked, pressing the gun deeper into his throat. "Let this be the last time you come anywhere near me talking shit about the past. What we had was a long time ago, and I don't love you, Carmelo. You pressing your lips against mine in a last attempt to remind me of what we had was enough to remind me of why I want no parts of you."

Carmelo's eyes went from the gun against his throat to my dead eyes. "You got it, Gianna. Can you please move your gun?"

I obliged him because there was no way in hell I wanted my wedding day plagued by tragedy. Carmelo ambled over to the door, humbled at my words, and glanced over his shoulder at me. With a shake of his head he was out the door. My attendants came from the corner they were hiding in and proceeded to help me into my second wedding gown. I secured my gun into the second garter belt, with one being for show, and headed out into the festivities. There was a small bit of commotion coming from the dance floor. Hasani, Zeus, Cash, Savion, and Lauren were standing in awe of whatever they were looking at. The crowd parted for me, revealing a beautiful sight. Kendrick Lamar's "Loyalty" was bumping through the speakers, amping up the crowd, but there were two people in particular having more fun than the rest. Quade and Yara stole the show, singing and rapping the verses to each other. Ever since they lost their baby boy they had been distant with each other. From what Hasani had told me they weren't even living in the same house with each other. Now they were sharing an expensive bottle of champagne and dancing in the middle of the dancefloor like no one was watching. They were in their own little world, coming together after being mentally apart for so long.

That's what marriage was, and I wanted a piece of that for myself.

Hasani locked eyes with me from across the room, warming me in the places where Carmelo had left me feeling cold. There wasn't a doubt in my mind that he was the one for me. Whatever obstacles we would have to overcome, I was ready for them. Marriage wasn't fair weathered. Nothing would keep me from the love of my life.

LAUREN

It was crazy what you would do for love and even crazier what you would do to keep a secret from being exposed. Sadan made sure to call me up everyday, reminding me that the deadline to pay him was drawing closer. This morning I received a text stating that he would text me with the address at a moment's notice to keep me from being able to have the upper hand. I knew I should tell Cash what was going on for my protection but watching her have a good time with Savion gave me pause. This was my secret to bear and I couldn't risk her life for the sake of keeping it.

"Crazy, ain't it?" Zeus said, nudging his head in the direction of the dance floor. "Who would've thought these conservative Italian folks would like Cardi B?"

"Look at grandpa. He's over there dabbing. Ayyye," I joked, smiling as a man that had to be in his late 80's was taking dance lessons from the children.

Zeus rose from his seat and extended his hand to me. I allowed him to pull me onto a small spot on the edge of the dance floor. Yara and Quade were still going strong on the floor an hour later. The resignation I had once seen in Yara's face had disappeared, showing her inner glow, which was infectious judging by the way it morphed

Quade into a new man. Happiness emanated from them, enough to light up the room. I was so taken aback by their transformation that all I could do was a weak little two step.

"They look happy, don't they?" Zeus said with a self-satisfied smile. "I found that song on repeat in Quade's Spotify history. Who knew it was so sentimental?"

I rested my head on his chest. "Maybe one day we can be that sentimental. You know, like us having a huge fight and then you put on 'Back That Azz Up.' I start twerking on you and we forget why we were mad in the first place."

"We don't have to wait until tonight to do that," Zeus whispered in my ear, pressing himself against me, allowing me to feel his erection in its entirety. I wasn't sure how much champagne he had to drink, but it had him acting really out of character and I was loving every single minute of it. "Ain't nothing stopping you from twerking on this—"

"Zeus! Not in front of all these people," I said, slapping him on the chest and looking around to make sure no one heard his freaky ass.

He caught my hand in his and showered it with kisses. I thought it was sweet until he bit the tips of each finger. They had the right amount of pain to send pleasure surging through my body, ending right in the sensitive spot between my legs. Zeus saw the yearning in my eyes and acted on it. With a devilish wink, he stole me from the dance floor. He grabbed a bottle of champagne from a passing waiter on our way out of the ballroom.

The castle was beautiful at this time of night, with pools of moonlight providing supplemental lighting that the candles lining the hallways couldn't provide. A gentle breeze crept up on us, ruffling my hair and tickling my flushed skin. I dipped underneath Zeus' arm and snuggled against his warm body to keep myself warm.

"You seem to know this place like the back of your hand," I noted as we arrived on the second floor, which had a more modern feel.

"I had some time to explore while everyone was getting ready," Zeus explained as he led me down another dimly lit hallway. "Most of the rooms are modern, but I found one that's still old fashioned."

What he failed to mention was that it was a room out of a fairytale. A king-sized bed adorned with red and gold bedding sat on a platform overlooking the spacious room. I ran my hand across the antique dressers, fingering the aged wood. Zeus sat on the edge of the bed, his eyes following me around the room as I sat on each sofa in the sitting area and opened every dresser drawer, looking to see if anything was left behind. I had always been a curious spirit with a love of exploring historical dwellings. Zeus knew this, which was why he chose this room when he could've easily found a better equipped room. My last stop was the balcony, where I found a breathtaking view. Zeus' cologne reached me before he did, mingled with the smell of his sweat. The mixture was intoxication; I placed my nose in the crook of his neck, breathing him in as if it would be the last time we'd ever be like this again.

"Could you imagine waking up to this view everyday?" Zeus asked, interrupting my sniff session.

The view wasn't Zeus, but it had its own special beauty. The setting sun retreated behind the lush trees covering the grounds, only revealing itself on the lake, dancing off the waves of opaque water and creating a dazzling effect. With the entrance of the summer breeze everything shifted slightly, sending the smell of grass and the good time below to join us up high. Zeus ran his hands down my arms, creating a trail of goosebumps where the tips of his fingers touched my skin, until our hands intertwined. He closed the space between us. I laid my head on his chest, listening to his heart beat. This was the first time in months it was just the two of us—no drama, no work, nobody—and it was one of the most peaceful moments of my life.

"In Paris."

"Hmm?"

"You asked me if I could wake up to this view everyday. I would love to in Paris. It's one of my dream destinations. When I found out how dangerous it was, that only made me want to go even more. You know, to see if I could get taken or meet some Romanian gypsies."

Zeus' rich laughter filled my ear. "Of course your crazy ass would go to Paris for the crime. What about cruising the Sienne? Or visiting the Louvre? You know, normal tourist shit?"

"You can enjoy the sophisticated activities while I'm on my hood rat shit," I rationalized. "Then at the end of the day we meet up at that bridge with all the locks and add one of our own. Doesn't that sound perfect?"

"Anything involving you is perfect, Lauren." Zeus reached into his pocket and emerged with a large, black ring box.

I started trembling so bad my teeth were chattering. I knew we would get to this level eventually, but I wasn't expecting for it to happen tonight. Zeus got down on bended knee, popped the box open with a dramatic *crack,* and there was the ring of my dreams.

"I'm a little fucked up right now, so instead of the speech I had planned, I'll speak from the heart. I love you, Lauren. I'm ready to make Grammy proud and put a ring on your finger. She was absolutely right to demand that I make an honest woman out of you because a woman like you only comes along once in a lifetime. Will you marry me?"

"Yes! Yes, yes, yes!"

Zeus slid the ring on my finger and kissed it. He was barely on his feet when I pounced on him, sending us backwards into the bedroom. Zeus' balance improved at the last minute, which was all we needed for him to make it up the two steps and onto the bed with a thud. The bed might've been old, but this was a new mattress, a springy one at that. I pulled my dress over my head and tossed it behind me. Zeus ran his hands up my sides, heating me up in places I was cold. His fingers teased my aching nipples before taking one into his mouth. My hand snaked down to his pants, unbuttoning them with haste so I could take him into my hands.

"I want you right now," I said between strangled breaths. "No foreplay, no lovemaking—just you."

Gone was the sensual Zeus that treated my body like a palace, replaced with the other Zeus, the one that came out on a rare occasion. We made passionate love that night, the kind of love you make when you're not sure if you'll ever see the person again. I wept tears of joy because never in a million years did I imagine after living in hell with Steez that I would have my own happiness. The million dollars I could pay to Sadan would be worth it, but I knew he wasn't going to go away that easy. I had to protect my peace at any cost.

I LAY in bed watching Zeus sleep from our wild night. We had made it home and continued throughout the house, leaving no place untouched. For a man nearing forty, Zeus worked me better than any man I had been with, including Steez, who bragged about being able to put it on a woman, yet I could count on one hand how many times he'd made me orgasm during our five-year relationship. He was a selfish lover, the worst of the worst, and Zeus entering my life, showing me that sex was more than a physical connection, felt like a reward after years of suffering. I never let a day pass without telling him how much I loved him, but the only way I could let Zeus know how much he meant to me was through show.

Like right now.

"Had to handle some business. I'll be back in a few. I love you," I wrote on the notepad he kept on the nightstand. I sprayed it with some of my favorite perfume, gave him a quick kiss on the lips, and slipped out of the room before I woke him up.

Compared to yesterday's bright sun, Monday morning was bleak. I could barely stay awake as I cut through the early morning traffic. Sadan wasn't shit for picking this early morning meet. To top it off, he chose a hotel in one of the busiest sections of Brooklyn. Discretion was a big part of my role as distributor; I didn't like handling business in broad daylight while people were refreshed from a night of sleep and more likely to remember me. It was all I could think of as I slipped through the front door, making sure not to make eye contact with any of the staff at the front desk.

"Room 208..." I said under my breath, pressing the corresponding elevator button.

I gave the book bag on my shoulder a little shift. One million dollars wasn't heavy on a normal day, but when you were working on no hours of sleep it felt like a boulder. The elevator doors sprung open, letting me off onto a deserted hallway. I could hear the sound of a vacuum cleaner somewhere on the floor. As it turned out, it was right next to the room I was meeting in. I could see the maid dancing to the music playing in her headphones as she cleaned the carpet. Knowing someone was only a room away gave me some solace. I knocked on the door and waited patiently. Something moved in the corner of my eye but was gone the second I turned to look.

"Right on time."

Sadan stood in the doorway with a devilish grin on his face. I stepped inside, getting a good look at my surroundings. The bed was neatly made with only a dent made by Sadan sitting at the edge. I noticed two other dents and immediately reached behind my back for my piece when I felt the cool metal press against my neck.

"Surprise, bitch," a cold feminine voice said, using her gun to push me deeper into the room. "I can't believe you really brought your dumb ass here thinking some money was going to silence us."

I closed my eyes, mentally cursing myself for being so stupid. During my entire relationship with Steez, I learned a lot about his brothers. Ghetto was stupid, Ahmad was sneaky, Salim was lethal, and Saaid was all three wrapped together. But Sadan? His biggest weakness was that although he was ruthless, he wasn't the smartest. That phone call from Sadan had Ivy written all over it. He always had a soft spot for her, and if they weren't siblings I'd swear they were on some strange incestuous shit. Ivy snatched my gun from my waistband and shoved me into the bed. I righted myself with the quickness to find that the duo was a trio. Standing to the side of Ivy was their younger sister, Quincy. I hadn't seen her since her high school graduation. She was blessed with the opportunity to study abroad and had spent the seven years living in London before returning back to the States to pursue a career with an MBA from Cambridge. Out of the Assan clan, if there was one person with a modicum of decency, it was Quincy. Her gray eyes were wide with fear, a stark contrast to Ivy's cool orbs.

"Really, Sadan?" I willed him to look me in the eye, but he refused and opted to stare around the room. "You said you wanted money, and I came through on my end. What happened to being a man of your word? Did that die when you went into jail?"

Ivy scoffed. "I know you aren't sitting here preaching about anyone being honest when you started fucking with the Townsend Brothers heavily after my brother's death. This was a war, Lauren, a war for our birthright, and you chose dick over family."

"Family? You've never liked me Ivy!"

"Because I could smell the disloyalty on your ass. I told my brother you would be his undoing, and I'll be damned if I wasn't right."

"Your brother's undoing was not being able to keep his dick in his fucking pants. He raped a woman and she put his ass down like the sick bitch he was."

Ivy advanced on me and pressed her gun into my forehead. "Watch how the fuck you talk about my brother."

I pressed the gun deeper into my head. "Do it. You know you want to. Might as well because even if I was to walk out of this room, I'm coming for you and the rest of your sisters. I'm sure they're somewhere around here. You never were able to do anything alone."

"For the first time in your life you're right about something. Saidya's next door keeping that vacuum cleaner going so no one will hear what's going to happen." Ivy removed her weapon from my forehead and sauntered back over to her siblings. She pressed the gun into a nervous Quincy's hand. "Do it exactly like I taught you. Right in the chest. Make it quick; there's but so much longer Sai can keep vacuuming that room."

"No," I said, shaking my head at the exchange. "Ivy, don't make her do this. I expect this heartless shit from you because like your brothers, all you are is a blind sheep unable to accept your father's death. Don't turn Quincy into that kind of monster."

"I'm sorry, at what point did I ask for your opinion on how to handle my sister? Quincy, handle your business."

Quincy choked back the silent tears streaming down her cheeks. "Okay…"

Sadan watched as his little sister struggled to do the dirty work. "Ivy, I think you should let me do it. Look at how she's—"

"Didn't you just hear me tell this bitch to mind her business on how I handle our sister? Shut the fuck up and let me take care of this," Ivy barked, her nostrils flaring. "Quincy, you got until the count of ten to pull that trigger. Do you understand me?"

"Yes, Ivy," Quincy choked out. She mouthed to me, "I'm sorry."

"What are you sorry about?" Ivy hissed, taking a menacing step towards Quincy. "She's been sleeping with the enemy for how many years now? She cheated on Steez with one of the men who killed our father. I know for a fact that she had something to do with Ahmad's death. Lauren doesn't deserve an apology for a damn thing; what she needs is to be put down like the animal that she is. So put her down—now!"

Sadan placed a hand on Ivy's shoulder. "Ivy, let me handle it."

"Didn't I tell you to shut up?" Ivy replied, raising my gun and shooting her brother dead in the face.

Quincy let out a strangled scream at the sight of Sadan's headless body crashing into the table behind him. I used that second of distraction to make a grab for the gun in Quincy's hand. Ivy anticipated my move and snatched Quincy's hand, placing her finger over her sister's, and firing off three shots. They tore through my body, slicing my neck, splintering bones in my chest, and hitting my left lung. My legs gave out at the sudden loss of air, slamming me face first into the hotel carpet.

"Grab the bag from her," I heard Ivy bark at Quincy.

Quincy bent down to grab the bag from my shoulder. We locked eyes for a second and she whispered, "I'm so sorry, Lauren."

"Hurry up!"

Quincy removed the bag gently from my arms. I used the momentum to shift myself onto my side. Ivy came back around the corner to get one last look at me wheezing on the floor. She stared down at me as if contemplating what her next move would be, and kicked me in the stomach, stealing the last bit of air I had left. My eyes rolled into the back of my head as my lungs worked overtime to deliver oxygen. Air crept in slowly, righting my eyes once again, at the exact moment a familiar face appeared.

"Lauren," Cash mouthed, dropping to her knees and pulling me into her lap.

I felt numb all over, and it was with that stark realization I knew she wasn't mouthing anything; my body was shutting down. Everything felt like it was closing in on me as I felt myself suffocate to death. The end was near, and I knew I couldn't leave this Earth without telling Cash my truth. I spoke her name through the blood and bits of lung pouring from my mouth. It had been so long since it passed through my lips that my vision blurred as tears flooded my eyes.

"Zoelle?" Cash mouthed. "Who's Zoelle?"

She was the reason why I walked into a room full of my enemies without pause. The reason I was afraid to bear a child for Zeus. She was the bright light I saw as I took my last breath. Her smiled welcomed me into a bright light as everything faded into eternal darkness.

ZEUS

I knew something had to be wrong the second I saw Quade's face. He was always calm in the face of tragedy. The last time he looked like this was when we "lost" Hasani. I sat up in bed, wiping the dried crust out of my eyes, which was my way of stalling to have one last minute of peace. It took a few blinks for me to see that he wasn't alone. Savion, Cash, and Yara stood behind him. Cash's face was swollen and her eyes puffy as if she had been crying for quite some time. There was one person missing from the group.

"Where's Lauren?" I said, patting the empty spot next to me.

Quade's mouth opened and shut a few times before he finally managed to get out, "Zeus…Lauren is dead."

"What?" I sunk into my pillows at the weight of the news. "Lauren isn't dead. We went to sleep last night. She's in the bathroom or maybe she went to get something to eat down the block…"

Cash shaking her head killed the explanations pouring from my lips. She was close to Lauren, close enough to know if Lauren really was… "Zeus, I found her bleeding out in a hotel room. Three shots to the chest. They might've been able to save her if not for one of the bullets puncturing her lung. I held her until she…"

"No," I said, balling myself up into the sheets and making a beeline for the bathroom, where I used my speakers to call Lauren.

Her phone went straight to voicemail.

"Her phone's dead," I rationalized as I turned on the shower. I stepped in blindly, immune to the scalding hot water piercing my skin. "She's not gone, she just let her phone die. Nah, she's not dead. She ain't dead."

I kept repeating the mantra to myself over and over, hoping that would make it untrue, but when I called her for a second, third, and fourth time I felt that familiar feeling setting in. It was the same gut wrenching feeling I had when I found out about my mother. The churning I had at the news my father was murdered. The way my heart dropped at the news Hasani was killed.

"Alexa," I said to the Amazon virtual assistant I had placed throughout my home. "What's on the local news?"

Alexa gave me the rundown of the events happening in Manhattan. She covered politics, traffic changes...and a double murder in a Brooklyn hotel room. A man and woman were both shot and killed. One of the victims had yet to be identified, but the woman was rushed to Brooklyn Methodist Hospital where she was pronounced dead.

"Her name is being withheld until the family has been—"

"Thank you, Alexa," I barked.

I took a seat on the edge of the bathtub, numb at the news. My first question was what she was doing there, and my second was—

"If you knew she was acting weird, why didn't you tell me?" I asked Cash.

Everyone jumped at my sudden reappearance. Cash, who was sitting on the edge of the bed playing with her hands, stifled a sob, and replied, "She told me she would tell me what was going on when she was ready. I told her she should tell you, but she refused."

"You didn't tell me anything and now she's dead."

Savion stood in front of Cash. "I understand you're grieving, but you won't blame my wife for what happened to Lauren. She was the one holding the secret, not Cash."

"And if Cash would've been a real friend and told me none of this would have happened!"

"Cash's loyalty is to her business partner at the end of the day," Savion shot back, slowly advancing on me. "I shouldn't have to explain this to you because you already know how it is. So instead of jumping on Cash, what we need to focus on is making sense of this mess."

"There is no 'we,'" I said, motioning between the two of us. "There's a me, and I'll sort this out myself. Lauren's grandmother is going to get the news and I don't want her to be—"

My phone started buzzing on the nightstand. I saw Grammy's name light up the screen. *They already got to her,* I thought as I answered my phone. The resolve I had dissolved at the sound of Lauren's grandmother crying out to me.

"Zeus, they're saying my grandbaby is gone," Grammy wailed. "Don't tell me that it's true. Please don't tell me someone hurt her."

I turned away from the group, refusing to let them see the silent tears that flowed from my eyes. "Yeah," I choked out. "She's gone. It's all over the news. Someone killed her."

"You were supposed to protect her! You promised me that you would keep her safe and now these people are at my home telling me that she's gone!"

My phone hit the floor with a clatter. I staggered to my closet, barely making it inside before I let out a sob deep in my chest. My brothers weren't supposed to see me like this—I was supposed to be their rock and I couldn't even keep it together long enough to comfort Lauren's grandmother. The automatic lights came on at my entrance. If there was ever a place I didn't need to be, it was here with Lauren's clothes. The same jackets I was complaining about were neatly lined up, waiting for her to slip into them once again. I was waiting for her to slip into my arms once again.

"Zeus, we're going to head over to Lauren's grandmother's house. We'll meet you there," Quade said through the door.

For someone that was so out of touch with other people's emotions, Quade understood what I needed right now was to be alone with my thoughts. I took my time getting dressed, preparing myself for life on the other side of the closet door. Any vulnerability I had died the second I stepped out of my bedroom. I had to be strong when all I wanted was to call on God to get down to the bottom of this. Having me fall in love with Lauren only to snatch her away.

EVERYTHING WAS WHITE. The Calla lilies lining the pews of the Baptist church, the roses surrounding the snow-white casket Lauren rested peacefully in, and the gloves I had on my hands for when we had to lift her casket. There was an outpouring of people at her funeral, and I wasn't sure whether they knew her in real life or if they were drawn to her funeral due to the media hype. I spent the last week dodging reporters asking me for a quote or comment on the case, none of which I was willing to give. It wasn't until Quade broke three cameras, slashed the tires of every news van in front of my house, and threatened to find out where they lived did reporters begin to back off. Those threats wouldn't matter today; everyone wanted to see the woman who was gunned down in cold blood.

"And now it is time for Lauren's friends and family to say goodbye to her," the bishop said in his rumbling baritone. "Ladies and gentlemen, out of respect for the family, I ask that you refrain from taking any flash photography..."

The two front pews rose. Lauren's family traveled from all over the country and her native home of Haiti to say goodbye. Her parents died when she was younger, but she had plenty of aunts and uncles who loved her like she was their own. I met them on a few occasions, mainly weddings and birthdays, however, like my relationship with Lauren, this was the last time I would ever see them again. Grammy held on to me tight as we approached Lauren's casket first. Her makeup was immaculate, not a single hair was out of place, and to the naked eye she could've been Sleeping Beauty with the crown of white roses on her head. Her hands were placed across the front of the white Versace gown she wore. Grammy fingered her engagement ring on her finger, shaking her head with sadness.

"You had it all, my darling. I am going to miss you with all my heart." Grammy placed her handkerchief to her mouth, stifling the tears that threatened to fall. I placed a comforting hand on her shoulder to keep her tiny frame from falling over. "I love you, Lauren, and soon we'll be together again."

There were no words that would bring her back to me, so I said nothing. I stared at her, memorizing the curves of her face, the wrinkles in her brow whenever she was mad, the way her now cold lips would turn up in a smile at the sight of me, how her closed eyes would watch me shave every morning. A hand clamped down on my shoulder after some time. Hasani's eyes locked with mine. He gave a small nod, which I returned after a minute more of observing her. He led me back to my seat, where Grammy sat being comforted by one of Lauren's cousins. They made room for the both of us on the front pew. I zoned out again, only coming back when it was time to take Lauren to the hearse. My brothers appeared on either side of the casket along with two of Lauren's uncles. They saved a spot in the front for me. The entire congregation stood as I took my place. The shutter of cameras overpowered "Amazing Grace" overhead. We lifted the casket, and I felt like I was hurdled back in time to when I did the same for my mother except it was an empty church.

White flower petals cascaded from overhead as we exited the church. Gasps of surprise filled the air as people looked up to see where they were coming from. A member of the congregation was placed in charge of scattering the flowers from the roof of the church until we pulled off. We placed Lauren gently into the hearse, and with the help of several bodyguards, climbed into the fleet of cars waiting to take us to the cemetery. I rode with my brothers while the women rode in a separate car.

"You planned a real nice service for Lauren, Zeus. The flower petals raining from the sky was a nice touch," Savion said, interrupting the silence as we cleared the crowds.

"It was nice for a funeral. When I die, I want to be burned and for my ashes to be turned into artillery. Knife handles, gun butts, bullets, and grenades. I want to take niggas out from beyond the grave," Quade said with a hint of wistfulness. "Rotting in the ground for the rest of time ain't for me."

Hasani and Savion stared at Quade, widening their eyes as if to tell him to shut up. On the contrary; I welcomed some type of normalcy. That wasn't Lauren riding in front of us—it was a physical memory of her that we would place in the ground as a way to reconnect with her whenever the need arose. I clapped him on the shoulder and replied, "Note taken. I'll even pop some shots of you at the gun range on your birthday."

The tension in the car eased at my forgiving tone. I spent the rest of the ride staring out the window watching how people's expressions changed at the sight of the procession. Smiles dropped at the sight of the hearse. Some looked genuinely saddened while others may have been reliving a time when they watched their loved one being driven to their final resting place. They remained living proof that this scar could scab but it would never heal.

~

SUMMER RAIN SPRINKLED the white casket, rolling down the sides and slipping into the six-foot hole to never be seen again. The rain started upon our entrance into the cemetery. Some might call it a coincidence, but I believed Lauren was here with us, crying tears at the realization that this was it: we were really saying goodbye to her. I refused to take refuge underneath the umbrellas provided the same way I donned an ink black suit to the funeral while everyone opted to wear white. This suit was a gift from Lauren for my birthday. I was comforted by the rain drops wetting the wool material, connecting us one last time. I squeezed the rose in my hand so tight an uncut thorn pierced my skin. I stared at my blood on the stem, thinking I could leave her with part of me as well.

"Goodbye, Lauren," everyone murmured as they tossed their roses onto the casket.

I leaned over, staring down into the hole, and said, "Later, Lauren."

The group dissipated as Lauren's grave was filled. Everyone was making their way towards the cars except Savion and Cash, who was kneeling over a tiny tombstone. Her body shook with quiet sobs. Savion hovered protectively over her, patting her back as she stared down at the tiny tombstone. I approached with Savion's permission and bent down to see what she was crying over. On a marble tombstone covered in ornate flowers read:

Zoelle Townsend
December 3, 2016 – December 7, 2016
"A flower bloomed already wilting. Beginning its life with an early ending."

"HER LAST WORDS WERE ZOELLE," Cash said between sobs. "I planned to ask her family later on at the repast when I saw this...she died to keep this a secret from you. I know I should've told you sooner but I had no idea this is what she meant..."

I embraced Cash, smoothing her hair as she broke down in my arms. "You didn't know any better. None of this is your fault."

The news that I had a little girl for no matter how short an amount of time shook me to my core. Lauren smiled in my face everyday for three years hiding this secret from me, which had me thinking: what else was she hiding? I would only have to wait until I arrived home to a message on my house phone from my private investigator asking me to call him back. Judging by the tone of his voice, the news wasn't good.

"Were you able to find out who it was?"

"Mr. Townsend," Pete said after a long sigh, "take a seat."

I complied, plopping down into my chair. "Who is it?"

"A law enforcement buddy of mine was able to give me an ID on the body before the name was released to the public. It belongs to a Sadan Assan."

My blood ran cold. "Come again?"

"The body belongs to Sadan Assan. Lauren had been corresponding with Assan from the day he was released from prison. I also saw that Lauren moved around a significant amount of assets over the days preceding her death, somewhere in the excess of half a million dollars. If I had to make an educated guess—"

"She was paying him off," I finished, my lips barely moving. "Pete, I'm going to need you to find out some information on a Zoelle Townsend. She was born on December 3, 2016 and died a few days later. I want to know the cause of death."

"Can do. I'll be in touch, Mr. Townsend."

The call ended, leaving me sitting in a stunned silence. I had spent the better part of a week trying to figure out what Lauren was trying to hide from me, why she would risk her entire life to keep a secret, and now that I knew, I felt like she made the right decision. Every day we spent together without her revealing the truth to me was a stab in the heart. I couldn't think of a single reason for her hiding this from me for all these years other than selfishness. She took away my option to decide if I still wanted to be with her. I was sleeping with a stranger, in love with someone that used to be the woman I fell in love with. And somehow, that wasn't enough to stop me from missing her. More than angry, I was hurt, cut deep by Lauren's deception. I would spend the rest of my life wondering what happened to my daughter, never receiving closure on her brief existence. Staring down at Zoelle's headstone, I not only lost my trust in women, but my ability to love was no more.

QUINCY

My face slammed against the wooden table, the force enough to make my teeth chatter. Blood poured from my nose, dipping into the creases of my lips, and filling my mouth with that familiar salty taste. The center of my forehead throbbed from the impact. I winced as I rubbed it, praying a knot wouldn't form overnight. Ivy watched with mild interest, sipping on her milkshake like she was enjoying a good show. Tears stung my eyes, but I wouldn't give her the satisfaction of knowing she made me cry. I didn't have to though; Ivy was always good at gauging my emotions. It was how she bent me to her will and made me do whatever she wanted.

"Are you finished staring into space?" Ivy asked in an offhand manner.

I accepted a napkin from my sister, Kaia, who shot me a sympathetic look. Unfortunately for me, her sympathy was fleeting; Ivy didn't tolerate any kind of dissent, whether it be words or emotions. Right now, by not giving her my undivided attention, I had unintentionally said fuck her when in fact I was preoccupied with what today was.

"I'm sorry, Ivy. Today is my mother's birthday," I apologized as I dabbed at my nose.

Ivy's expression softened. "You should've said something. Take the rest of the day off. Saidya will bring you up to speed tomorrow," she said, nudging her head at our other sister, who sat across the table popping crispy french fries into her mouth one by one.

"No, I'm fine. If I take the day off all I'll do is think about her. I'd rather be with family," I replied, which was a half truth.

I didn't want to be alone, but I would rather be around anyone except my family. When my mother died of cervical cancer, I was left with no one. She was an only child and my grandparents died long before I was born. I thought her memory would be able to live on with the home her parents left her, but it was foreclosed due to several missed payments. As it turned out, my mother was paying my tuition and bills instead of taking care of herself, which was another added stressor that led to her death. Homeless, jobless, and without any living relatives on my maternal side, I started doing some digging on my father's side, looking for an offer of help from anyone. That's where my older sister, Ivy, came in. She welcomed me with open arms and promised to take care of me. She became a motherly figure to me right off the bat, and I felt safe with her. However, I learned that safety came from her being the person everyone needed saving from, myself included.

"If you're going to stay, then you need to pay attention," Ivy replied, placing her empty cup on the kitchen table. She gave her undivided attention to Saidya and Kaia, who were looking especially satisfied with themselves. "Where are we so far with Hasani?"

Kaia took a delicate sip of her caramel macchiato. "Everything went exactly as planned. He came faster than I expected, but I was able to get a decent amount of his nut into the condom. Saidya shot it inside of me with a turkey baster and we'll know whether or not I'm having little Baby Townsend in a couple weeks."

"With as much as we paid for In Vitro you better be pregnant. We can't afford another round of that shit, and even if we could, I don't see us being able to get close to Hasani again. He's the weakest when it comes to the flesh. The rest of them are too damn faithful for their own good."

"Not necessarily. I think with the right setting I could break Quade," Saidya said, playfully sticking out her tongue. "Ever since they lost their baby, him and Yara have been on the outs. He needs a shoulder to lean on, a confidante, and once a nigga starts confiding in you, he's hooked."

Ivy smirked. "That would work if it weren't for the fact that you don't know how to separate your emotions from fucking. How many niggas have you killed because they refuse to leave their wives for you, Sai? Every time I turn around you're fucking a taken man and hoping your pussy and a few conversations is enough to make them choose you. No, bitch, I refuse to get this far only for you to fuck it up for everyone. You'll stay on standby."

"I'm not a little fucking kid, Ivy. I know how to do more than wait on the sidelines! Instead of passing up on me you need to use me instead of using her." Saidya pointed a bejeweled fingernail in my direction. "Had I been in that hotel room instead of her we would still have our brother. But no, you had to take her little scary ass in there with you."

"She had to get her feet wet," Ivy rationalized. "Everyone freezes up during their first kill."

"Not me!"

"Because you lack common fucking sense!" Ivy replied through gritted teeth. She rose from her seat and leaned over the kitchen table until her nose kissed Saidya's. "Sadan isn't dead because of Quincy—he's dead because he didn't know how to obey my orders. If you can't learn to listen, you can leave in a body bag or out of that window. Blood sister or not, I don't do loose ends. So are you going to follow my orders or do you need a little motivation?"

Ivy started reaching for the Beretta she kept tucked in the back of her pants. Saidya swallowed, and answered, "I'm here to follow orders."

"That's what the fuck I thought," Ivy barked, backing away and grabbing her phone from the table. "Kaia, I want you laying down for the rest of the day; Saidya, clean up this fucking house from top to bottom; Quincy, grab some money from the cookie jar and take yourself out for a drink."

Saidya eyed me with hate: out of the trio she was the least welcoming. I chalked it up to jealousy. Whereas Ivy was a gorgeous honey hued bombshell and Kaia resembled an African goddess, Saidya was easily overlooked because of her plain jane features. She was pretty—with smooth brown skin, a pert nose, and small eyes—but the only way she got half the attention her sisters did was by putting on twice as much makeup. If life wasn't hard enough for her, I came along, unintentionally stirring the pot. I didn't think I was as pretty as my older sisters, but I was smart, and Ivy said smarts was a missing niche on her team. Kaia welcomed the idea of me joining them, but Saidya couldn't stand me. After trying to win her over, I decided there were some people who were destined to be hateful.

"What can I get you?" the bartender at The Monkey Bar asked with a polite smile.

I skimmed the menu for a third time and replied, "I'll have a Little Gems Caesar Salad and a Cosmo to start."

Placing my thoughts of my sisters aside, I focused on having a good time by myself. The black Zimmerman dress I wore fit in with the ambiance of the expensive restaurant. Other than family heirlooms, my clothes were the only items I had left from my previous life. My mother prided herself on dressing me for success, which meant making sure I stepped out in nothing but the best designer labels. Too bad I didn't notice her signs of financial instability until it was too late. I would give anything to be back in my childhood home wearing rags. Memories of my mother continued to run through my mind, leaving me crying well into my third drink. My food remained untouched; I spent my dinner watching a slideshow of her on my phone.

"She's beautiful," a smooth voice said to the left of me.

I pressed pause on the slideshow to see who had the nerve to be minding my business. The verbal assault I had geared up died on my lips at the sight of the handsome man sitting one seat over from me.

He wasn't regular fine either—he was 'my panties are moist at the smell of his cologne' fine. More like 'what does that mouth do' fine. Better yet: 'I'm willing to risk it all to get even a taste of what he was packing in those pants' fine. I had been living in New York City for a few months and hadn't ran into a man this fine yet, and now here was a supermodel talking to me.

"She *was* beautiful," I replied, shooting a nervous smile his way. "She died a few months ago. Today's her birthday; she would've been celebrating her 50th. I had an entire party planned for her. It would've meant the world to me to have one last birthday with her."

His eyes filled with concern. "I'm sorry for your loss. You're not the only one mourning someone: I lost my fiancée a week ago. I find myself unable to stay home because everything there reminds me of her, so I've been staying here for the time being."

"Lucky you," I said, downing the rest of my drink. "I'm living with my sisters for the time being. The company is nice, but days like this all you want is to—"

"Be alone," he finished.

An awkward silence lapsed between the two of us. My handsome stranger ordered us both another drink. I sipped mine as daintily as I could, except the liquor was slowly creeping up on me, lowering my inhibitions. My heart was beating a mile a minute as his presence overtook me. Just from his aura I knew he commanded whatever room he set foot in the way he was currently commanding my heart.

"How about we be alone together?" The words tumbled from my lips before I could stop them. He just told me that his fiancée died days ago and here I am trying to fuck a kind of widower because he bought me a drink.

His eyes never left mine when he said to the bartender, "Charge the lady's meal to my room."

I finished my drink with haste, knowing I would need some more liquid courage to get me through. His glass of scotch was already finished. Like a gentleman, he helped me from my seat. His hand rested on my waist with a hint of possession as we made our way through the now packed bar and into the main lobby of Hotel

Elysée. He was greeted with smiles from the hotel staff on our way to the elevator. Nerves shot through my body as we rode up to his room in silence. I nearly leapt off of the elevator when the doors slid open on the top floor where the presidential suites were located.

We had barely cleared the threshold when his lips crashed against mine, sending shockwaves of pleasure through my body. I reacted instantly, my fingers grabbing at the buttons on his shirt as he hiked my dress up. My jacket and purse hit the white shag, joining the suit jacket he shed. His hands traced from the backs of my kneecaps to my thighs before reaching my ass, which he cupped, pressing me against his growing erection. I wrapped my legs around his waist, grinding against him in anticipation of what was to come. He propped me up against the foyer wall, peppering my neck with soft bites while I worked on unbuckling his pants.

"Fuck," he moaned as he entered me roughly, stretching my walls with the right amount of pleasure and pain.

I moaned in reply, gyrating my hips to match his tempo. Our lips explored each other's faces, biting cheeks, licking the curves of ears, and finally locking in a fevered frenzy. I clawed at my dress, begging to free my breasts straining against the semi sheer fabric. He obliged me, unzipping the dress and taking one of my taut nipples into his mouth, swirling his tongue around it and pinching the other. I clenched at the feeling of ecstasy, the feeling enough to push him over the edge. He bounced me up and down on his dick until he came, filling me with his seed. We collapsed on the floor in a heap.

"Stay the night?" he asked after some time.

I nodded.

We spent the rest of the night fucking in silence, with nothing but sounds of our bodies filling the air. I returned home with a smile on my face, the first one I had since my mother had passed away. Even Ivy noticed on my walk of shame upstairs. She let herself into my bedroom as I undressed to get some sleep.

"Someone smells like expensive body wash," she noted, taking a seat on the edge of the full-sized bed. "I see you took your little bougie ass uptown and met you a Wall Street type, huh? Must've been good to have you come in here walking funny."

My cheeks reddened at the accuracy of her statement. "It was nice."

"Don't downplay it; there's nothing wrong with getting some dick every now and again. Just make sure you don't get caught up in those sweet words niggas like to ply you with so they can have convenient pussy," she replied, tugging at the strap of my panties, making it snap against my skin.

"That won't happen in this case. I don't know his name."

Ivy looked more than pleased—she was impressed that I was able to get a nut without investing any feelings. "Little Quincy out here fucking niggas and leaving them? Reminds me of myself when I was your age except I already had a few bodies under my belt. We'll get you there though. Taking care of these Townsend Brothers will turn you into a different type of savage. You ready for that?"

With my mother's birthday behind me and one great night fueling me, I had no problem answering, "No doubt."

HASANI

"Hasani, why are you looking at me like that?" Gia asked without looking up from her textbook.

I snaked my arm around her waist and pulled her close, kissing on her stomach. "I can't look at my wife? Is that a crime now? Hmmm? Hmmm?" I asked, blowing into her stomach and giving it a playful bite.

Gia may play tough on the streets when she was handling business, but she was extremely ticklish, her stomach being one of her sensitive spots. She dissolved into a fit of giggles as I squeezed her sides, tickling her senseless. The bed shook from the tussle, with her books, glasses, and phone falling onto the floor. Once I felt her nails gliding down my arms I knew it was time to move because she was getting ready to hit one of my ticklish spots. No sooner had I thought it did she lock her legs around my torso and proceed to tickle the fuck out of my underarms. I tried wiggling free, but she was too strong. The only way to get her off of me was to fight dirty.

"Hasani," Gia yelped as I gave her pussy a squeeze.

That moment of surprise was enough to turn the tables. I flipped Gia onto her back and pressed my lips against hers before she could object. She responded by tugging my pajama bottoms down with her feet. I broke the kiss and hovered above her, marveling at how beautiful she was. *This is my wife,* I thought as I stroked her soft skin.

"What?" Gia asked.

"This entire situation with Lauren has me scared for you to leave my side. I don't know what I would do if I ever lost you," I said, more to myself than to her.

Gia leaned up and pecked me on the lips. "Is that why you've been withholding the D from me? I didn't know this situation traumatized you that bad."

The morning after my bachelor party, I woke up sprawled out in the car on our way to the castle. I asked Zeus if he knew who those strippers I went into the back with were, and to my complete shock, he had no idea what I was talking about. According to him, I was sprawled out on the sofa in the VIP section with a drink in my hand. Unable to tell whether the events were a figment of my imagination or not, I decided to play it safe and have a doctor set me up with a shot of antibiotics hours before the ceremony. Part of me wanted to come clean to Gia when she asked to have a word with me on the balcony, but I knew if I told her the truth she wouldn't believe me. Hell, I wouldn't believe me either. Lauren's death provided the perfect cover for me to secure a clean bill of health. I couldn't come up with any more excuses now; either I was going to give it to Gia or she was going to take it.

"Anything that would have me thinking of life without you is trauma is enough," I said, leaning down and planting another kiss on her lips, this time deeper.

Gia was hot and ready for me. She had been pressing her ass against me every night in the hopes that I would take it. I wanted to, believe me I did, but the thought of doing Gia the way Boyd did my mother was enough to quell those cravings.

"You need some motivation?" Gia asked, sliding down the bed and expertly placing the tip of my dick in her mouth.

I nearly collapsed on top of her at the feeling of her warm mouth sucking me off. Gia placed me on my back and got down to business, bobbing on my shit as she stroked it using the saliva that poured from her mouth. That shit drove me wild. I gave her three carats because I love her, but that fourth one was for the crazy shit she could do with her tongue. I was on the verge of busting a nut when my phone started going off.

"G-G-G-Gia," I said, sounding like the narrator of the Chia Pet commercial, "I gotta take that, baby. It might be an emergency."

Gia's response to my pleas to stop were met with her taking her thumb and kneading the skin right underneath my balls. She told me it was something called the perineum, and when I asked what that was she replied, "That's how I make you my bitch." She sure had me screaming like one as I came in her mouth. I lay there trembling, watching her as she swallowed every last drop. I married a fucking beast and maybe she should be worrying about something happening to me.

"Take your phone call and when I come back, you better be ready to return the favor," Gia replied, sliding out of bed like she ain't just snatch my soul.

I picked my phone up off the nightstand and saw that I had a few calls from an unknown number. Gia was in the bathroom singing to herself over the sound of running bathwater. *She must be drawing a bath,* I thought, thinking of Gia's favorite go-to when it came to setting the mood. We didn't have a romantic honeymoon due to Lauren's death, and she had to return to work after the funeral, so this was the only time we could have some fun with each other. I would handle this real quick and get back to my lady.

"Yo," I said, stepping into the privacy of my office.

"Damn, what type of greeting is that for your baby momma?" a slick voice asked.

I checked the bottom of my bedroom door to make sure Gia hadn't come looking for me. "Who the fuck is this?"

"I said it's your baby momma. Damn, nigga: I give you some of the best pussy you've ever had and you already forgot about me?"

"Listen, bitch. I don't know who the fuck you are, but stop playing on my motherfucking phone," I hissed into the phone. "I ain't fuck you or that bitch you was with."

My thumb was hovering over the end button when shorty had the nerve to clap back with, "That's not what these pictures say. I can send them right over to Gia and let her be the judge. Or you can stop playing games and have an adult conversation with me, Hasani."

"What do you want?"

"I want you."

"Name something else because that ain't happening."

She sighed. "All I want is for me and my child to be taken care of."

"You're not pregnant by me."

"That's not what this pregnancy test says. I'll even send it over as proof."

Seconds later, my phone received a message from the same number. I clicked on the picture and clear as day were pregnancy test results from Planned Parenthood. "You can't have this baby. If you have an abortion, I'll set you up with something nice, but I'm not raising a child with a bitch I don't even remember fucking."

"Mmmm...I'm not having the abortion until I get my first payment of $100,000."

"You want what?" I barked. "Nah, fuck outta here with that—"

"Like I said, I have no problem sending these pictures to Gia. Either you pay me and keep this charade going, or you look your wife of not even a month in the face and tell her that you got a stripper from your bachelor party pregnant. So which one will it be?"

I was in no place to bargain with this bitch and she knew it. "I'll call you with the details on when you can pick up your money."

"Don't keep me waiting too long. I might get an itchy finger and hit send if I even feel like you're playing me."

I hung up. Gia's voice traveled down the hall of our brand new three-story house. As much as I wanted our wedding day to be the happiest day of my life, moving Gia out of her apartment and into our home was a true celebration for me . Living in a house had its advantages, with the main one being that at night it talked to you. I could hear Gia's footsteps as she traveled down the hall calling out for me. I opened the door before she could knock.

"Is everything okay?" she asked, searching my eyes for the answer.

"I know there were some problems with the *primeros* beefing over territory..."

"Just some bullshit with these young niggas on the block. I'll handle it tomorrow, but for tonight I wanna get a taste of my baby," I replied, pulling her into my arms.

Gia stood on her tiptoes and tongued me down. I carried her back down the hall to our bedroom where we took a romantic bath and possibly made another little Townsend. As I lay there watching her sleep, I couldn't stop thinking of the irony of me being stressed over losing Gia to the game when I just might lose her to my foolish decisions.

~

I SPENT the entire night tossing and turning over this paternity situation. Gia woke me up three times to ask if I was alright, and each time I lied in her face. It was bad enough that I would be forced to spend the rest of my life lying to my wife over this situation, I didn't want to keep lying to her about the small stuff either. Sleep evaded me until nine in the morning, and I had slipped into a light slumber when I heard the screams.

"No," I whispered, drawing out the word as I thrashed around in bed.

The screams grew quiet, and just when I thought they were over, more shrill shouts traveled upstairs. Leave it to Gia's loud ass family to turn a bad night into an even worse morning. Yesterday, Gia mentioned her sister and cousins stopping by to look at the house so they could start decorating. I planned to be gone by eight, but this bullshit set back my sleep pattern. My phone started buzzing on the nightstand. Another set of screaming was motivation to hop out of bed and get out of here. I showered, dressed, and shaved in record time, halfway to the door when I was stopped by Gia.

"Hasani, where do you think you're going without greeting your wife?" Giada, Gia's pesky sister, said to my back. "Gia, I know you're not about to let him get away with that."

I turned in time to see Gia playfully cut her eyes at her sister. "He wasn't leaving, Giada. As the man of the house, Hasani likes to grab the mail first thing in the morning."

Gia knew damn well I was ducking out the door to avoid this hen house but was willing to cover for me in the name of love. That was another reason why I married her: it was rare to find that type of loyalty. I pressed Gia against the kitchen counter she was posted up against and gave her a kiss deep enough to carry her through the day. Nothing made my heart swell like turning around to find Giada and Gia's two annoying ass cousins, Martina and Iris, frowning up their faces in mild disgust.

"What are you getting into today?" Gia asked, wrapping her arms around my neck.

"I'mma go visit Zeus and make sure he's good. After that I'll see what's going on with these li'l niggas."

"And then you're coming home?"

I pecked her on the lips. "And then I'm coming home. See you ladies."

"Bye, Hasani," they replied back all stank.

I didn't mean to drag Zeus into my deception, but the longer I gave it thought, Zeus was probably the only person I knew that could get me out of this situation. Lauren's death had done a number on him, and I knew he might need some more emotional support no matter how much he claimed he was fine. I could see him now, sitting at home in the same pajamas, staring at pictures of her while drinking scotch straight from the bottle. Laden with breakfast and a pick-me-up basket of his favorite bougie ass chocolates, I let myself into his house.

"Zeus?" I shouted throughout the silent house.

I placed the items on the table in the foyer and made my way through each room in the house, searching for my brother. I finally heard something when I hit the second landing. *Somebody must be watching basketball,* I thought as I walked past the empty bedrooms to the final story of the Harlem brownstone. The television grew louder, almost deafening, as I approached Zeus' bedroom. I opened the door and instantly wished I hadn't. Sitting on a mountain of women's clothing was Zeus playing NBA 2K18.

"Fuck!" he shouted, throwing his remote control down in defeat.

"Fuck is right," I said, noticing that the clothing looked familiar. "Nigga, what the fuck are you doing sitting on a pile of Lauren's clothing playing a video game?"

"She's dead, Hasani. I don't think she'll give a fuck about me using her clothes as a cushion. I been playing this game for the past five hours and my ass started hurting. Turns out my bed is a piece of fucking shit, so I gotta get rid of that too. Without these clothes I don't think I would've made it to the next level."

I rubbed my eyes to make sure I wasn't hallucinating due to sleep deprivation. Not only was Zeus sitting on top of his dead fiancée's clothing, he was dressed in sweats and a wrinkled shirt. This was some *Twilight Zone* type shit, and I was considering calling for backup. Then again, I didn't want to share my infidelity with my other brothers just yet.

"Zeus, I need your help with something," I said, picking up one of Lauren's jackets and neatly folding it.

"Aight, talk to me," Zeus said without taking his eyes off of the game.

I gave him the complete rundown of my situation, making sure not to leave out a single detail. Zeus, who was a natural when it came to crisis control, stressed the importance of having every tidbit of information. Leaving out one detail could be the difference between having a situation handled or spiraling out of control. He listened without interrupting, and I thought he wasn't listening at all until he replied, "Call her and set up a meeting for today."

"Zeus, I don't have a hundred grand just lying around. I recently washed a load of money through the construction of my house. I could take it out the bank but I don't want to leave a paper trail."

"We're not taking it out the bank. I have the money. Set the meeting and let me worry about the rest," Zeus asserted. He glanced back at me to see what I was doing. "Are you folding this stuff up?"

"You think I'mma let you continue to disrespect Lauren's clothes like this? I know she was hiding a kid from you and everything, but I'm sure she had a good explanation for—"

Zeus climbed off of the bed and padded to the bathroom, tossing the remote into the closet on his way. "Hasani, make the call."

I guess fixing Zeus would have to wait because as of right now, I couldn't afford to piss off the one person who had the potential to get me out of this mess. I set up the meeting and spent the rest of my time folding Lauren's clothes. The messy pile was neatly packed away into garbage bags when Zeus emerged from the bathroom. He made a beeline for his closet, and minutes later, emerged dressed in a pair of slacks paired with a black cashmere shirt and cable knit sweater. In his hand was a small, black satchel. This was the Zeus I grew up with; I don't know who that other nigga was. My initial concerns ebbed on our way to the meeting. Zeus zoned out to his favorite old school playlist on the train ride and was the picture of calm when we approached the three-story brickhouse in the Rego Park section of Queens. Very few cars were parked on the street, which let us know this was a working-class neighborhood. No neighbors meant no problems. The door opened as we walked up the steps, revealing a familiar smug face.

"Nice baby mama," Zeus said, eyeing the tiny running shorts shorty had on with a white wife beater sans bra. "You sure know how to pick 'em."

I cut my eyes at him. "I ain't pick this bitch. If I didn't know any better, I'd say she drugged me."

"Glad to see you took me seriously and came through, Hasani. And you brought some company," she said, welcoming us into the silent house.

To be quite honest, I was expecting shorty to live in a trap house filled with all types of niggas, because it was obvious she was using me for a come up. Instead, I was alarmed to find that her house was normal. The living room was tastefully decorated with oversized sofas, a ceiling to floor bookcase, and smelled of lemon furniture polish. Zeus explored the room, perusing the books and eyeing the artwork while I got down to business.

"You got my money?"

"Are you going to tell me your name?" I countered, taking a seat on the arm of the sofa. "You think I'm gon' hand over a hundred grand to a stranger claiming to be pregnant by me without any solid proof? On the way here I picked up a test. If it's positive, we talk abortions. If not—"

"There is no if not, nigga. I'm not a liar. I'll take your stupid pregnancy test just to wipe that smug ass look off of your face. Hand it over." I tossed her the Duane Reade plastic bag containing a Clear Blue pregnancy test. "Ah, you got the good stuff. Wanna watch me piss on the stick too?"

"I might as well 'cause you obviously can't be trusted."

Zeus continued looking over the room, still silent. I thought I was doing him a solid by getting him out of the house, but I was starting to think I was wrong. His eyes were glazed over and I was pretty sure he was in his own world. A call to Savion and Quade was on the schedule once we handled this situation.

"I hope for your sake this test comes out positive..." I warned, posting up in the doorway and watching her shimmy down her shorts from between her ass cheeks.

"Kaia. My name is Kaia. I guess you need to know that since we're going to be tied to each other for a really long time."

Kaia followed the instructions to the tee, peeing on the stick, placing on the top, and setting a timer on her phone. I did the same for mine. *She doesn't appear to be nervous at the idea of the test coming up negative,* I thought as I watched her stare at her toes, wiggling them every now and again. This had to be the longest fifteen minutes of my life. Gia and I had a few pregnancy scares, but each time through our nerves there was a hint of excitement.

Beep! Beep! Beep!

Kaia picked up the pregnancy test, glanced at the results, and handed it over to me with a poker face. Positive. I looked from the digital results to the Cheshire grin on her face. The smile increased on our walk to the living room where Zeus sat waiting, his satchel at his feet. I took a seat beside him. Kaia plopped down where she was seated and made a "gimme my money" motion with her hand. Zeus looked over at me, waiting for my confirmation.

"She's pregnant, Zeus. Give her the money so she can set the appointment for this abortion," I said, rubbing my hand over my face.

Zeus chuckled at the request. "We ain't giving her shit."

"Zeus, give her the money—"

He silenced me with a look. "I'm not giving her anything. You think this is the first time she'll have her hand out to you? Nah, she'll have the abortion or she'll find herself floating along the Hudson."

"You think you can get rid of me that easily?" Kaia asked, shaking with silent laughter. "Nigga, you have absolutely no idea who the fuck I am and who my sisters are. The fear we bring through these streets. The trail of bodies we've left behind us. You think you can kill me and they'll let you get away with that shit? Ain't a chance in hell. Do it, go on and make my sister's motherfucking day. She'll like playing with a pretty nigga like you before she hits you with two to the chest."

"I'll make sure to have that bitch suck my dick the way you gon' suck this bullet."

Kaia's mouth opened to come back with a smart reply and swallowed two bullets from the end of Zeus' silenced Glock. Her head jerked back and she slumped over in her seat. Zeus placed the gun into his satchel, which was empty save for an extra pair of gloves and another gun.

"You were going to kill her regardless of whether the test was positive or not," I said, watching in disbelief as Zeus wiped imaginary sweat off his forehead with a handkerchief and tossed it into the satchel along with the gun. "Don't you think I should've known something that important?"

Zeus opened his mouth to reply when we heard a car pull up in the driveway. With a glance at each other, we booked it for the backdoor, dashing past a patch of fresh dirt. We jumped over the fence separating the yards and had barely cleared the neighbors house when we heard a faint scream. I was coughing and wheezing as I tried my best to keep up with Zeus, who was in perfect form as we grew closer to the train station. The train pulled into the station the second we hit the bottom row of stairs. I breathed a sigh of relief the second we boarded the empty car and took a seat.

"What the fuck is wrong with you?" I asked through gritted teeth. "You could've gotten us killed back there or worse. What if she wasn't alone in the house?"

"I spent the fifteen minutes the two of you were in the bathroom casing the place. There was nothing to worry about," Zeus replied as he pulled his AirPods from his jacket pocket and placed them in his ears.

My mouth flopped open and shut in disbelief. Not too long ago, it would be Zeus cautioning us against making any rash decisions that could have us end up in jail or worse. Now he was unhinged, acting irrational when he was the one we relied on to be the voice of reason. He was acting like...Quade, except much worse because for all of his shortcomings, Quade knew how to pick his battles. Zeus was lashing out at the world and if we didn't save him, we might be burying a brother for real this time. It was all I could think of on the way home, and had I been paying closer attention I would've noticed the change of energy in my house. The smell of steak pizzaiola wafted through the house.

"Damn, baby, what you—"

I stopped at the sight of Gia sitting at the kitchen sipping a glass of red wine as she stroked her chin with a Walther CPP. She used it to motion to the chair in front of her. "Have a seat, Hasani."

"Gia, you need to put down the motherfucking—"

"I SAID HAVE A SEAT HASANI!" Gia shouted at the top of her lungs and took a calm sip of wine like nothing happened.

I took a seat in the chair across from her. Placed on one of the plates we received as a wedding gift was a picture of me at my bachelor party with Kaia sucking my dick. When I didn't say anything, Gia picked up a spoonful of her food and replied, "Bon Appetite, motherfucker."

GIANNA

When Hasani cheated on me with Sade, part of me felt like it was my fault. I had spent so much time handling my arms business and med school that I let my relationship with him take a backseat. Even though I made him beg for my forgiveness, I knew I had to accept a small amount of blame for his infidelity, but this shit right here? Him fucking a stripper the night before we were supposed to be married? None of this was my fault.

"Gia, what are you over there looking at that has you so pissed?" Giada asked, craning her neck from the other side of the kitchen island to see what had changed my mood so drastically.

I looked up from the pictures of Hasani having a threesome with two strippers and played it off like my world wasn't crumbling around me. "Nothing. I'm supposed to be going back to work this week and they messed up my schedule by placing me on a rotation in clinical when I'm supposed to be in the emergency room. I'll take care of it later on. What were you saying?"

"I was saying that I might talk a lot of shit about Hasani, but I love the two of you together. You complete each other in a way I never would've imagined," Giada replied wistfully. "After that situation with that hoe I cancelled him and was ready for you to get back with Carmelo. I'm happy everything worked itself out."

"Me too."

I started focusing on making dinner, my mother's famous steak pizzaiola. My mother may have been black, but she mastered Italian cuisine to the point that my grandmother, an extremely conservative Italian woman, asked her to help with Sunday dinner from time to time. The day after I was engaged, I started taking lessons from both women and could cook soul food as well as Italian. Giada was still young—she was turning twenty-three next month—and eager to learn how to cook so she could snag her own husband before she turned twenty-five, which was fifty in Italian years. I looked out for her the same way my mom did for me: by teaching her a recipe every now and again. However, today I wasn't on my A game.

"Gia, don't lie to me. It's just the two of us now," she said in reference to our cousins that left an hour ago. "What's wrong? Work wouldn't have you this upset but a certain Townsend Brother would. Did Hasani do something?"

"No, he didn't. It was a message from Carmelo asking if he could see me again. I thought me pointing a gun at him during my wedding reception was enough to keep him away but I guess not," I half-lied.

"You did what?"

I spent the rest of the prep telling Giada the details on Carmelo's pop up. She listened intently, giving her input on how trash he was for trying to show up after I was a married woman, and I lived for it. While I wasn't discussing the issues I currently had on my mind, I was able to vent to my little sister, blow off some of the steam that would be shooting from my ears if she wasn't here.

"He fucked up when he cheated on a real one like you, Gia," Giada replied as she helped me set the table. "You're smart, beautiful, and independent with the right amount of traditional. Plus, you're a doctor. As your little sister and biggest advocator, I'm here to say that no man will ever be good enough for you, but I think Hasani will be the best."

All I could do was nod. "I think so too."

Giada glanced at her Apple Watch. "My girls are texting me to hit up this new club in the city. I'll see you tomorrow, Gia. We're going furniture shopping, right?"

"Yeah, I'll pick you up around ten."

Five minutes into chopping up a garden salad for dinner I noticed that Giada had taken her positive vibes with her. The more lettuce I chopped the angrier I became. I pictured Hasani fucking those bitches and then having the nerve to stand up in front of our families and profess his love to me. That was the lowest thing he could have possibly done. Nah, there was no way I was letting this slide. He was going to have to answer to me for his sins. I finished setting the table and printed out the pictures sent to me, placing them on a plate where his table setting was. I made myself a plate, poured a glass of wine, and patiently waited for my philandering husband to show up with his no-good ass. He showed up ten minutes later, creeping through the dark house with a goofy ass grin on his face. It dropped at the sight of my gun and disappeared when he laid eyes on the picture sitting on his plate. Yeah, nigga. You got a lot of explaining to do.

"Gia, you gotta let me explain—"

"You waited two weeks to have sex with me. Yes, I did the math, Hasani. Two weeks is more than enough time for whatever either one of those hoes gave you to clear out of your system. I'm a doctor, or did you forget that?"

Hasani ran a hand over his hair. "I didn't have sex with either one of those women—"

"HASANI THOSE FUCKING PICTURES TELL A COMPLETELY DIFFERENT STORY—"

"GIA DO YOU REALLY THINK I WOULD BE THAT FUCKING SLOPPY!" Hasani shouted over me, picking up the plate and tossing it against the wall.

I flinched at the sound of glass splattering all over the kitchen tile. Like a solar eclipse or blue moon, an angry Hasani was a rare sight. Known for being the more lighthearted one out of his brothers, Hasani's anger issues rivaled Quade's when he got started. He could be as mad as he wanted to, but I wasn't backing down.

"I think you got caught, and instead of owning up to it, you're deflecting like a bitch! There's no rationalizing you having a threesome the night before we took vows," I barked, slamming my gun on the table.

Hasani's eyes lingered on the gun for a second. "You think you bad because you got a burner? Either you gon' shoot me or listen to what the fuck I got to say."

I pulled the trigger, sending a bullet slicing right through Hasani's hair and into the wall right behind him. He glanced back at the hole in the wall behind him as he patted his hair and back at me.

"You got one minute to speak your peace. The next one won't miss, I promise you that," I said, finishing off my glass of wine and pouring another one.

"Gia, the night of my bachelor party I got fucked up off some Patrón. I'm sitting at the bar and a stripper approaches me. I ain't wanna go with her but I can't control myself because everything keeps going in and out of focus. She takes me to the back room where I feel everything go dark. Before I pass out she's sucking my dick real wild like while her friend records."

If he was telling the truth, then it sounded like he was drugged at some point during the interaction. No one at that party would be able to tell the difference because everyone was fucked up. Hasani could tell he was winning me over and decided to hit me with the next part of his story.

"Ask for the videos."

"The what?"

Hasani sighed. "If I really was having sex with two women at once, wouldn't it hurt more to send you a video instead of some pictures? They can't send you a video because I was passed out the whole time."

"I am going to text this number and ask for the video footage," I said slowly, pulling out my phone and doing exactly what I said. "Let these bitches send me a video of you doing anything other than being passed out and you will regret it..."

"They won't because after what I did to you with Sade, I promised myself to never do you wrong again." Hasani reached out for my hand, which I gave to him reluctantly. He gave it a gentle squeeze and kissed each finger, paying special attention to my wedding bands. "Also, there ain't no need to worry about that bitch because Zeus clipped her ass. Her people were probably the ones that sent you those pictures to make good on that blackmail scheme they had going."

"Blackmail?"

"Yes, blackmail. She was...she was pregnant. Whether or not it was by me we'll never know, but she was shaking me down for a big payout. Zeus nipped that shit in the bud," Hasani said, staring me in the eye. "Do you believe me?"

Sincerity shined in Hasani's eyes. Like anyone, he had his shortcomings, but Hasani had always been upfront with me. Even right now he laid everything on the line. Those pictures and his actions over the last two weeks should've have me calling my father to get that grave he had dug on our grounds ready, but my love for Hasani had me reply, "I believe you."

~

HASANI and I spent the rest of the night sleeping in the same bed, but in our own different worlds. I knew he was set up by whoever took those pictures and the main culprit was out of the picture, but that didn't stop me from shrinking away at his touch every time he tried to hold me. It was no surprise to me that I woke up in bed alone. The smell of eggs and bacon wafted past my nose. My stomach growled loudly, begging me to wake up and fill it with something after starving it last night. Sometime during the middle of the night, the few bites of steak pizzaiola I had came up with the full bottle of wine I demolished. A plate of greasy food would quell my aching stomach.

"Good morning, Gianna," Giada said with forced kindness as she plated me some scrambled eggs with bacon and two pancakes. "Judging by those bags under your eyes and the smell of throw up on your breath, I take it your romantic dinner didn't go too well? Did it have something to do with those pictures of Hasani fucking some hoes?"

I slapped my hand on my forehead. "Giada—"

"Gia, how could you look me dead in the eye and lie to me? I'm your sister! You don't ever have to worry about me judging you for anything."

"The pictures came through to my phone and I was in a state of shock. I didn't want you yelling in my ear encouraging me to make any rash decisions, okay? It's easy for someone unmarried to make snap decisions when they aren't invested in a relationship."

Giada dropped the plate on the table in front of me, sending eggs splashing down the front of my nightgown. "You've been married for five minutes and all of a sudden you've got more invested than me? I never thought in a million years you would become one of *those* married women, the ones that look down on everyone else because they have a ring on their finger."

"Giada, I didn't mean for it to come out like—"

"I don't give a fuck what you wanted it to come out like! You sound like all of our relatives that spent your entire wedding asking me when it was going to be my turn. I get that pressure from everyone and now I have to worry about my sister pulling the same shit? Fuck you, Gia."

Giada stormed off, cussing me out in Italian as she stormed down the hall. I followed behind her, tugging at her arm for her to hear me out. My apologies fell upon deaf ears as she grabbed the first jacket her hand touched, which happened to be mine. She swung the front door open and turned to face me, revealing a fresh coat of tears.

"I wouldn't have told you to leave him," Giada said, wiping at her tears. "Unlike you, I believe in fighting for love."

I never would've imagined that seconds later my sister would be fighting for her life. The sound of squealing tires filled the empty street, competing with the sound of spraying bullets. Giada bucked as they pierced her skin. I yanked her to the ground and dug in her purse for the .38 she kept on her person. I took off the safety as I raced from the house, popping off shots at the car speeding down the street. Each one missed, hitting the trees or a neighboring car. Knowing I wouldn't be able to catch them, I ran back to Giada, who was wheezing on the floor. I checked her body for bullets and saw that most were grazes, but two hit her, one puncturing her lung, the other somewhere in her back. I placed her on her side to get her air in her one good lung and grabbed my supplies from my coat closet. She was stabilized when the paramedics arrived.

"Giada, you gotta stay with me," I said, stroking her cheeks as we climbed into the ambulance. "I'm not letting anything happen to you, you hear me?"

Giada, who was staring around the ambulance in confusion, gave my hand a squeeze. That was all I needed to know everything was going to be okay.

Arriving at my job on the other side of the emergency call was a memory that would never leave me. The nurses I worked with did a double take at the sight of me standing in the waiting area in a bloody nightgown and Giada's jacket because she had mine on. Dried blood the color of rust covered my legs, turning them a dirty shade of red. I paced the emergency room making calls, some in Italian while others were in garbled English. The first person to arrive was Hasani. I leapt into his arms, breaking down after being strong for so long. I told him the same story I recounted to the police. Whereas they were confused, Hasani picked up on a point I wasn't able to because of the shock I was in.

"They thought she was you," he said after a minute. "They came looking for revenge for Kaia."

Why hadn't I thought of that? From our curly hair to our curvy figures, Giada and I were identical from behind. Her wearing my jacket made the situation even worse. "Well now they've got the mafia coming for them because I won't stand for this shit, and neither will my family. You might've started this, but I'm finishing it. Them bitches are dead on sight."

ZEUS

Every time I came home, I kept thinking something would be different. Some days I was looking for Lauren playing in the living room with Little Quade. Other days I could smell her whipping up some of her favorite Caribbean dishes. Most days I could smell her perfume in the air like she was here minutes before I showed up. Today that smell came from her clothes piled up on my bed. I stripped out of my clothes and laid on top of the pile, wiggling around until I was comfortable, and placed one of her T-Shirts over my face. I had been holding on to her clothes for longer than I should've, and Hasani walking in on me sitting on top of the pile helped me face the fact that I was holding on too tight. In an effort to not appear weak I played nonchalant, even cold, because I couldn't tell my brother I was holding on to my dead fiancée by spending time with her clothes. I guess I wouldn't have to because for the second time today I was caught in the act.

"Hasani told me to come and talk with you because you're acting a little...weird," Quade said, taking a seat at the edge of the bed.

I removed the shirt from my face long enough to gauge his expression. He was studying me, picking me apart so he could figure out which chord to strike. I knew that look because I gave it to him once upon a time. "Hasani's a crybaby. I did what I had to do to keep that bitch from talking, and I'd do it again if I had to. You would've done the same thing if you were in my shoes."

"You're right. I would have done the same thing, except being like me shouldn't be a goal for you." Quade fingered the edge of a jacket sitting on top of the pile. I could tell he was teetering between sitting with me in this room and being a million miles away. "You're my conscience, Zeus. I can't have my conscience running around doing wild shit."

"So you're the only one that gets to make irrational decisions? Quade, get the fuck out of my house."

Quade's eyes flashed with anger. "Zeus—"

"Don't 'Zeus' me. I said get the fuck out of my house." Shirts and jeans flew all over the place as I clamored out of bed to get a good look at Quade, who was on his feet the second I had moved. "How dare you come up in here and tell me how to deal with my grief because it's an inconvenience to you? I took care of your son for months, put my own life on the backburner for you and your wife, and you think you got the right to tell me I'm overreacting? I lost everything when Lauren died! EVERYTHING! She had a baby by me and I lost that too, so I'm fucking sorry if I don't have time to coddle you and Yara, but I'm currently trying to stay sane for myself since it's been made pretty clear that none of my brothers give a fuck about me!"

"You think me telling you to keep it together is me not giving a fuck about you?" Quade countered with a smile that didn't reach his eyes. "I'm telling you so you don't become me! When Mommy died I slept in her closet every night, smelling her clothes and stuff trying to remember her before she was a skeleton. You remember what you did right?"

"Quade—"

"You packed up all her shit and told me it was time to let go. I told you I let go, but I didn't. Nah, that would be too simple. I started popping pills and killing people to fill the void in my heart from her being gone. Something in me died and I became heartless. I don't want the same thing to happen to you."

I chuckled at his stupidity. "Quade, there has been something wrong with you since the day you were born. I used to think it might have something to do with the time I dropped you on your head. The reason why you started running around on a drug induced rage is because you have always been CRAZY! I am not weak like you. I've got my life under control and you need to focus on yours because I can't do that right now."

I never thought it would be possible to hurt Quade—he was a rock after all—but the look in his eyes told me I'd done just that. Everyone called him crazy or weird, but the second the words left my lips, he believed them. I had cut my brother deeper than I intended to as a way to push him and everyone else away for the sake of my sanity. He took the jab in stride, nodding his head on his way out of my bedroom.

"You know what the difference is between you and me?" he asked with his hand on the knob. "I know I'm crazy, which keeps me in check. You won't know until you're staring at yourself in the mirror trying to figure out what you've become."

The door slammed shut. I stood there, chest heaving, trying to figure out what my next move was. Quade disrupted whatever sleep I had planned for the night and the thought of spending another night with Lauren's clothes felt like too much. I called Hotel Elysée and reserved my favorite suite. Being there would help me get some rest, but it would do nothing for the attention I craved right now. We had agreed it would be a one night only kind of situation, but there was something about her touch that left me craving more. I stole her number from her phone while she slept and swore I would only use it when the time felt right. I called her, only to get her voicemail, which was her soft voice directing callers to leave an answer at the beep. She was probably a screener like myself. Not one to give up easily, I texted her the room number and left the rest up to fate. She arrived in the middle of my shower, wrapping her arms around my waist and kissing the planes of my back. My resolve weakened with each one until the barrier I kept up came crashing down. I fucked her up against the shower wall, taking out every ounce of frustration I had on her body. There wasn't an ounce of fight in her; if anything, it felt like she was punishing herself for something. I would've asked, should've asked at the pain shadowed in her eyes, except I didn't care. It's all about me for once.

All about me.

"WHY DID YOU CALL ME?"

I was sure that she had fallen asleep, especially after the way I tore her ass up. Somewhere around round four we made it to the bed and slipped into a light slumber. Or at least I did. I rolled over and found her propped up on her elbow, watching me with those doe eyes of hers. A pool of light from the living room slid through the cracked door, reminding me of what attracted me to her in the first place. The illuminated half was absolutely beautiful, showing off her high cheekbones, pert nose, pouty lips, and that cute little dimple in her chin. I reached out and ran my fingers along the side of her face, warming at the feeling of her silky, soft skin. She rubbed against them like a kitten in heat, her bottom lip trembling at my touch.

"Are you going to answer my question or not?" she breathed, backing out of my touch long enough to regain her composure. "I don't recall giving you my phone number."

"I stole it."

"Do you steal the phone number of all your one-night stands?"

"I haven't had one in a long time."

Her cheeks flushed with embarrassment. "I'm sorry, I didn't mean to—"

"There's no need to apologize." I laid on my back and stared up at the ceiling. "To answer your question…I called you because you're the only person that makes me feel normal. My brothers expect me to always be this rock and have everything under control when all I want is to be free. I spent the better part of my youth making sure they're good, and just when I thought it was my time it was snatched away from me. I don't think I'll ever find love again."

This time it was her turn to offer comfort. She stroked my cheek with those tiny hands of hers and said, "The only way you lose out on finding love is if you stop looking."

I didn't know how to respond to that, so I didn't, instead I focused on her. "Why did you come?"

"Excuse me?"

"You asked me why I called, now I want to know why you came."

She climbed out of bed and sashayed across the room to the dark corner her overnight bag was placed in. I admired the view from behind just as much as I did the front on her way back to the bed with a makeup bag in her hand. My heart skipped a beat at the sight of the bag; in my line of work I knew exactly what some women kept in their makeup bags. Fucking a cokehead was not on the menu. I was poised to kick her out when she pulled a freshly rolled blunt.

"Mind if I blaze one?" she asked, wiggling the blunt.

"Go ahead."

She perched the blunt between her two lips, flicked the rose gold lighter with her freshly manicured fingers, and took a deep pull. A plume of smoke passed her lips, creating a small cloud of smoke. She took another, this time creating smoke rings. She held the blunt out to me. I wasn't a big smoker—Savion smoked enough for all of us—but it wouldn't hurt to indulge. Like any unseasoned smoker, my first pull was hell. I damn near hacked up a lung as I coughed into my elbow.

"Had I known you didn't smoke much I would have at least given you a shot or something," she said, watching as I downed half a bottle of water. "Gimme the blunt before you hurt yourself. I don't need another body on my conscience."

I could tell she regretted the words the second they tumbled from her lips. The temperature in the room dropped ten degrees. Several explanations for what she said had came and left her lips. I could practically hear her brain whirring to come up with a plausible excuse. This time I took my time puffing on the blunt, allowing the smoke to seep into my lungs.

"Take a pull," I suggested, extending the blunt to her. "Relax. No judgment here."

The weed had the exact effect I hoped it had on her. A few pulls later she was able to get out a coherent sentence. "You asked me why I came to see you, and the reason is because I feel like I'm stuck in this hole. The more I try to pull myself out, the deeper it becomes. My sister is sucking the life out of me. Every time I think she can't become any worse, she proves me wrong."

"What happened today?"

She took another pull, longer this time around. "I think I killed someone. I tried not to, believe me I tried my best, but I think I took the life of an innocent human being. Each pull of the trigger, I prayed the bullets missed. I can't take having that kind of guilt weighing on my chest. All I could do at home was sit there and think 'how do people do this and still sleep at night?'"

"You find your own inner peace."

Her eyes found mine in the darkness. "What?"

"The only way you'll ever be able to sleep is if you learn to live with yourself and the decision you made. Whether it was for a good or bad reason, it happened. There's no undoing it, so you can accept it and move on or allow it to haunt you." I could feel the unasked question hanging in the air, keeping the smoke company. "You're not the only one to take a life today."

I expected her to run off, or at least grow uncomfortable at the fact that I didn't regret my kill today. My words had the opposite effect; her shoulders slackened, and I could see her let out a breath she was holding in. She passed the blunt back to me. I placed it in the ashtray and sat up in bed, staring at her as I considered my next move. While she might not have outright admitted it, I knew her reason for coming when I called had something to do with needing someone to tell her everything was going to be all right. I held my arms out to her and she leapt into them, dissolving into a fit of tears. If I was being real with myself, I would admit that was the reason why I called her too.

I WOKE up to an empty bed once again. Somewhere between pouring out pieces of our souls to each other, we still had no clue what each other's names were. I would like to save her under my phone as something else other than Cosmo, the drink she was sipping on when we met. Just when I was ready to charge it to the game did I spot a piece of paper on the pillow next to me. In neat, slanted handwriting was a letter addressed to me by name:

This time around I decided to do a little snooping around, Zeus. Last night was...different. A good kind of different. I don't know about you, but I'm kind of tired of crying every time I see you. Maybe we can meet under better circumstances the next time around. I certainly hope there is a next time. And since you don't seem too keen on asking, my name is Quincy.

Quincy. With such delicate features I would've never pictured her name being Quincy. Maybe Maxine, Janice, Ella, or even Jasmine. On second thought, there wasn't anything remotely bland about her, which made a unique choice like Quincy fitting. I wondered if she went by Quinn for short. Was she named after her father? Did she like having a male name? I guess we were due for a meeting under lighter circumstances. However, the thought of being out with another woman so soon after Lauren's death felt wrong. This was supposed to be strictly physical, nothing more, nothing less. I was so caught up in figuring out where I stood with Quincy when I noticed the same car from five blocks ago following me. Before I led with paranoia, I decided to take an alternative route home. Three lights and two avenues later the same car was following me.

"Shit," I muttered, making a sharp right and heading towards one of our warehouses.

The car continued tailing me the entire way. With each passing block I had to ask myself, how long has this car been following you? Could this have something to do with Kaia's murder? I would find out the second I got them right where I wanted them. Slowing to a stop as we approached the warehouse, I jumped from my car and ran up on the other car with my piece in hand. The window rolled down, revealing a nervous man. I reached inside of the car and opened his door with one hand while pointing my gun at him with the other.

"Who sent you?" I barked, pressing the barrel into his head.

He raised his hands in the air. "Listen, I don't want no problems—"

"'*I don't want no problems,*'" I mocked, yanking him out of the car and knocking him across the face with the grip of the Glock. "Motherfucker, what did you think you would get by following me? I'm not asking you a second time. Explain why the fuck you were tailing me before I put two bullets in your skull and my size 12 loafers up your ass. Speak!"

"I thought you would be the nicest of them all," dude spat, earning him another kick. He hit the side of his car with a thump and hit the pavement for a second time in a matter of seconds. This time he chose his words better, replying with forced politeness, "No one has me following you. I came looking for you myself."

Grabbing him by the collar, I pulled him to his feet and pressed him against his car. The early morning sunlight chose that moment to illuminate his eyes, turning them from dark brown to a bright hazel with flecks of pumpkinseed green. There was only one other person I knew in the world with those eyes.

"Who are you?" I asked although I already knew the answer.

"Grayson," he replied. "Grayson Townsend. Your brother."

QUINCY

Zeus. His name was Zeus.

Zeus Townsend.

I kept replaying his name on the ride home, the sound of it cancelling out my R&B playlist. *I wonder what kind of music Zeus likes to listen to,* I thought as I scrolled through the old school love songs. *He's older than me by at least ten years, which means his taste is more Jodeci than Jaquees.* Everything was old school about Zeus down to the way he fucked. I never had a man learn my body the way he did. We had only known each other for a short amount of time, but I felt a connection with him. What sucked was that my feelings were unrequited. I was falling for a man who lost his fiancée not even a month ago. All he was looking for was a fuck and a decent conversation. He said as much when he mentioned giving up on love. Maybe I could change his mind? Thoughts of Zeus put a smile on my face for the rest of the trip. It was wiped away at the sight of Ivy sitting on the stoop of our new place smoking a cigarette. Her hand was shaking so bad that embers flew in the air with each flick.

"Where you been?" she asked, taking a sip of coffee from the paper cup sitting beside her. Her red rimmed eyes stared up at me, boring straight into mine, which were red for a more lighthearted reason. "Answer me!"

"I was out with my friend. He invited me over to his place," I half-lied. I was sure Zeus lived somewhere as nice as Hotel Elysée, he just wasn't ready for me to know exactly where. "I would've told you but you were sleeping, and I didn't want to disturb you. That wasn't a problem, was it?"

Ivy took a pull of her cigarette. "No. Somebody around here should be smiling while our sister is rotting on a sidewalk until someone notices the stench."

Guilt curdled in my stomach at the thought of poor Kaia laid out on the couch missing the back of her head. What fucked us up the most was that her body was still warm, which meant we missed her killer by minutes. Ivy tore the house apart, searching every nook and cranny for the possible killer. Saidya dropped to her knees at the sight of our slain sister. A gut wrenching wail emitted from her, scaring the fuck out of me. Ivy returned from her search of the house with a murderous glint in her eyes. She told us she knew who was responsible for this, and they would pay the price for taking our sister. We placed Kaia's body into a suitcase, dumped her in a mess of garbage bags, and made a stop to the other side of Queens, where the houses were kept on manicured lawns and luxury cars filled each driveway. It was there that Ivy showed me a picture of a beautiful woman, handed me a gun, and told me to shoot the second she walked out the door. Who knew such simple directions would lead to chaos.

"Ivy, I'm sorry, I—"

"What are you sorry for? Kaia brought this all on herself by being fucking stupid. How hard was it to wait a couple months and then spring this baby on him? No, she had to run a play by herself and it cost her, her life." Ivy spoke the words with hate, but I could hear that tremble in her voice. She was hurting. Like magic, she pulled herself together with the help of another sip of coffee. "I hope you're well rested because tonight we're handling business."

"What kind of business?"

Ivy gave me a thorough once over, starting at the black Yves Saint

Laurent pumps I wore, up to the matching Norma Kamali dress hugging my curves, and stopping at the messy bun I wore my hair in. "The kind of business that requires you not looking like you've been getting it in every orifice all night. Put on some sweats and sneakers. We'll be waiting."

Saidya was sitting in the living room talking on the phone when I entered. She whispered into the receiver and hung up the second our eyes met. I wasn't sure what she was up to, but I didn't want to be involved when Ivy found out. Whether she was around or not, Ivy had a knack for reading people and picking up on any signs of disloyalty from a mile away. For that reason, I saved Zeus' number under my ex Marcus' name. If she came across my phone she wouldn't look twice at the correspondence. Checking my phone one last time, I turned it off and placed it into my nightstand. Ivy had banned us from taking any electronic devices with us anywhere except for burner phones. Fully dressed in a pair of cheap H&M sweats with a matching hoodie and some black on black Roshe's, I returned to find Saidya standing in the foyer talking to Ivy.

"We should've left her at the house," Saidya said, pointing upwards. "Ever since you took her in, everything's been fucked up. She fucked up with Lauren, she couldn't even manage to hit Gia, you really think she's going to be a success today? This isn't a simple job: one fuck up could have us all laid out."

"For that reason, I'm going to have her shadow this time around. Why are you so damn hard on her anyway? Jealous?"

Saidya frowned her face up like she smelled a healthy dose of shit. "Never that."

"Then what's the problem?"

"She has no idea." They both turned to see me standing at the foot of the stairs. "That's how hating ass bitches operate. They don't have anything to be mad about so they just stay mad. I frankly don't give a fuck."

Ivy jumped in front of Saidya before she could advance. "Quincy, I suggest that unless you're ready to throw hands you watch how you talk to people. I can fight your battles outside, but if Sai decides to drag your ass up and down this house I'm not getting in the middle of it."

"I don't need you to," I spat. "I am sick and tired of her shit. We're supposed to be a team, Ivy. How am I supposed to ride out with someone I can't trust to have my back?"

Saidya scoffed. "You think I can't say the same for you, little miss bougie? Coming in here with your designer clothes and college education like you're better than somebody? No matter how much you try to pretend, you're a bastard just like the rest of us!"

"I KNOW THAT! My mother knew it too, and instead of having me live that reality, she pushed me to do better. I won't allow you to make me feel bad about who I am and where I came from, because guess what? We're all in this together," I finished, worn out from this argument. "We ride together, we fight together, and we'll die together. Or did you take the wrong pledge?"

Ivy beamed with pride; my very first night here she made me take a pledge to ride with my sisters until the very end. Every opportunity I was given to show my loyalty failed, but no one was perfect.

"She's had plenty of chances to leave, but she hasn't," Ivy said after a minute. "We're connected by everything we do, down to the bodies we share. Let's not forget what the goal is here."

"I still don't know what the goal is," I replied.

Ivy tossed me a black ski mask. "You'll soon find out."

She walked out the front door without a backwards glance, leaving me and Saidya there to sort out our feelings. I didn't expect anything less than attitude from her as she shrugged into her jacket without taking her eyes off of me. Saidya waited until I was within earshot to say, "Don't let Ivy taking you under her wing have you thinking you're invincible. She won't always be around to protect you."

"Lucky for me I've been protecting myself my whole life."

The ride to our destination was spent in silence save for the radio playing on low. Saidya sat in the front with Ivy, who looked like she was in another world. Kaia's death had messed her up more than she cared to admit. Walking in and seeing her like that did a number on me as well. The real reason I came when Zeus called was because every time I tried closing my eyes to sleep, I would see her lying on the couch and it haunted me. Being in his arms was the temporary fix I needed. Too bad I didn't have enough courage to call him—or the deep pockets for a presidential suite. I was in the middle of replaying our night when we pulled up to a housing project in the industrial section of Brooklyn.

"Where are we?" Saidya asked, looking around the streets sprinkled with people posted up enjoying the summer night air.

"Red Hook."

Ivy was always careful—she never put us in a situation that could get us in trouble—but something about tonight felt different. With all these people around, how were we supposed to get in and out without any detection? I received my answer by a knock on the window. A man appeared at Ivy's window, puffing on a cigarette as he took in his surroundings. A thick plume of smoke entered the car as she rolled the window down.

"They're in the big building. Fifth floor. The back door will be open within the next five minutes. After that you're on your own," he said, reaching his hand into the window.

Ivy reached into one of the compartments and pulled out a thick wad of cash. She placed it into his hand with a, "We'll be in contact. Make sure you have everything set up on your side by the end of the night."

"You got it."

He disappeared with one more puff of smoke. Ivy popped open the glove compartment and doled out guns. I accepted the Glock she handed me along with an extra clip and placed it into my waistband. Saidya did the same, placing her gun in the arch of her back. Ivy placed her phone between the two of us, giving us a clear look at a picture of a group of men. The three center ones were circled with a red markup pen.

"The second you lay eyes on any three of these niggas, pop them and keep it moving because at the sound of that first shot you can expect an entire army to be on your ass. Saidya, I want you to the left of me, Quincy, I want you on the right as close to the door as possible.

Since you've got a white woman's voice, the second we hit our targets I want you to use this"—she handed me a brand new burner phone —"to report gunshots over at T park. No need to worry, those shots will happen. Everyone good on their roles?"

Saidya gave her back a pat. "Hell yeah, let's do this."

Somehow during the brief conversation we had, the entire block cleared. There wasn't a soul in sight on our walk to the fifteen-story building. As promised, the back door was opened with a bottle top pressed to the door magnet.

We pulled our masks on and started up the stairs at a steady pace, making sure to pause if we heard someone coming. I wasn't sure if it was chance or luck, but we hadn't ran into anyone on the trek. Ivy let us out on the fifth floor and led us down a long, winding hall to the last door on the right. Music blasted from the house, the noise deafening the closer we grew. She turned the knob and opened the door. Her profile lit up with a smile; paired with her beauty, Ivy's smile could disarm anyone faster than she physically could. Her gun was second. She pulled it from her waist and fired three shots into the house with a silenced Glock. Saidya and I hurried along at the beckoning of her hand.

"Quincy, shoot whoever walks through this door," Ivy ordered. "I don't give a fuck who it is, you kill them where they stand. You hear me?"

I posted up in the wall facing the door with my gun pointed at it. "Yes, ma'am."

Ivy and Saidya disappeared down the hall, entering rooms and firing off shots while I stood there with my gun pointed, ready for anything. A waving motion happened in my peripheral. I turned to see a man, one of the three in the picture, waving at me. Against my better judgment, I walked towards him, peeking in the hallway every so often to make sure Ivy couldn't see me. I could see his life leaving his eyes and knew I wouldn't have to worry about him identifying me. Pulling my mask off my face, I asked him what he wanted.

"My daughter," he said over the din. "Please let me send a message to my daughter."

I glanced back. Still no Ivy. Reaching into his pants pocket, I pulled out his iPhone X. "I'll make it a video. What's her name?" I asked as I placed the phone on video mode.

His reply was something with a "la" at the end of it. I recorded him speaking into the camera and sent it to Shayla, who had a princess crown next to her name. I finished placing it into his pocket and was halfway to my feet when a pair of hands dug into my scalp, lifting me to my feet and placing me eye to eye with an enraged Ivy.

"What—the fuck—are you doing?" she said through gritted teeth.

"Killing him!" I lied, pointing down at him. "He was trying to reach for his phone so I stopped him and was in the middle of turning it off when you came over here grabbing me by my hair."

Ivy glanced down at him. "If I check his phone, it's off?"

"Yes," I lied. "Go ahead and look, but that just shows how little faith you have in me. What the fuck happened to us being in this together?"

Ivy's hard eyes traveled back up to meet mine. "Let's get the fuck out of here."

The fresh night air soothed my trembling skin. I kept my head low on the jog back to the car. Shots fired in the distance send a jolt of panic through my body. Ivy slapped me on the arm as a reminder of my job. I called the police using the burner phone, dumped it into a trashcan, and hopped in the car. Saidya drove on the ride back home while Ivy relaxed in the passenger seat making phone calls. Her volume was up high, making it easier to listen in on the conversation she was having with the deep male voice on the other end.

"You made sure all them niggas is laid out, right?" he asked.

"I haven't missed a target yet. Sylvester cried and begged like a little bitch for us not to kill him. I hope the bitch you had sucking his dick ain't mean too much to you because she had to go too...It was your daughter's mother? Nigga, you cold," Ivy laughed. I could tell she sensed us being nosy and decided to cut the conversation short. "Be ready to make that deal, you hear me? I'll talk to you later."

Saidya stole a furtive glance in Ivy's direction. I'd rather her get a slap in the back of the neck for asking the question I was dying to hear. "What's next?"

"What the fuck do you mean 'what's next?'" Ivy countered. "Why can't you be more like Quincy? I'm sure she's sitting back there itching to ask what the next part of the plan is, but she hasn't. Why do you think that is?"

"I don't know..."

"Because she's smart enough to wait for orders, unlike you. Smart people always want to know the bigger picture, not what's next. Quincy, are you looking to know what's next or do you want to know what tonight was about?"

Saidya's hands clenched the steering wheel so tight that her knuckles turned white. I could feel the anger radiating off of her, but if I had to place their wraths side by side, Ivy's would always win out. "I would like to know how tonight configures into the ultimate goal we have," I answered honestly.

"You'll find out as soon as we get home."

The news left me reeling. Ivy was playing her plan close; as of right now we had been following her orders under nothing more than blind loyalty, and tonight was the night we would receive answers to the questions we had. Even Saidya couldn't stay mad too long at the thought of finally learning the plan. My theory was that Ivy wanted a hand at building her own empire; she had more than enough money to start thanks to the book bag filled with money she took from Lauren. It was the only reason that made sense for us to still be in New York when we could be lying on a beach in the Caribbean sunbathing while people brought us fruity drinks. I felt my spirits lift when Ivy confirmed my theory over dinner.

"Quincy, you might be too young and sheltered to remember this, but our father was one of the greatest drug dealers of his time. Boyd moved so much coke for the Columbians that they considered giving him a prestigious position in their cartel. If he was still alive today, he would be the connect for the East Coast. My mother wouldn't have died a crackwhore because she didn't have the money to keep food on the table. Saidya, your mother wouldn't be working all of those minimum wage jobs to keep her lights on. Quincy, your mother could've fought harder with the right treatments." Ivy gave this passionate speech in front of a corkboard. I couldn't lie; she knew how to captivate an audience, and in another world, she could've been a motivational speaker. "Tonight, we succeeded in getting back a piece of his territory that our father owned. It will be ran by a really good friend of mine, but we're bankrolling everything until it's time for us to claim our seats on the throne. This is an uphill battle we're fighting, and if we do it right, we will be the connects for all of the East Coast. The only thing standing in the way of our success is the Townsend Brothers."

"Townsend?" I piped up, thinking the world couldn't be this small. I thought Zeus' name looked familiar, but the trauma of watching Lauren die before my eyes erased the conversation prior to her demise. However, it was all coming back to me now as Ivy broke down her plan with visual aids.

Ivy flipped over the corkboard to reveal four covered squares. She removed the paper from the first one, revealing a handsome boy that had to be no older than 21. "This one right here is Quade Townsend. Don't let the baby face fool you; this motherfucker is lethal. He's paranoid by nature, which makes him our last target on the list. The next one is Hasani. Saidya, you should remember him because you were at his bachelor party where he fucked Kaia. She was going to add on to our cash flow until she started making boss moves on her own. Quincy, you shot his wife, Gia's, sister because both them mixed bitches look alike from the back," Ivy continued in an offhand manner. She pulled off the penultimate sheet, revealing yet another handsome man. "Savion Townsend. He's a family man. Him and his wife just had a baby. She's a distributor who is currently short on a partner since we killed Lauren. That baby is wearing her out and it's only a matter of time before she hires a nanny, a position that Saidya will apply for since she's got that gullible, trusting look. And now for the head of the snake—Zeus Townsend."

I nearly swallowed my tongue at the sight of the man I had been sleeping with pinned to a corkboard, staring at me with those mesmerizing eyes of his. This couldn't be happening. This was a really sick joke being played by Ivy. At least that's what I had to keep telling myself because there was no way any of this made sense.

"He's the oldest Townsend Brother, and although he shares the position of connect with his brothers, he's the real one in charge. No kids, dead fiancée, nothing for us to really use to get close to him because he isn't trusting by nature. That means we don't have to waste our time plotting on how to get to him. Without him, everything they've built crumbles to the ground and we take over."

Saidya tentatively raised her hand. "Is that the plan? To kill the Townsend Brothers?"

"Yup," Ivy replied, whipping out her handy switchblade and stabbing it into Zeus' face. "We're going to kill them and everything they hold dear, but for right now the goal is Zeus. We're going to kill Zeus Townsend."

HASANI

I laid in bed watching Gia pace back and forth, the mess of curls bouncing up and down with each revolution. A mix of Italian and English filled the room, with the only recognizable words being the names of guns. She had been on 100 since Giada got out of surgery early this morning. According to the doctors, most of her wounds were superficial, but there was some damage done to her left lung. As of right now, she had a tube inside of her chest removing excess air and blood that accumulated as she healed. The entire Luchesi family was waiting at the hospital for her to wake up. Gia broke down every time she laid eyes on her sister, forcing me to take her home for the night before she had to be admitted as well. We went to sleep and I woke to this sight.

"You found the car abandoned in Brooklyn? Have someone check the surveillance and street cameras to see if we can get a visual." She slowed to a stop. "What do you mean we lost someone in the traffic department? Money's not a factor here, Marco. I want to know who shot my sister by the end of the day!" Gia hung up her iPhone and threw it to the ground. She stopped in her tracks at the sight of me sitting there watching her. "I know; I'm supposed to be sleeping…"

"Then get ya ass back in bed," I said, flinging the blanket back. "You won't be any good to Giada on a few hours of sleep."

Gia dragged her feet on her way to the bed and begrudgingly climbed in, snuggling up under me. I closed my eyes, dozing off back to sleep, when Gia slapped me on the chest. "Hasani, you have to remember something from that night. Anything could help."

"I gave you the address—"

"My cousins checked the place out. They said there was nothing but a couple of bodies buried in the backyard. Probably the owners. You don't remember the name of the other woman that was with her?"

I closed my eyes in an effort to jog my memory. "I got nothing, Gia. If I knew, I would tell you. Now close your eyes and at least pretend to get some rest."

Gia relaxed in my arms the best she could. I knew she was going to lay here long enough for me to fall asleep and would be right back to pacing the second she heard me snoring. For that reason alone I locked my arms around her like she was a toddler. Knowing she wasn't going to break free, she sucked her teeth and settled in. Fifteen minutes later I heard her soft snores in my ear, tickling my neck. I was halfway asleep when I heard my phone vibrating on the dresser. Gia's snores stopped and she stiffened in my arms.

"Yo," I greeted Zeus.

"6-1-7."

I hung up and jumped out of bed like I had been electrocuted. I felt like I had since Zeus used the code for a level five emergency. Gia, who I had tossed when I jumped out of bed, sat up looking at me through a mess of curls.

"Where are you going?" she asked, sliding out of bed and following me into the closet. She posted up in the doorway and watched as I rummaged through boxes of clothes to find my sweats. "Hasani? Is someone hurt? I've heard of 9-1-1, but I've never heard of 6-1-7. If you're looking for sweats, check that box over there."

"It's"—I threw on a pair of black sweats, shrugged into the matching hoodie, and placed a lightweight vest over the outfit— "the day my mother died. We agreed from that day on that when you get the code 6-1-7 you come to the meetup spot with no questions asked."

Gia placed a hand over her chest. "Do you think one of your brothers—"

"I hope not."

Gia beckoned for me to follow her. We ended up in the basement, where she planned on starting her own private practice in a few years. Right now medical supplies were being brought in slowly, but by the end of next year Gia would have her very own state-of-the-art facility. Can you say tax write off? She stopped at a medical cabinet where she would keep all of her supplies. Or at least that's where I thought she was going with this. Gia popped the cabinet open, pressed a few buttons and the whole entire wall came out, revealing a small arms room. There was enough guns and ammo to take out a small town. Gia stepped into the room, went over to a small shelf filled with duffle bags, and proceeded to fill it with some of the best heat this side of the country had to offer.

"If this isn't enough, call me and I'll be on my way," she said, handing me the bag along with a kiss on the cheek.

I was halfway to the front door when I turned around to see Gia standing there watching me. "Gianna, promise me that you won't go anywhere."

"I can make you that promise but I think we both know it'll be a lie," Gia replied with a crooked smile. It faltered when it wasn't returned. "Hasani, you're not serious. You want me to sit in the fucking house while you go to war?"

"I don't want you out there running around with an unknown threat trying to kill you. For once in your life, I need you to follow simple directions."

Gia scoffed. "'Follow directions'? This isn't the 1950's, Hasani. You can't make me do a damn thing I don't want to. I'll walk out the house right behind you and handle business if I want."

"And by doing so you'll put a bunch of people's lives in danger all because you wanna prove a point! Gianna, I swore in front of our friends and family that I would love and protect you. I can't do that if you won't listen to me!"

"You mean obey!" Gia countered, stomping over to me with her fists balled up. "You want me to obey you like a faithful wife when you haven't been a faithful husband. That was always your shortcoming, Hasani. Wonderful man, but weak as fuck when it comes to some pussy."

I can't even lie—that shit hurt me. I had caused Gia more heartbreak over the course of our relationship than she deserved. Maybe I should've told her the truth on the balcony instead of hiding it from her like I hid everything else. "I knew you didn't believe me."

"Hasani, that's not what I was trying to—"

"Don't worry, you don't have to. I'm sure a divorce lawyer will be able to get you that independence you need. Ain't no need to have me holding you back any longer."

Gia clamped her hand around my arm. "Hasani, don't leave like this—"

"Let go of my arm, Gia. I gotta get to my brothers before they think something is wrong. You already know how family comes first."

Gia's grip on my arm loosened enough for me to break free and dip out before she started crying. I could only stomach the thought of leaving my wife behind if I didn't see the pain she was in. My phone lit up with apology after apology from Gia. I texted her back with the truth, that she shouldn't apologize for her feelings because they came from a valid place. No matter how far we came from that situation, Gia would always have a hint of suspicion after every kiss or touch we shared. There was no point in dragging this entire situation out.

It was time for us to move on.

~

THE SILENCE in the warehouse was so loud that my ears popped. I would've thought I was here alone if not for the three cars parked out front. *Why is everyone so quiet?* I thought as I walked deeper into the warehouse looking for any type of life. Even during times of emergency we'd still speak to each other. I guess the reason why was because even one sneeze would set off a hail of gunfire. Quade held a man in a headlock made awkward by the gun he pointed at his head. Zeus had his gun pointed at Quade like that wasn't our little brother and Savion had his gun trained on Zeus, ready to pull the trigger the second Zeus made the wrong move. I dropped my duffle in front of the group, rummaged through it, and came up with two AR-15s. Eight pairs of eyes widened at the sight of the rifles pointed at them.

"Somebody better tell me what the fuck is going on or else we're all dying!" I shouted, giving the rifles a little wiggle to let them know I was equally serious. "Zeus, why the fuck do you have a gun pointed at Quade's head?"

"Because he has a gun pointed at our brother's head," Zeus said without looking at me. To Quade, he added, "Quade, let go of him and put the fucking gun down!"

"Fuck you, nigga! I ain't doing shit. You walk up in here with some stranger claiming he's our brother and we're supposed to believe you? Ever since Lauren died you've been out of your fucking mind. Fuck you, fuck this nigga, and if you press your gun into my head any harder I'mma shoot him just because."

Savion adjusted the grip on his gun. "Zeus, if you remove your gun Quade will remove his gun. Right, Quade?"

"Don't believe him," Quade said with a shake of his head. "Instead of egg, you'll be wiping blood off your face. I'm not moving the gun from his head until someone gives me a valid explanation on why the fuck y'all got some stranger here claiming he's our brother."

Everyone started arguing at once, Zeus and Quade going in on each other while Savion tried to be the voice of reason. The man Quade held stared up at the group with fear in his eyes. I pointed the rifles in the air and fired off a barrage of shots. The arguing stopped, and I had their undivided attention again.

"He *is* our brother," I admitted.

The guns they had pointed on each other were now pointed on me. I pointed mine back, showing them I wasn't with the shits. They could be as mad as they wanted to but if I was dead, how would they hear the truth?

"A week after he ended up in jail, I got this call from Pops asking me to come to the prison to meet him," I started, reliving the moment my world was blown over a decade ago. "He gave me an account number, told me to take a set amount out every month, and write a check to Victoria Sheppard. I was to send it to the same address every month on the same date. No questions asked."

"Our father had an outside child and you never thought that might be something we needed to know?" Quade barked. He gave Grayson a rough shake. "How old are you?"

"He's twenty-eight," I said at the same time Grayson said, "Twenty-nine."

Quade's face turned to granite. "He's…the same age as me? Pops fucked around on Moms while she was pregnant with me? And you've been holding on to this how long?"

"She was pregnant?" Zeus said to no one in particular. Three pairs of eyes traveled to him. "I met her once. Pops was grooming me to take over for him, so he started taking me on runs. One was to a beauty salon. He left me in the car but I could see the two of them talking. Moms called his phone so I had to go in and give it to him. We spoke while he went outside to talk to her. She lined me up while he spoke on the phone. She was asking me all types of questions, most of them being if Pops was a good dad. I guess now I know why."

"He must not have been that good, using one of his kids to lie for him all these years. Then again, he chose right," Savion conceded.

I bristled at the remark. "What the fuck you tryna say, Savion?"

"He's saying that since you don't know how to be faithful it makes sense that you had no problem hiding Pops' bastard from us. It doesn't take a degree to figure that out," Quade answered through gritted teeth; Grayson fought back and ended up being choked by Quade even more. "You cheated on Gia the night before you got married! Yeah, Savion told me 'cause he knew if I found out I would've fucked you up."

"I didn't cheat on Gia! I was…I was drugged."

"Drugged or drunk?" Quade mocked. He let go of Grayson and shoved him at me. "Take your fucking brother who you obviously give a fuck about more than us!"

"Where are you getting this from? I'm sorry, but none of you are my fucking father! He asked me to do him a favor and I did it."

"How much money?" Quade asked, pointing menacingly at me. "How much money have you sent him over the course of his life?"

"You don't have to answer that," Zeus and Savion said, but I answered, "It was a quarter of a million in the account. I sent five grand a month."

"So when we lost everything because of Boyd you let this nigga and his mother eat good?"

"Quade," Zeus cut in warningly.

"Don't 'Quade' me, Zeus. Mommy died in the house alone and hurt! She started fucking Boyd to hurt Pops and look where it got her. The fact that you knew he hurt our mother and still did for them says a lot about you. You ain't even worth a bullet. I'm out of here," Quade said, placing his gun into his waistband and walking off.

His actions triggered a domino effect; we lowered our guns at the same time. Grayson crawled over to me and sat at my feet, chest heaving as he took in his first full gulps of air in five minutes. I took a step away from him in an effort to keep our association far and few.

"Why did you come looking for us anyway?" Zeus asked.

"My mother died a week ago. Heart attack. She was the last person alive in her family. No brothers, no aunts or uncles. Just her and her parents, who died when I was younger. I was going through a few photo albums and came across a few pictures of me and our father." Our father. The way he claimed ownership on my father had me sick to my stomach. "I always wanted to meet all of you but I was afraid of how you would receive me. You definitely didn't disappoint."

Savion let out a dry laugh that didn't reach his eyes. "Well, you got what you wanted: to meet your other brothers. Now you can get the fuck up outta here. We don't want anything to do with you."

"Savion," Zeus said warningly. "We can't abandon him. Remember how we were after losing Moms? Fucked up in the head, making reckless decisions. We need to take him in."

"Why? Why the fuck should we give him our grace? As far as I'm concerned, I have three brothers. Better yet, two-and-a-half considering that Hasani straddles the fence whenever it's convenient for him." The venom in Savion's voice was enough to make me cringe. Two weeks ago, we were playing checkers and now he couldn't even look me in the eye. "You can deal with this nigga, but I'm not. I'll catch you later, Zeus."

Zeus placed his gun inside of the shoulder holster he wore and walked over to us, his expression unreadable. He held out a hand to Grayson, who accepted it reluctantly. I knew if I had Zeus on my side it was only a matter of time before the other two came around. They could be mad all they want, but we all know if they were placed in the same position they would've kept the secret too. Or maybe they wouldn't have and that was the reason why Pops chose me. We would never find out the truth.

"You ran out of money?" Zeus asked, clapping Grayson on the back. "You need somewhere to stay? I have a reserved room at Hotel Elysée you can use until you get on your feet."

I knew that was Zeus' way of keeping a close eye on him until he could verify Grayson's story. The Assan Brothers brought out a whole new level of paranoia in all of us. Anyone stepping a foot into our inner circle had to be vetted better than the FBI did its agents. I knew he would check out; I had kept an eye on Grayson all of these years. He was a good guy: graduated from high school two years early, went to school for Sports Medicine and finished his residency last year. Overall, Grayson was the normal Townsend Brother.

"I appreciate the gesture, but you don't have to. I'm staying at a hotel in Brooklyn until I find an apartment. My reason for finding you guys has nothing to do with financial gain," Grayson asserted as he rubbed his throat. "However, I would appreciate a ride to my car."

Zeus' phone went off. His thumb hovered over the accept button. "I gotta take this call. Hasani, can you give him a ride?"

"No problem."

The ride back to Grayson's car was awkward. I had questions for him—with how well he knew our father being the main one—yet I didn't utter a word to him. I should've since we were going to be heavily acquainted being that I gave up two brothers for him.

"I appreciate what you did for me back there. You didn't have to go to bat for me like that. I'm sorry it meant causing this fallout with you and the rest of our brothers."

"Aren't you rather comfortable," I declared with a heavy dose of sarcasm. "I know you like to think of us as your second chance at having a family, but I can promise you that it ain't happening. Savion might come around after having a long talk with Zeus, but Quade? You'll never exist to him so please do us all a favor and keep that 'our' shit to yourself when in their presence."

Grayson sucked his teeth. "So I'm going to be punished for what our parents did? I didn't ask to be born a love child. You think I wanted to spend my childhood seeing my dad the day after major holidays? Having Thanksgiving dinner on Black Friday? Having to watch the kids in my neighborhood play with their toys on Christmas day while I had to wait for the next day? Everyone's pissed at me thinking I had it easy because of some child support when that wasn't the case. My mother was lonely as fuck. She really believed in her heart that our father was going to leave your mother to be with her. When he died she lost her mind. Literally. It triggered a sedentary case of schizophrenia."

"What?" I spent so much time researching Grayson that I never thought to look into his mother.

"She hid it well in the beginning, but I noticed her mental deterioration as time went on. Some days, she would sit in the living room window looking like a lost puppy. I'd ask her what she was looking for and her reply was that she was waiting...she was waiting for Zeus to come home. He'd already been dead a few years. I tried getting help for her, but she insisted that she didn't need it. That money you sent every month? She wasted it every time. Some months there was barely any food and sometimes we went without lights. I grew to resent her. I finished school early so I could get out of her house as soon as possible. I chose a full ride scholarship to Stanford and never looked back. I still kept in contact with her, making sure she was good. She sounded like she was getting better, taking her medicine and cleaning herself up. I really thought we were getting somewhere before she..."

I wasn't going to make him relive his mother's death. Not when I had just relived mine at the expense of my feelings. A switch in gears would help him right about now. "Did you know she was having heart problems?"

"She had high blood pressure. The thing is, with schizophrenia, once she gets to a level of paranoia where she won't eat food, she stops taking her medicine as well because she thinks someone's trying to poison her. It resulted in a heart attack. I came home the next day and found her on the floor, inches away from her phone." Grayson pinched the bridge of his nose. I could tell he was trying his hardest not to cry in front of me. "I will live with the regret of letting her die alone on a cold linoleum floor for the rest of my life. I came looking for you guys because I thought—"

"We might be able to relate."

Silence enveloped the car. A suppressed sob sounded from Grayson's throat, one I could tell he was trying his hardest to push down because once that dam came crashing down, that was it. I couldn't let him go home alone in this mental state. The rejection of our brothers left him in a dark place. My phone lit up with a message from Gia telling me that Giada was awake.

"Grayson, you mind if we make a stop real quick? My wife's sister was shot and she woke up. I want to make sure she's good," I said, hoping that bringing Grayson around Gia and her people might brighten him up a little.

Grayson agreed with a choked "sure," and we were off to the hospital. The entire Luchesi family was there as well as Gia's mother's family, the Donovans. I was man enough to put aside our argument from earlier for the sake of Giada, and embraced my wife, who was crying tears of joy. Grayson, who had pulled himself together in the hospital's parking lot, was introduced as my brother, which gained him an overload of attention. He was being passed from family member to family member, some asking him why he wasn't at the wedding while others wanted his entire life's history for one of the many single women in Gia's family. Gia used their infatuation with the newest Townsend addition to speak on our argument from earlier.

"I know we didn't leave off on the best terms earlier, but I appreciate you coming," Gia said, leaning her forehead on my chest. "Hasani, I'm sorry for earlier. I shouldn't have said those things to you."

I thought of my brothers spewing the same words at me in a fit of anger. Maybe the way Zeus got his business mind, Quade got his anger, and Savion received his bright spirit, I received my father's infidelity. "Don't apologize for the truth, Gia," I said, and proceeded to tell her what I planned to tell my brothers at a later date. "I have this problem where I'm loyal to myself before everyone else, which is a good thing, but it can't be that good when it's at the expense of the people I love. It's a curse more than it's been a gift. I need to work on finding a middle ground, one where I don't sacrifice myself for the sake of everyone and vice versa. I'mma make it happen."

Gia stood on her tip toes and kissed me on the lips. "Of course you will because you'll have me right by your side."

GIANNA

Giada was sitting up listening to our maternal grandmother, Etta, anoint her in prayers. Her hair was in a tangled mess, her creamy brown skin was flushed, and I could see the exhaustion in her eyes. Tears welled up each time I saw my sister lying in a bed that was meant for me. It could've been worse—she could be in a casket. Instead she was hooked up to machines providing her nutrients and aiding her breathing, a better fate any of us could've asked for considering the circumstances. Whatever issues Hasani and I had were left at the hospital door. He went from sullen to a bright ray of sunshine for Giada.

"Wassup, Gigi," he greeted her, using the nickname he gave her that she hated. Those once exhausted eyes narrowed and rolled. I laughed at the sight. "Looking real good. I remember this one time I was shot back when I was younger. It was a through and through. The recovery was long, I nearly gave up, but I had so many people rooting for me, like we are for you." He took her free hand into his. The action was subtle, but I saw her hand squeeze his. "I promise you that whoever did this is going to be handled. I might not be the best person when it comes to other stuff, but I keep every promise I make, even if I shouldn't. We're all praying for you, baby girl."

Part of his statement gave me pause. What promise did he keep that he shouldn't have? Did it have something to do with Grayson, who stood near the entrance trying not to intrude on what he felt was a personal moment? I pulled him into the hallway to find out.

"My brothers are pissed with me, Gia. Not normal pissed either," Hasani admitted, and the strong façade he put up for my sister came crumbling down. "I've known about Grayson for a long time. After my pops got sent to prison, I was the one who made sure he was financially taken care of. While my brothers and I had nothing I made sure he always had because that's what my father told me to do. We were corner boys looking for our next come up, trying to make ends meet, I was sending Grayson's mother five G's a month. In their eyes I betrayed them, and I can't even argue it because they're right. The same way I hid the truth from you because it benefitted me, I did the same to them."

"No, you didn't." I grabbed him by the front of his jacket and gave him a little shake to bring him back to reality. "In my family, what the boss says goes. Your loyalty is to your brothers, yes. But your father was the boss and you were obeying his last orders. He chose you for a reason, Hasani—"

"Because I'm a cheater like him. Somehow, I feel like he knew I would be the only one to handle this because I couldn't be faithful either."

I shook him again. "He chose you because he knew you could separate your feelings from what needs to be done. You didn't flinch at the request, did you?" I hadn't. I didn't ask any questions either. "Everyone is falling apart at the seams over this new brother and you haven't missed a beat. You never do. You keep moving, keep adapting, and that's why I fell in love with you. So stop with the self-doubt. Your brothers will go home and think about the situation you were placed in, and I promise you that no matter how much they didn't want to, they would do the same thing you did. They'll come around."

Hasani engulfed me in a bear-like hug. I could tell he needed to hear those words, that reassurance that everything was going to be okay. He had provided me with the same comfort over the past twenty-four hours. We were each other's rock, and I knew us breaking apart would make us crumble. Too bad this wasn't the only situation we would have to deal with. My phone started going off, interrupting the moment. It was Cash, and I thought she was calling to talk about the situation between the brothers. Instead, a song played on the other line, a war cry. U2's "Sunday, Bloody Sunday" pumped from my phone and into the silent hospital hallway.

"And the battle's just begun
There's many lost, but tell me who has won
The trench is dug within our hearts
And mothers, children, brothers, sisters
Torn apart."

We were at war.

And just like that, shit started changing.

~

IN THE MIDST OF TRAUMA, betrayal, and healing, someone came through like a thief in the night and took out Sylvester Parks along with his entire team. The house was filled with at least fifteen men, each killed with a single bullet to the head or chest. Word on the street is that it was Toussaint, the Haitian that runs shit over in Queens. The two gang leaders had been beefing ever since Sly started gaining traction and amassing more territory, territory that happened to border Toussaint's. According to Cash, she had a sit down with the leaders days after Lauren's death and they agreed to a set boundary.

"We shook hands and they gave me their word that whatever beef they had was squashed," Cash said, running a hand through her mane of curls. "I can't believe this shit. I've never known Toussaint not to be a man of his word. Sly came a long way from where he was three years ago. The idea of him risking it all doesn't make sense to me."

"Have you spoken to Toussaint? This could be someone else," I suggested, running my fingers along the crate of AK47's that were fresh from my Bronx warehouse.

The second I got word from Cash that a war was brewing, Hasani and I went our separate ways. He went to meet up with his brothers to discuss their next steps while I put together an arsenal large enough to take out a small city. I had found Cash sitting in her warehouse puffing on a blunt while her lieutenant, Joel, stood to the side, texting on his phone at rapid speed. My first thought was how Lauren's death caused a ripple in the way the two worked. Cash never said it, but Lauren's death shook her in a way she might never recover from. The light in her eyes had dimmed, and, at the rate she was going, her time in the game would soon come to a close.

"Who else would've had knowledge of their beef? Nobody," Cash conceded, accepting he blunt Joel held out to her. She had it halfway to her lips when she said to me, "Please don't tell Savion I was out here sharing a blunt with another man. It would be nice to share one with him, but he quit for Chenille. He wants me to do the same except it's hard to give away your Zen when you're taking care of a baby all day."

I held up my right hand to God. "Your secret is safe with me."

Cash took a deep pull of the blunt and let out a steady stream of smoke. "I'm praying to God that I don't have to make this call, Gia. We've had peace for a long time. I already know Sly's people are gonna be on the offense. Toussaint has to be taught what it means to go against my word."

"Cash, I think you're going about this the wrong way," Joel said after a minute of contemplation. "If Lauren was here—"

"'If Lauren was here'? Lauren is dead and she ain't coming back! So excuse me if I don't want to listen to what you think Lauren might have wanted to do!" Cash screamed at the top of her lungs, her voice bouncing off the walls of the warehouse. "I have been holding this shit together the best I can by myself and I think I've been doing a good job. I can't rely on the word of my dead partner, but I can rely on myself."

Everything in the change of Joel's demeanor said he wanted to clap back on her, but for the sake of keeping his job and life, he kept his comments to himself. I, on the other hand, could speak to Cash businesswoman-to-businesswoman. She puffed on the blunt with shaky fingers.

"Cash, you have to consider both sides of the chessboard. What if this wasn't Toussaint? What if this was someone who wanted Sly's territory? It could be a takeover," I said to Cash, who was staring off into space at this point. "I'm not telling you how to make this call, but what I will say is there was a reason why you and Lauren worked so well together: you kept each other in check. With her gone, who keeps you in check?"

Cash ashed the blunt and said to Joel, "What would you do, Joel?"

"Wait for them to find you."

"Whoever took over will need product. They could have their own connect, but even if they do, it won't be hard to find out who." I could see the wheels spinning in Cash's head. She was finding her footing even though it took her a little time to get there. "Toussaint wouldn't pull some shit like this and risk me cutting him off."

My phone went off in my pocket. It was a message from one of my police connects. The second Cash called, I set up a line between me and everyone involved in handling the case with Sylvester and his men. Cash and Joel watched as my face when from neutral to shocked. I tried to play it off, but there was no fooling either one of them. Cash was the first one to speak up when I got off the phone.

"Gia," Cash said slowly, "what happened? Is it about the shooting?"

I replied with a stiff nod, still digesting the information. "There was a survivor from the shooting. One man. He hasn't told the police much, but he said three women were responsible for the hit."

"Didn't some women hit Sly and Toussaint?" Joel questioned, looking to Cash for confirmation, which she gave with a curt nod of her head.

"Both of you were right. It's not Toussaint. Do you know how long it took him to trust me enough to buy from me? He's not sending women to handle a hit for him." She climbed off the table and walked over to me, taking the phone out of my shaking hand. "Gia, what's wrong? Did he tell you anything else?"

"Giada. The car. When Giada was shot it was by a woman. I saw their profiles in the rearview mirror. It's the same women. Cash, now you're looking like you know something I don't."

Cash looked me in the eye and said, "The last time funny shit started happening, who was behind it?"

"The Assan Brothers."

"Who was found with Lauren?"

"The last Assan Brother."

"You sure them niggas ain't got no sisters?" Our heads snapped to Joel so fast they cracked. "I mean we know Boyd had sons. Did he have any daughters?"

Cash pulled out her phone and got to business. "We don't know, but we're about to find out."

I received a text telling me where the lone survivor was. Fortunately for me, it was the hospital Giada was recovering, the same hospital where I worked and could make myself his attending physician. "Damn right. Assan Brothers, Sisters, Cousins or whoever-the-fuck-else. We're coming for them. The funny part is that they didn't fuck up by making a mistake. Their fuck up was by making no mistakes. I'mma correct that shit though. These bitches want some static, wait until they see my Beretta's cling game."

ZEUS

My head sat between my knees, sending the blood that pumped feverishly through my veins to my head. I had been sitting in this position since I arrived hours ago when I got the call from my goddaughter concerning the news about her father, who was currently laid up in a hospital bed pulling through after an eight-hour long surgery. Shayla was on the couch behind me slumbering peacefully. She was an emotional wreck when I arrived at the Bed Stuy apartment she shared with her father and my close friend, Sean. I hadn't seen them since Lauren's funeral. Sean was the only person that gave me the space I needed to heal; he lost his wife a few years ago to cancer. The bills had eaten up their nest egg, leaving him with a pile of debt and an empty nest egg. I offered him a position at one of the many businesses we owned around the city, but Sean needed fast money to dig himself out of the financial hole he was in. I wouldn't have my friend, who was pushing forty, on the corner. Instead, I gave him a position as a lieutenant for Sylvester, who inherited the Red Hook territory from us when took over as connects. As I sat here watching him, heavily bandaged and breathing with the help of machines, I felt guilt plague me. I was the one that got him caught up in the middle of this mess.

"Zeus, is my dad going to die?"

Sometime during my deep thoughts, Shayla pulled up a chair beside me. She was a cute kid, no older than sixteen with Sean's dark skin and doe eyes paired perfectly with her mother's kinky, curly hair and heart shaped face. I wish Kyla was here to see how beautiful of a young woman her daughter had grown into. Fucking around with me, Shayla was going to end up an orphan if Sean didn't pull through.

"Not if I can help it," I said, slinging an arm around her shoulder and pulling her close. She still shook with residual sobs from crying so hard. Her tears varied from sadness at the mention of a video Sean sent her to relief when the doctor said he pulled through. I was the only family she had here in the city and it was my job to keep her calm. "Shayla, what did you tell the police about the video your father sent you?"

"I didn't tell them anything. He said if anything ever happened to him that you would handle it. That's why I showed you the video," Shayla replied.

Sean had raised a smart one. Shayla grew up in the suburbs of Florida and never stepped foot in the hood, but she adapted to her new surroundings quickly. It was a reminder of how suffering a loss builds a bond between family that nothing can shake. That bond was formed between me and my brothers after we lost our second parent. I thought Shayla was a great kid, but I didn't want her childhood ruined by having to create that bond with a man as broken as I was. She needed Sean more than anything.

"You wiped your father's phone, right?"

She nodded. "Right after I received the video."

"Good girl." I gave her a gentle squeeze. "You want anything from the vending machines? A soda or some tea?"

"A cup of tea would be nice. My throat's pretty dry," Shayla said as if it were an afterthought.

"One cup of tea coming right up. You keep watch over your dad and let me know if anything changes, alright?"

I had several missed calls from Savion, who was the only person I was on speaking terms with as of right now. I texted him with an update on Sean's condition and promised to keep him posted. Against my better judgment, I called Quincy to see what was happening with her. We were supposed to be nothing more than fuck buddies but something changed between us from our last encounter. I needed someone to confide in, if only for a few minutes, before I went back to being the rock Shayla was leaning on. She picked up on the first ring sounding like I caught her in the middle of a deep sleep.

"I didn't mean to wake you up," I apologized, stealing a glance at my watch. It was going on five in the morning.

Quincy let out something between a grunt and a yawn. "You're fine. You wouldn't call at this time unless it was for a really good reason."

"It is. I'm at the hospital right now. A friend of mine was shot yesterday. I'm here taking care of his daughter, my goddaughter. I'm scared, Quincy. I keep reassuring her that he's going to wake up, but if he doesn't..." I boarded the elevator and pressed the lobby button. "For the first time in a real long time, I have no idea what I'm doing. My life has been spiraling out of control and now I'm adding another human being I'm responsible for."

"I'm so sorry to hear that." A pregnant pause followed her statement. "When was the last time you prayed?"

"Excuse me?"

"When was the last time you said a prayer, Zeus?"

The doors sprang open in welcome. I stepped off and into the lobby, which was bustling with first shift employees. Quincy's question still hung in the air. "I don't know," was all I could say because in reality, I couldn't think of the last time I spoke to God.

"How about we pray?"

I was tempted to tell her that no amount of prayer could fix the fucked up situations I found myself in, but after all, I was the one that reached out to her in the first place. Taking a steadying breath, I made a beeline for the chapel. The pews were empty save for the lingering prayers left behind occupying seats here and there. I stood in the middle of the church, immobile, unable to drop to my knees in submission.

"I don't know what to say, Quincy. I shouldn't have even come in here…"

I had turned around and was halfway to the door when her words stopped me in my tracks.

"That is the beautiful part of faith: you don't have to be perfect. You don't have to know the right words to say. You came seeking guidance. God doesn't expect you to have all the answers. What he does want is for you to accept him into your heart and allow him to lead you on the path he has made for you."

"What if I don't know what that path is?"

The saddest laugh escaped Quincy's lips. "I lost my path recently. I have spent some nights worried that I'll stray so far off of it that I'll never be able to return to it. Tonight, after weeks of not praying, I finally spoke to God. I broke down and had a conversation I desperately needed to have and the weight that's been on my shoulders has been lifted. All you have to do is let him in and he'll take care of the rest."

I walked back to the altar and, with the help of Quincy's reassuring words, dropped to my knees. A wave of emotion nearly knocked me over. Feelings I had suppressed, thoughts I had given away, and unshed tears I fought back everyday overcame me. Now I remembered the last time I prayed. My mother was on her deathbed and I prayed to God for a miracle, something that would save her from the fate Boyd had dealt her. Those prayers went unanswered and I never allowed myself to be controlled by religion ever again. However, tonight felt different. I let God in and felt like a better man for it. I wasn't expecting anything to be quite honest, but when Shayla shook me awake to tell me that her father was awake I was in a state of shock. Sean's recovery wasn't the only thing I prayed for this morning. Someone to help me heal the hole that Lauren left in my heart was on the list, and after today, I had a feeling Quincy was the one.

QUINCY

I woke the next morning to swollen eyes and tear-soaked pillows. Praying with Zeus reminded me that I was the reason for his pain and heartbreak. Did I pull the trigger to the gun that killed Lauren in cold blood? No, but I pledged my loyalty to the person who did. Ivy left me in a fucked up predicament when it came to my situation with Zeus. Seeing his face on that corkboard and hearing Ivy state without a tremble in her voice that we were going to kill the man I was falling in love with broke me. Everything I was involved in since arriving to New York had ruined his life. Was I supposed to be the consolation prize? I spent the entire night and day praying for some type of solution that would give Zeus the peace he deserved.

"You could come clean to him," I said to myself in the privacy of the shower, the only place I could voice my thoughts without being overheard. "No, if you come clean he'll kill you. Shit, I would kill me too. Fuck, there's gotta be some way to fix this."

Maybe if I stopped thinking of a way where Zeus and I ended up together I would end up closer to a solution. My heart was making it impossible to make sound choices. Staring at myself in the mirror, I said to myself, "You and him will never be together. He will never love you no matter how much you want him to. The most important thing right now is saving him because it's the least you can do."

The apartment was quiet, which was strange considering that Ivy was an early bird. It was going on noon and she hadn't made her typical rounds. I took my time getting dressed—a luxury I wasn't given unless I was going to see Zeus—and didn't emerge from my room until I looked perfect. I styled my hair in a high bun, applied my favorite Chanel makeup, and put on a cute New York and Company jumpsuit from Gabrielle Union's collection. The emerald green was stunning against my lightly tanned skin. I was on my way to the kitchen when I heard a piece of the conversation coming from Saidya's bedroom.

"Babe, like I'm so tired of her shit. Ivy thinks she can talk to everyone however she pleases, and we're supposed to take that shit because she's her. Like, bitch, you ain't the only one with a mouth." I would love a front row seat to that show. Saidya was throwing a lot of shots at our sister and if confronted would hide her hand. "She's been like this since we were younger, thinking that everything has to go her way. I went along because Kaia would, but with her gone I'm ready to break out and get away from Ivy."

"What's holding you here?" I heard a male voice ask.

"Money. I don't have any. Ivy controls our finances. Everyone gets a weekly allowance and if we need anything between then there's a jar kept in the kitchen. At the most there's like a grand in there, which ain't enough to do shit. What I need to do is get my hands on the million dollars she has hidden somewhere."

I heard the bed squeak as the mystery man sat up. "Shorty got a million dollars hidden in this house and we just sitting here? Didn't you say she went to handle some business? How much longer do we have before she gets back? We can have this apartment searched in an hour tops."

"Ivy tells us one time and will return hours earlier or later. We can't go looking around anyway because my other sister is here. I don't fuck with her like that either. That bitch can't seem to get shit right, but Ivy's always sticking up for her." Saidya sucked her teeth.

"Half the shit Quincy does would've had any one of us six-feet under. If I didn't know any better I'd think she was saving her to be the fall guy in the event that all of this goes south."

"Stop stressing yourself over what your sisters are doing. You're better than them, Sai. You need to start believing it, you hear me? Now, about this money..."

"Rome, I don't wanna talk about the money anymore. The only way we would ever get to it was if we tied Ivy up and made her tell us where it was. Even then I don't see her giving it up. Ivy's a rock. I don't even think she gets dicked down on the regular. Actually, I wouldn't be surprised if she was into women. I've never seen her with a nigga."

Loud sounds of lips sucking on skin filled the bedroom. "Sounds like she might need some D to loosen her up. I could solve that problem if you don't mind sharing. You know, just to get whatever information we need from her..."

"I don't share," Saidya moaned.

The conversation about Ivy died at the sound of grunts and moans. I tip toed down the hall to the kitchen, where I made myself a turkey sandwich with all the fixings and a large glass of Pepsi. I wasn't a huge fan of soft drinks but today I had to have something fizzy. I was polishing off the last bit of my sandwich and a plate of onion and garlic potato chips when Saidya and her boyfriend emerged from her bedroom. She stopped short at the sight of me, and I could tell that she was wondering if I overheard her conversation. Not one to give away anything, I continued munching on my chips, only acknowledging the pair when they grew closer. The sexy voice was fitting for Rome, who was as fine and chocolate as he wanted to be. Saidya made sure to keep her eyes on me as if I was the one ogling her man and not the other way around.

"Hey," Rome said, waving at me. "You must be Quincy. Saidya's told me a lot about you."

I snorted. "Nothing good I'm sure. It's nice to meet you..."

"Rome."

"Nice to meet you, Rome," I said to his retreating back.

Saidya nearly pulled his arm out the socket in an attempt to keep me from engaging in any conversation with him. I continued eating my food and ignoring her silly ass. She made sure to loudly proclaim her love for him. Too bad I could barely hear it over munching on these chips. Speaking of, I couldn't get enough of them. I poured myself another plate and grabbed the onion dip from the fridge. Saidya eyed the combo with mild disgust but didn't say anything as she made herself a sandwich.

"Your boyfriend seems nice," I said in a weak effort to make conversation. "How long have the two of you been dating?"

"First off: he's not my boyfriend. You already know Ivy doesn't allow us to create any type of attachments unless it's for her"—Saidya stopped short, regretting her choice of pronoun—"*our* gain. Second: we've been seeing each other for a couple of months. I met him at a bar in the city and we hit it off."

"Do you want to be more?"

Saidya was in a good mood after that thorough dick down Rome had given her because she opened up more in the last five minutes than she had since we met. "Yes, I'd like more with him. This isn't the life I wanted for myself. You're not the only one with dreams and shit. I wanna meet a nice nigga and settle down one day."

"Nothing is stopping you. I'm sure when we're done with this whole situation Ivy would be more than willing to let you go off and do your own thing. Have you considered talking to her about it? Ivy's logical; if you come to her with a plan she's more likely to hear you out. Give it some thought."

Saidya took a bite of her sandwich, mulling over my idea. "Maybe. Don't think just because we're sitting here talking that we're friends or something."

"Why would I think something crazy like that?"

The front door swung open and in walked Ivy laden with shopping bags. For someone that spent most of their time in nondescript clothing, it felt strange to see Ivy holding bags from Bloomingdale's, Barney's, Neiman's, and more of the best stores that Fifth Avenue had to offer. Saidya eyed the bags with a hint of jealousy. How Ivy never picked up on her jealousy was a mystery to me. She reeked it at times. I retched at the thought.

"You good?" Ivy asked, dumping her bags by the couch and coming over to where we sat. "Looking a little green, Quincy. I hope all that fucking you've been doing involves condoms because at this point in the game we can't afford a baby."

I laughed at the thought of being pregnant by a man I barely knew. I gave my thigh a tap. "I'm on the patch. My mother put the fear of God in me when it came to making a baby out of wedlock. I can promise you she would resurrect herself from the grave and give me a down home ass whupping if I came up pregnant."

Saidya scoffed. "You? Ass whupping? You seem like more of the 'time out' type."

"Time out? My mother whipped my ass so many times I became immune to it. I got hit with shoes, belts, extension cords, pulled my own switches from the backyard, and when none of that worked she called Daddy."

Ivy let out a low whistle. "You got an ass whupping from Daddy and lived to tell about it? I got one once when I was like fourteen for wearing a miniskirt to school. He tore my legs up. I didn't wear skirts for two years because of the scars. What the fuck did he do to you?"

I held up my hand and showed them the hard scar tissue on my right palm. "I stole my mother's rent money when I was in junior high. Spent it all on clothes and shit trying to impress some boy. He burned the fuck out of my hand, placed it on the kitchen table, and hit it with a mallet. Told me where he came from they did worse to thieves. Broke my hand in five places then gave me an uppercut just to make sure I got the message. After that, my mother only called him when she really couldn't get a handle on me."

"Damn, maybe I misjudged you," Saidya decided.

Ivy grabbed a seat next to her. "You think I would have someone around us that I didn't fully trust? I told you Quincy is one of us, just with different packaging." She grabbed a chip from my plate and munched on it thoughtfully. "Have either of you seen the news?"

"I've been in bed sleeping all day," Saidya said with the right amount of innocence. "They don't have any leads on the shooting, do they?"

"Worse. One of those niggas lived. His condition is unknown, but if he wakes up..."

"We're screwed," we all said at the same time.

Ivy slammed her hand on the table. "I've already got someone working on finding out where he is. Once I get that information I'll be sure to handle him personally. What I need from the two of you is to be ready tonight to head out. We're handling a loose end tonight."

"The guy you paid?" I could see from Ivy's standpoint why he would have to go; if word got back that he had anything to do with it, we'd be sold out with the quickness.

"If he could sell his friends out for their territory, he'll sell us out if it means keeping the profits for himself. Be ready tonight around ten. I spent this morning watching him spend the money I gave him for our first order on some clothes for a party he's throwing tonight. We're handling that nigga tonight. No mistakes this time, right Quincy?"

"No mistakes," I repeated, holding my hands in the air.

"Good. Tonight, you're going to handle our problem for us. I got a Glock with your name on it, baby girl. You catch your first body tonight without the help of us," Ivy said with a smirk.

I knew it was only a matter of time before I had to prove my loyalty with more than words. Ivy had divulged her plan and she wanted a way of keeping me in line, and what better way than having me commit a murder. Up until this point I failed at every chance I got, but something told me if I fucked around and missed tonight, Ivy would cash in on the target she had painted on my back.

~

THE LINE at Club X was deep, with the entire hood in attendance for Deon's birthday celebration. Ivy wasn't lying when she said this nigga went all out with her re-up money. According to the videos he made on Facebook and Instagram, there was an open bar in the VIP section, strippers flown in from King of Diamonds to dance, and a buffet catered from one of the best soul food restaurants in Brooklyn. With this being one of the hottest events of the year, it was hard to get in. The hostess was being extra picky when it came to who was able to get in. Minor infractions like having chipped nail polish or dirty sneakers had people walking off the line with a heavy heart. I pulled my fur jacket close in an effort to stave off the cool night air. I could see Saidya a few people ahead of me, waiting as impatiently as everyone else. It was Ivy's idea to have us show up separate tonight. I was dying to know why, but after all this time I knew there was a method to Ivy's madness.

"Who the fuck is that?"

"Damn, Deon already inside, who pulling up in the Wraith?"

People were speculating at who was arriving in an icy white Wraith that had come to a stop in front of the club. The driver, who was dressed in an immaculate suit, came around to open the door for his client. A bejeweled Louboutin Pigalle heel hit the pavement, attached to a long, mocha colored leg. The hens behind me were pressed at the sight of a leg so I could imagine the hate this woman was going to get for the rest of her ensemble. The other foot touched down and out stepped Ivy dressed like she was going to a movie premiere instead of this party in the middle of Brooklyn. The form fitting, black, silk, ruffled romper she wore with elbow length gloves had these hoes mad. I had to pick my mouth up from the ground as Ivy sashayed into the club, bypassing the line Saidya and I had been standing on for the better part of an hour. I hid my frustration well, but Saidya was a completely different story. She pulled out her phone and I heard her going in on Ivy to her boyfriend.

"This bitch has us standing on line for nearly a fucking hour and she pulled up like a damn boss. I can't believe this shit right now. We get a measly $300 per week and this bitch is out here wearing the latest designer shit? Shining bright with diamond earrings while we're treated like peasants? I'm sick of this shit, babe. Remember that plan you came up with? I think I'm ready to go through with it."

Plan? I know Ivy had her ways, and she was no one's victim, but I didn't like the idea of Saidya plotting on her. I saw her turning around to look back at me to possibly gauge my reaction and I didn't plan on giving her the satisfaction. I buried my face into my phone, scrolling through Zeus' Instagram. He treated it more like a business—there were more pictures of insightful quotes than there were pictures of him—except every now and again there was a picture of him that would send a wave of butterflies through my stomach. In a perfect world this could've been my man.

"I guess I'm the only that sees a problem with this. I don't even know why I considered bringing her in on this. We vibed earlier, but it's obvious she willing to live at Ivy's fucking feet." My shoulders sagged in relief when she turned back around. "Babe, I gotta go. I'm next on line."

The appearance of Ivy had this weird effect on time; the long line moved with the quickness as groups were either permitted entry or dismissed. Saidya was almost one of the rejected because the hostess didn't like the Lucite heels she wore with a sequined dress. When she asked me what I thought I told her she should consider pairing the dress with some thigh high boots, but she wouldn't listen. Her bad. I feared I would be met with the same fate, which was why I kept my outfit simple and dressed it up. I wore a black bodycon dress with a pair of blush furry Aquazzura sandals. My matching fur set the whole look off. To my surprise, when I reached the hostess she took one good look at me from head-to-toe and let me in without question. The second I stepped inside of the club, I found myself wishing I was back outside. It was hot as fuck in here from all the ass shaking going on, on the dance floor. I made a beeline for the bar, where I planned to wait for Ivy's next orders. My butt barely grazed the seat when I received a message from her telling me to come up to the roof. I thought I would run into some type of trouble, but no one stopped me from sneaking through the exit door and heading up to the roof. I nearly tripped and broke my neck at the sight in front of me.

Saidya held Ivy—the same Ivy who could pull her piece at a moment's notice—at gunpoint.

I reached into my purse and pulled out the gun Ivy had given me earlier, pointing it at the one person who swore I'd never be able to pull the trigger.

"You think this uppity bitch is going to kill me, Ivy? She'd have a better chance of hitting me if she was aiming at you," Saidya sneered, pressing her gun into Ivy's chin. "I am sick of your shit, Ivy. I have been your lap dog and punching bag for too fucking long! Following behind you like some fucking minion while you always seem to come out on top. Tonight was the icing on the cake."

Ivy laughed. "Then go on and shoot me. Quincy, put your gun down. This is between me and who I thought was my sister. I guess blood ain't always thicker, huh?"

"I guess not."

I lowered my gun. Don't get me wrong, I would've shot Saidya, but I was relieved that I didn't have to. Ivy would never make a call she wasn't completely confident on, so I guess at this point I was waiting to see what she pulled from up her sleeve. The exit door opened, and Rome appeared. He was dressed in a charcoal colored Armani suit, a signature Thomas Pink shirt, and matching loafers. Even during a tense time like this I could admire how good he looked. Saidya shot Ivy a triumphant look as Rome approached. I trained my gun on Saidya at the same time Rome brandished his own weapon—a Beretta the same color as his suit—and pointed it at Saidya's head. I pointed my gun at him, protecting Saidya even though she didn't deserve my grace.

"Rome...Rome, why are you pointing your gun at my head?" Saidya asked as if it wasn't obvious.

Now it was Ivy's turn to smile triumphantly. She had played this game better than I ever could. "Did you really think a nigga like Rome would ever settle for someone like you?" Ivy let out a howl of laughter at the hurt on Saidya's face. I felt my own flushing with embarrassment. "Rome is my man, and he's been fucking you because I told him to. You see, at this point of my plan I needed to know everyone that is for and against me. The same way I knew Kaia's greed would screw her over in the end was the same way I knew all it would take was some dick and sweet promises of forever to turn you against me. And look, you proved me right like you always do."

"I didn't prove shit but how ruthless of a bitch you are. I didn't wake up like this, Ivy—you made me this way! Your mother broke you and you've been breaking people ever since," Saidya shot back, tears falling down her cheeks. "Fuck you, Ivy. Do what you've been dying to do. Take me out of my fucking misery."

Saidya's arms dropped as Ivy's rose with the quickness, hitting her with two shots in the chest. She was dead before she touched the ground. Rome lowered his own weapon and accepted the smoking gun from Ivy, who didn't flinch at taking our sister's life. They made small talk as Ivy rummaged through Saidya pockets, taking her phone, wallet, and any other identifying items. I didn't even realize I was standing there with my gun still in the air until Ivy asked me to put it down.

"I know you're in shock and shit, but you might fuck around and hurt someone, Quincy. Unlike yours, my gun has a silencer." Ivy placed her hand over the gun and lowered my arm like a patient mother assisting her child. "Let Rome get rid of that gun for you. Quincy, I need you to let go of the gun."

I loosened my grip enough for her to pry it from my trembling hand. Rome placed it in his waistband and we made our way back to the party. Thunder sounded overhead, warning of an impending storm. Depending on how long it rained, Saidya could be up there for a day before someone noticed her. Ivy planned this to the tee. The VIP section was still bumping. I don't even think anyone noticed we left. I checked the time on my watch, and to my surprise, only ten minutes had passed. Up there it felt like forever. We took a seat on the sofa, with Ivy in the middle.

"Quincy, can you stop looking like a witness to a crime?" Ivy said, pouring me a hefty glass of the Cîroc that sat on our table. "Drink half of this. Come on, take it to the head."

I did as I was told, ignoring the burning feeling in my chest. She pressed down on it when it was time for me to stop. My cheeks burned, my head spun, and I knew it was only a matter of time I started bawling like a baby. My mood prior to drinking always determined what kind of drunk I would be.

"I appreciate you having my back up there," Ivy said, giving my leg a gentle squeeze. "I'm not the easiest person to get along with and it would've been nothing for you to let Saidya kill me and split our nest egg with her. You haven't said it, but I know you're falling in love with that guy you're fucking around with. Half of that money could have bought you your happily ever after. Instead of going with the choice you wanted, you made the choice I would've made if the tables were turned. Thank you."

Thank you.

Two words I've never heard Ivy speak to anyone. Not at restaurants when she was served, never to anyone who holds the door open for her, and I was convinced she had no clue what the words were up until now. I wasn't grateful for her gratitude—it turned my stomach. With Kaia and Saidya gone that meant it was just the two of us. Ivy would be depending on me to have her back for the duration of her plan. However, I knew it was an act. She had killed her sister she grew up with; ending my life whenever I was no longer useful was nothing to a savage like her.

"You're welcome," I replied with a small nod.

Ivy observed me over the rim of her glass. "Why don't you call him? I'm sure he can use some company tonight. I'll see you tomorrow and we'll discuss how we're moving forward from here on out."

Rain fell in sheets from the night sky, obscuring everything beyond an arm's length. I dialed Zeus with shaky fingers, praying he wasn't in the middle of sleeping. My heart almost leapt from my chest at the sound of his voice. He didn't sound asleep, but he didn't sound quite awake either.

"I know this is last minute and um...you're really private...we're only supposed to be fucking...I don't have anyone else that I could call—"

"Where are you?" he asked without hesitation.

I gave him the address to the deli I passed on the walk to the club.

It was a few blocks away, far enough to keep anyone from seeing who I left with. My hair, jacket, and pumps squished with falling rain as I made a mad dash down the two blocks. I was starting to regret giving him such a far address. That feeling was fleeting at the thought of Saidya, who was lying on a roof cold and drenched, forgotten for the night but soon to be discovered once day broke. Suddenly, I didn't feel so cold. The deli was closed, but its awning provided shelter from the downpour, which had reached nor'easter status. Through the haze of rain I saw a familiar pair of headlights pull up in front of the store. Seconds later, Zeus appeared with an umbrella in one hand and a coat in another.

"Come on, lets get you somewhere dry," he said, helping me place the coat over my shoulders.

Heat blasted from the car vents. My body let out an involuntary shudder at the warmth. Even the seats were heated. I closed my eyes and fell into a light slumber, only to be gently shaken awake.

"I need you to hold the umbrella," he said.

I accepted the umbrella from him and was shocked as he lifted me from the car bridal style. I could barely see where I was, but I knew it was fancy. Zeus carried me up the flight of brownstone steps with ease. He entered a code into the door, one I peeped out the corner of my eye, and next thing I know, I'm in the middle of a foyer that's a replica of home and garden magazine. If I had to describe Zeus' esthetic for his home, it would be "Old Money in a New Time." Every table was handmade, the couches were plush and covered in expensive fabrics, and expensive art hung in the halls. He led me upstairs to a guest bedroom.

"The bathroom is down the hall, there's a linen closet inside with everything you need. I also set you out something to wear," Zeus said from the doorway, pointing in the direction of everything he named.

I took in the guest bedroom, another well decorated room with a comfy, queen sized bed. Kicking off my heels and shrugging out of both coats, I replied with a thick, "Thank you."

I spent the next hour trying to scrub the night off of me. The straight vodka picked the perfect time to kick in. Tears mixed with the soap and water I saturated myself in. I was nothing but a pruned drunken shell of myself as I slipped into the T-Shirt and sweatpants Zeus left for me. He even included a pair of boxers with the tag still attached.

"Two-hundred dollars for a pair of drawers?" I said to myself as I slipped the silky boxers on. "I'm all for good taste, but damn. Hmmm…they do feel really nice though…"

I pictured Zeus walking around in silk drawers and my kitty thumped. There was a knock at the door. With my permission, Zeus entered the bedroom with a mug of tea and a sandwich on a tray. He was dressed in a pair of navy blue pajama pants with a matching shirt with "ZT" embroidered on the chest. I made myself comfortable on the bed and lifted my arms as he placed the tray onto my lap. He took a seat at the foot of the bed, watching me sip the tea and play with the sandwich.

"What's wrong, you don't like turkey?" he asked, pulling my feet onto his lap and beginning to rub them.

I was going to tell him that I did like turkey, but this kind tasted funny when the pain of my heels was relieved by Zeus' kneading of my arches. I squirmed in ecstasy; every part of my body had been pampered by Zeus, but my feet in his skillful hands was a feeling on another level. He laughed at the funny noises I started making as I sipped my tea. I should've known something this nice came with a price.

"What happened tonight?"

I sipped my tea loudly, using it as a way to buy myself time for an explanation. "I was out at the club with my sister and shit went left. You would think with how long I've been in this city I would have made at least one friend, but no, I've only managed to meet you."

"I'm not your friend?" Zeus asked with a laugh. "We have dinner together, share secrets, and call each other whenever we're in need. Where I'm from, that's a friend."

"I guess you are my friend." I smiled. I took another sip of tea, pondering how I was going to ask him for something that was outside of friend territory. "Zeus? I'm grateful for everything you've done tonight—especially this foot massage—and I feel terrible for asking you for one more favor."

"Name it."

"Can you hold me until I fall asleep?" He stopped rubbing, a sign that I had taken things too far. "You know what? I'm bugging. I'm sorry I even asked—"

"Are you finished?"

I held out the tray to him. Zeus appeared five minutes later with two bottles of water, mentioning that he likes to have a drink handy for the middle of the night. He slid into bed beside me, turned the lights off with a clap of his hands, and pulled me to him. Heat radiated from him, along with the smell of his Maison Martin Margiela cologne tickling my nose. I closed my eyes and with each passing breath, the events of tonight faded away to nothing. Zeus and I would never be, but at least I had one night of intimacy with him to last a lifetime.

~

ZEUS WAS GONE the next morning, taking his warmth with him. I slipped on my now dry dress, which was stiff from hanging all night, and gathered my stuff together. My search for Zeus began on the first floor in his immaculate kitchen. Next was his office, which was spotless as well. I recalled another set of stairs on the second level. I called Zeus' name on the walk up. Nothing. This final level was different than the rest. It had its own living room and bar. There was only one door, and it was slightly ajar. I called out Zeus' name once again and gave it a gentle push, nowhere near ready for the sight I set my eyes on. Compared to the rest of the house, the master bedroom was a pigsty. Women's clothing sat in a large pile on top of the bed, heels and purses littering the floor. A few garbage bags overflowing with more clothes sat next to the bed. I spotted a PS4 hooked up to a huge television with the remote sitting on top of the mountain of clothes. So...if I'm correct, Zeus sits in a pile of his dead fiancée's clothes and plays video games? I didn't have much longer to wonder because he appeared from his closet.

"I was looking all over for you. I started in the kitchen, I tried calling you—"

"But you never thought to use one of the many intercoms hooked up all over the house?" Zeus countered coldly.

My cheeks flushed with embarrassment. "You're right. I'm sorry. I don't think the clothes are weird—"

"I don't recall asking for your opinion on them. You ready to go?"

His cold tone chilled me to my core. I responded with a head nod and shrill, "Yeah, I'm ready to go."

No silence would ever compare to sharing one with a man whose privacy you invaded in a large way. I wouldn't call Zeus talkative, but it felt like all the air had been sucked from the interior of the car. Try apologizing, I mentally scolded myself.

"Sorry. I should've just sat on the couch waiting for you instead of wandering around your house," I said after some time. "I guess deep down, some part of me wanted to get a look at the other side of you. I'm sure that will never happen again because I fucked up big time."

Zeus chuckled. "Apology accepted. What do you mean 'the other side'?"

"You've always been a mystery to me, but I've always wondered about you. Your favorite foods, music, friends. Part of me should have prepared myself for the fact that another woman still lives with you."

"I love a good steak—medium rare. I'm an 80's baby, so I'm all about old school R&B and Rap. As for friends? I think I can show you better than I can tell you."

Twenty minutes later, we were parked in front of Brooklyn Methodist Hospital. I followed Zeus into the hospital, where he was greeted like a regular. *He must spend a lot of time here,* I thought as we boarded an elevator and took it to the fifth floor. I ran a nervous hand over my bun, making sure it was smooth. I didn't want to look a hot mess during my first meeting with one of Zeus' friends.

Too bad it wasn't our first meeting.

Our eyes locked and the recognition was instant. Zeus missed the exchange because he was too busy greeting the teenaged girl that sat in a chair beside her father's bed. Shayla was as beautiful as I thought she would be. Her eyes were puffy from crying, crying due to what my sister did to her father. I just knew he was going to out me to Zeus at the given opportunity, I could feel it in my bones.

"I know you're still recovering, Sean, but I wanted to introduce you to the friend I've been telling you about," Zeus said, bringing me over to the hospital bed. "This is Quincy. Quincy, this is my good friend Sean and his daughter, Shayla."

Sean's mouth opened, and I expected him to tell Zeus to call 9-1-1, but Sean said politely, "Nice to meet you, Quincy. Zeus mentioned how you've been a great help to him during such a dark point in his life. He's doing the same for me. I was shot in gang related shooting a few days ago. The doctors are calling my recovery a miracle. I like to believe that it wasn't my time, and everything happens for a reason."

"Never underestimate the power of prayer. It was Quincy who told me to pray for you," Zeus said, giving my shoulder a gentle squeeze. "Shayla, you hungry? I know you could use something to eat after being here all night."

Shayla rose from her chair into a deep stretch. "I could use something good to eat, and not none of that cafeteria food. I'm tired of it. I was thinking something from the café across the street?"

"You got it. Quincy, you want anything from across the street?"

I shook my head. "I'm not very hungry."

"With the way your stomach was growling on the way over here? I'll bring you something anyway. You mind staying behind with Sean and keeping him company?"

"I would appreciate it...Quincy," Sean added.

Shayla picked her jacket up from the couch where the rest of her stuff sat and skipped out of the room behind Zeus. Sean and I stared at each other, waiting for their retreating footsteps to disappear. He motioned at the seat next to his bed. Against my better judgment, I plopped down in the chair, never taking my eyes off of him.

"You're not a bad person," Sean declared in a matter-of-fact way. "How you ended up in such a bad situation is beyond me, but I can tell just by looking at you that you're not a monster. You offered a dying man one minute of mercy and for that reason alone I will give you a chance to tell him the truth before I do."

My eyes welled up with tears. I never intended on telling Zeus the truth; I was going to save him from Ivy, pack my bags, and run off never to be seen again. Sean was leaving me in a tough position. "If I tell him, he's going to hate me. You're not the only person she hurt. She...she's hurt other people he loves...loved."

It didn't take a genius to figure out what I meant. Sean closed his eyes and emitted a world-weary sigh. In a calm voice he replied, "You need to tell him by the end of the night. No excuses, Quincy. Zeus has been nothing but good to me and my daughter, looking out for us when not even my own family would. I can't look him in the eye knowing something this devastating and withholding it. Take this few minutes to think over what you're going to say."

I spent the next twenty minutes replaying the truth in my head, each time sounding worse than the last. Sean sat watching me with those wise eyes of his. At the sound of Zeus and Shayla's voices growing close, he asked for my number to make sure I kept my word. Then we switched the conversation to a lighter topic: the weather. I played along the best I could. As promised, Zeus brought me back a plate of delicious breakfast food. Under better circumstances, I would've tore up the eggs with bacon and french toast, but today that wasn't the case. I ate what I could and feigned sickness to get out of eating the rest.

"You've been quiet ever since we got to the hospital," Zeus said as we headed to the address I asked him to drop me off at. "Everything good with you?"

"I didn't mean to act so distant. I've got a lot on my mind from last night. Anyway," I drew out the word, hoping to veer away from my emotional state. "Since you still haven't asked me out on a date, I'm going to beat you to the punch. Dinner. Tonight."

Zeus laughed. "I've never had a woman ask me out. This is a new experience. I'll play along. Who knows? This might be the start of something..."

He peered over at me and that's when I saw it. Not love, but an intense like, one stop before falling in love with someone. Zeus played it cool most of the time, but today his eyes told a different story. The way he held me last night revealed a new truth. He was falling for me as hard as I fell for him. How was I supposed to look him in the eye and tell him that I was responsible for his pain, one of the reasons why he believed he would never love again and now, once the truth was revealed, the reason he would never trust again? I had to suck it up and tell him because I *did* love him. Sean shouldn't have to speak up on my truth. Zeus deserved better than that.

He deserved better than me.

GIANNA

Giada's eyes flickered from me to the phone in my hand, which had become an extension of me ever since Cash and I started on this Assan Sisters lead. Every spare minute I had was devoted to checking my phone to see if there was an update from the PI we hired to run a background check on Boyd. I wanted to know everything there was to know about him, more specifically, how many kids he had. Hasani mentioned having someone do a background check after the aftermath of their war with Boyd's sons. My reply was if he ever looked into if Boyd had any daughters and his reply was that he never considered it. He was already hurt by his brothers spurning him because of Grayson, so I kept my feelings on his slip up to myself. Speaking on the arrival of an additional Townsend Brother, I noticed that my little sister's improving condition had very little to do with medicine and everything to do with the makeup she wore. Her hair was up in a neat bun and on her lips was a thin layer of lip gloss.

"Are you expecting someone?" I asked, knowing damn well Giada wouldn't preen herself for any visiting relative. "Maybe a certain doctor who stayed with you last night? Oh, you thought I didn't know that Grayson spent the night to 'keep you safe'? Oh, Giada, big sis knows everything, including that you like him. A lot."

Giada rolled her eyes, trying to play cool, but the blush creeping up her neck said otherwise. Like I once did, my baby sister was falling for a Townsend Brother, and no matter how new he was to the family, he still had their charm. "I think he's a really nice person, and since my sister is spending all of her time chasing ghosts, having a doctor like Grayson around is beneficial to me."

"Where'd you get all this makeup from anyway?"

"Mommy brought it here for me."

I doubled over in laughter. "Why am I not surprised? Mommy tried to marry me off to a surgeon at one point in time. I'm not the least bit surprised that she's doing the same with you."

"Gia, you say it like Carmelo's a downgrade or something. He comes from a respected family, he's one of the best plastic surgeons on the East Coast, and he loved you with all his heart. You still never explained why you broke up with him."

"Never become so enamored by someone's exterior that you ignore their interior. Carmelo was the perfect boyfriend on paper, I was grateful to find someone I was equally yoked with, but on the inside, he was just like these no-good niggas. He cheated on me every chance he got to the point that I believed I was the problem. When I asked him how I could fix the situation, you know what he told me? Maybe if I got some work done he wouldn't have to chase fat asses because he would have one of his own. I told him he can kiss my flat ass and we went our separate ways."

Giada shook her head. "You met Hasani a week later, right?"

I thought of the arms meeting where I met Hasani's silly ass for the second time. Imagine my surprise when a guy I shared a raunchy dance with sauntered into a meeting where I had to be a respected businesswoman. He was standing in for one of his brothers and it showed by his lack of knowledge on what he was purchasing. The entire meeting was spent with him feigning interest over the guns I was showing while subtly trying to find out if I had a man. I rejected him and thought that would be the last I saw of him until he came to the next meeting with Quade. He kept showing up to meetings with a little more knowledge of guns than the last time. I was poised to tell him no again when he mentioned having tickets to a gun expo I was interested in. After that night I knew I wanted to spend the rest of my life with him. I could see the same in Giada's eyes.

"You really like him, don't you?"

Giada's eyes welled up with tears. "Gia...there's something I need to tell you."

"Giada...what is it?"

"Earlier, I got some news from my doctor. You know how the bullet pierced my lung? That's not the only place one of them hit." Giada swiped at the stray tears. "Part of my spine was damaged by a bullet and there's a good chance I'll never be able to walk again."

The weight of Giada's news pressed me into my seat. "No...that's not true. We'll get you another opinion, one of the best physical therapists in the country—"

"Grayson is one of the best physical therapists in the country. He was here when the doctor performed the test and offered to help with my recovery. Instead of looking at me like I was a paraplegic, Grayson saw me as a woman. I know it's stupid to think of him as something more, but I can't shake the feeling that...that I might get my Hasani."

What? Giada had always maintained a mild interest in Hasani. They've tolerated each other more than anything. "You want a Hasani? Like my Hasani? The one I'm married to?"

"Gia, he's a fuck up, we both know this for a fact, but that man has loved you since the day the two of you met. He's always wanted what's best for you even when you didn't have the sense to want it for yourself. Hasani's your rock, and no matter where life takes both of you, he'll always be there. I want someone who's going to love me that way."

I kissed Gia on the forehead. "Your time for love will soon come, you hear? I don't want you chasing anyone thinking they're going to cure the empty feeling in your heart. Love will come when you least expect it." My cellphone buzzed in my pocket, reminding me of my duties. "Now stop all that worry and focus on healing. You're going to come out on top, Giada. I gotta do my rounds. I'll be back when I'm finished, okay?"

I spotted Grayson walking towards Giada's room on my way to check on my patient, Sean. He was the man who was shot in a hit gone wrong a few days ago. An armed police officer was posted in front of his hospital door. This one was different than the rest, with his neatly trimmed beard and expensive smelling cologne. My gut instinct was to ask him who sent him over, but something told me to hold off just yet. There was no way the NYPD would be stupid enough to send over an unqualified cop. Inside of Sean's hospital room was a nurse readying herself to administer medication. The problem was that Sean wasn't due any medication for a few more hours. His daughter, who had remained by his side since he was brought in, was nowhere to be found. I walked over to the woman, who was wearing the teal scrubs our staff wore with a name badge that belonged to one of my close friends. They looked alike if you weren't paying any attention, but anyone that knew Allison would know this wasn't her. Not even Sean, who was slumbering peacefully, had any idea how close he was to losing his life had I not arrived when I did.

"Hi, I believe we haven't met," I said, placing my hand over her hand gripping an empty syringe. "I'm Giada, Sean's attending, and you are?"

She had the audacity to smile in my face and reply, "Allison Hawkins. I was transferred up here to take care of Sean since his nurse didn't come in today. I was told that you would be made aware of the change."

"Or," I said, dragging out the word as my hand tightened around hers, "you could be here to finish what the fuck you started."

She answered with a right hook strong enough to knock me off of my feet had I not dodged it at the last minute. I countered with one of my own, nearly knocking her off of her feet. Using my momentum against me, she freed her hand holding the needle and jabbed at me, missing my neck and slicing the side of my face. I shoved her against a wall by her neck. This was the woman that shot at my sister and I was going to find out who the fuck she was if it was the last thing I ever did.

"Who are you?" I hissed, increasing the pressure I had on her neck. "Hmm? Who the fuck sent you?"

She smiled wide, revealing a set of perfect white teeth, which was crazy because I always imagined whoever was behind this was a savage. "You'll find out when it's time, bitch."

I slammed her into the wall once, twice, three times. "You think you scare me? Tell me who sent you or else so help me God—"

"What? You're going to kill me in front of your white colleagues? Go ahead, bitch. Make my motherfucking day."

All it took was my second of hesitation for her to get the best of me. She head butted me, knocking me back into the tray of instruments, sending them flying everywhere. The noise was enough to rouse Sean from his slumber. He pressed call button on the side of his bed at the same time the NYPD officer entered the room and hit him with two shots to the chest. On her way out the door, the woman hit me with a swift kick to the gut. I knew she wouldn't be able to resist getting the last lick in and used it to my advantage. An agonizing scream filled the room as I dug a scalpel into her leg, making sure to hit tendons and muscle. The police officer, who I knew wasn't an officer by now, caught her before she could hit the floor and ran from the hospital room with a trail of blood following behind. Every nurse on the floor filled the tiny room, some helping me up while others stabilized Sean, who was hyperventilating.

"He's been hit with two bullets to the—" one screamed as she pulled off his hospital gown to reveal a bulletproof vest. "Where did this vest come from? I've never seen the police issue one of these to a victim."

"A friend of mine gave it to me," Sean said, failing to mention that friend was me.

One his first night here, I explained to him that I would be watching over him for the duration of his hospital visit. The first step was fitting him with a bulletproof vest in case whoever shot him the first time came back to handle him the same way. He thought it was crazy at first, but I could see the relief in his eyes as they set upon the two bullets stuck in the Kevlar vest.

"Someone call the police," one of the nurses shouted. "Gia, you need to have a seat so we can patch up your face. You're bleeding all over."

I swatted away their hands. This scratch was nothing and would be scabbed over in 24 hours time. What I needed was to have someone find this bitch and her partner before it was too late. On my way out the room, I spotted a plastic card on the floor. I picked it up and placed it into my coat pocket with one smooth swipe. My first call was to my cousin, Antoine, who was an NYPD detective.

"Antoine, I need a favor. I'm going to send you a picture of someone and I need you to get me a current address on them. When you have it, send it out to everyone. I want her and everyone she's associated with by the end of the night." I looked around the hallway to make sure no one was listening in on the conversation. "I believe she's the one that shot Giada."

Antoine let out a low whistle. "Say no more, cuz. I'll get back to you when I have something."

My next call was the police even though they had already proven themselves to be useless. Where was the one assigned to Sean? Coming back from lunch because he was too stupid to recognize the difference between a real uniform and fake one. In the middle of such a busy hospital it would be easier to trick him off of his post than kill him. His fuck up almost cost Sean his life. The severity of the situation didn't hit until his daughter reappeared, dressed in school clothes, asking what happened to her father. I could see it in his eyes that he didn't want to tell her the truth, but with this psycho running around she was better off informed than blissfully ignorant.

"I knew we shouldn't have moved here!" she screamed at the top of her lungs, catching the attention of every adult in the room. "Life wasn't great back home, but it was better than you being in danger every other day! You're all I have, Daddy. If something happens to you, I'm stuck here all alone with no one!"

My heart broke at the pain in her voice. I knew what it was like to wonder whether or not my father would make it home some nights. Every promotion he received was a new opening for him to be snatched away by enemies, with the police and Feds being on the frontline. What if Shayla was here to bear witness to her father being attacked? There wasn't a doubt in my mind that we would be wheeling her into the morgue. I had to nip this situation in the bud for the sake of not only my sister, but Shayla, who stormed off after her diatribe and took solace in the bathroom.

"There's something I need to tell you," Sean said with an evasive glance at one of the nurses that stayed behind to make sure he was good. "In private. About my condition."

"Nurse Joyner, can you give us a minute?" I asked with forced politeness; if she wasn't at the nurses' station running her mouth with the rest of those old hens they would've noticed an unfamiliar nurse walking around with the nametag of someone I worked with on the regular. A long talk with the administration was high on my To Do List once I was done here.

We watched her scurry from the room, her shoes slapping against the floor until the sound disappeared entirely. Sean leaned over to make sure she was completely gone before he said, "I never pictured this life for myself. A forty-year-old hustler? Shayla deserves better than the life I've given her so far. How much longer do you think I'll have to be in here? The second I'm cleared to go home we're leaving town." I could tell his body was waging a war with his mind. This was his second time starting over, and this time around he wasn't physically capable of taking care pf himself and his daughter. "If I had a cellphone number, could you track the location of the person?"

Antoine had tracked people with less information. "What's the number?"

I jotted down the number, texted it to Antoine, who sent me an address ten minutes later. My adrenaline was pumping as I sent out the mass text with orders to bring Bonnie and Clyde in alive. Sean looked on with an unsure expression on his face, which I found strange considering that whoever this number belonged to had something to do with him lying in a hospital.

"The number I gave you belongs to one of the women who was there when I was shot. You have to promise me that no harm will come to her," Sean said, sitting up in bed.

"As long as she's willing to give up her partner, nothing's going to happen to her," I said as my phone went off with a message from a lieutenant.

Completare.

"Gia, I didn't give you that number to harm an innocent person."

I pointed down the hall towards where Giada was. "Today my sister found out that there's a good chance she'll never walk again. All because of a bullet that wasn't meant for her. You might have forgiven her for what she did to you, but you have no right to tell me how to handle revenge for my sister. If this woman is as innocent as you claim, there's no need to worry about her."

Shayla exited from the bathroom rubbing her eyes. She stalked past me without a look in my direction and took a seat next to her father. I made a call for a lieutenant to stand guard up here. Another police officer had been placed in front of the room, but the NYPD proved tonight that they couldn't do shit right. With a curt nod to Sean, I was off to step on some necks and end a bitch or two.

QUINCY

The silence woke me as easily as it had put me to sleep. I was at home adding on the finishing touches of my makeup when my bedroom door opened with a creak. Thinking it was Ivy popping up on me like she usually does, I continued applying my lipstick until I felt the cool touch of a barrel underneath my chin. Three men filled the tiny bedroom, breathing up all the fresh air and replacing it with the smell of cigarettes, heady cologne, and perspiration. The leader, a man who fit every stereotype of the typical Italian boss, asked me one simple question: was I alone? I returned home to an empty house. There was no sign of Ivy—it didn't even appear that she returned home last night. I shook my head and my last memory up until now was having it slammed into my vanity mirror. The hissing of hushed voices started the second I opened my eyes.

"She's coming around," a woman's voice announced in a hushed whisper.

I opened my eyes expecting to see a few people, but instead, I was surrounded by six. Three men and three women. A few more blinks corrected my vision, and half of the faces became familiar. These were Zeus' brothers. Hasani studied me like I was a science project while Savion looked unsure of the situation. Quade...Quade was smiling at me, but not one of those comforting smiles. If I had to guess, this was what the big bad wolf looked like before trying to eat Little Red Riding Hood. I pressed myself into the table I was laying on, praying someone would stop him from hurting me if he got too close. The woman beside him laid her doe eyes on him and slapped his arm.

"Quade, you're scaring her. Stop looking at her like that," she hissed.

"If she's behind half the shit we believe she is, she better be scared," he replied, but he turned down the smile enough to ease my fears. For now.

The woman next to Hasani cosigned Quade with a curt nod of her head, causing her curls to bounce. Those curls…her hair…the picture Ivy showed me. Recognition must have shown on my face because she swung at me, the punch skimming the edge of my chin as Hasani pulled her away.

"You didn't see how she looked at me? She knows what the fuck her sister did! That bitch put her hands on mine? Wait until I get my hands on hers. Hasani, get the fuck off me, I'm good!"

"I'm not letting you go until you promise me you won't try to hurt her again," Hasani said with the patience of a saint. "Gia, we won't get anything resolved if we don't talk to her. Like you said, this isn't the woman from the hospital. We need to know where she is!"

Gia crumpled in his arms. A pain-filled sob escaped her. Hasani used his arms to hug her, rocking her back and forth until she had calmed down. I turned my head in shame; I was the reason why her sister was in the hospital. *Maybe I should say sorry,* I thought, and the words followed shortly after. Gia stared at me as if sizing me up.

"I don't want your fucking sorry. I want to know where your sister is. Tell us: where is Ivy?" My face betrayed me again. "Yeah, we know all about you and Ivy. You put a hit out on the leaders of our Red Hook territory and took over using the best friend of our *primero*? Deon squealed like a pig while we sliced his ass up. Told us all about your plans to disable our cartel so you could take over in the name of your father, that infected bastard. Now tell us where Ivy's hiding."

"Infected? My father wasn't infected with anything. He was

murdered in a drug related hit. We were taking back his territory from the people who stole it."

Six pairs of eyes looked at me like I was crazy. Gia shrugged out of Hasani's grip and walked away, proclaiming that she couldn't deal with this any longer. Everyone else glanced at each other as if deciding who was going to speak to me some unspoken truth. Quade was the one to speak up, and when he did, I felt like all of the air had been sucked out of my body.

"Boyd had AIDS. He gave it to our mother and countless other women. She died of it over a decade ago. Where the fuck have you been? On another planet?"

"Another country. The folder said she moved to London at…eighteen. Around the time Moms died," Hasani replied, motioning to a folder sitting on the table.

I covered my mouth to keep my sobs in check. "No…no…oh my god. It wasn't cancer. How could she lie to me like this?" Everyone waited for me to explain myself. "Throughout my childhood, my mother has had bouts of illness. Recently, she had to go into the hospital. She told me it was cervical cancer. How could I have not read the signs?"

"Your mother died of an AIDS related illness and you've been out here caping for this nigga, killing for him and shit. I bet you feel extremely stupid right now," Savion said, shaking his head in disgust. "You want to make this right? Where's your sister? We read all about you, Quincy, you're the smartest of the group, but you don't have the heart to pull this shit off. But Ivy, with her troubled past, does."

I dabbed at the tears at the corners of my eyes. "How did my father really die?"

"I killed him," Quade said with a self-accomplished smile. "Then, when your brothers came for us, we killed them motherfuckers too. Except Sadan."

"Ivy killed him right before she killed…right before she killed Lauren."

Everyone stilled. Two pairs of arms tried to grab Savion's wife, but she was too quick and two feet closer than Gia. I dodged the first punch but the second one knocked me dead across the face, snapping my head to the side. Sharp talons dug through my hair and gripped it, gaining the leverage to pummel me to death if possible.

"My fucking partner! You bitches murdered my fucking partner!" she screamed at the top of her lungs as she fought me and everyone dragging her away at the same time. "Get off of me! Fuck talking to her, I'm murking this bitch! Savion, get the hell off of me!"

"Cash, let go of her hair! Remember: we need her in order to get Ivy. That's who you want, that's who killed Lauren. Ivy killed Lauren," Savion rationalized to his wife while prying her fingers from my hair.

Cash let go of me, but she didn't do so without aiming a few slaps at my head, most of which I blocked. I sat up on the table this time around. They wouldn't get a third time to catch me off guard. Quade, who hadn't stepped in to save me from being attacked, pulled up a neighboring chair to the side of the table. He pulled a pack of cigarettes from his pocket and offered me one. I shook my head. He lit one and blew a plume of Newport smoke into my face.

"What was the next phase of the plan? We know the overall, but what was Ivy's next move? If you tell us, I'll make it quick. You won't feel a thing. If you don't tell us...I'll make it so long and drawn out that you will wish you could snap your own neck." Quade took another pull, this one long enough to give me an opportunity to mull over my options.

I wasn't ready to die and answering his question would be the proverbial nail in the coffin. "Please don't kill me. When I found Ivy, I was looking for family. My mother was dead, the childhood home I grew up in was gone, and I had nothing. Ivy took me in when there was no one else. You think this is the life I would've chosen for myself if I had the option? She wanted me to kill Lauren but I froze. She told me we were going to shoot Gia to avenge our sister's death. Even then, I aimed for anything but her. I swear on my dead mother, if you want Ivy I'll give you her, but please don't kill me."

"Speak."

"Are you going to kill me?"

"Of course I am, but after listening to your little speech, I've decided to make it quick." I broke down, crying and snotting all over the place. There was no point in acting cute when he was going to kill me anyway. "I don't know why you're holding on to her location so tight for anyway: she fucking left you behind to take the fall for her. If you ask me, she decided to let us handle this loose end for her. This is your opportunity to stick it to her by telling us where she is."

"I don't know. She has the million dollars she extorted from Lauren. She could be anywhere by now. Any plans she made, she kept close." I madly swiped at my eyes. "I can tell you where some of her people are in Florida, but it won't do you any good; Ivy stopped fucking with them a long time ago. They hate her as much as you do and she wouldn't hesitate to let you kill one of them if it means her getting away."

Quade put the cigarette out on the palm of his hand without flinching. "Is that your final answer?"

"Yeah," I choked out. "I don't know where she is."

"And the plan? What was the next part of the plan?"

"She was going to kill Zeus in the hopes that it would break all of you. He's the head of the cartel and his death would place a fracture in the organization that might not be able to be repaired."

Quade brandished a Glock and placed it right over my heart. From this angle he would kill me instantly. We locked eyes for a second, with him gauging the fear in my eyes. "She's wrong. Zeus isn't the head anymore. I am. When Lauren died he turned everything over to me."

This time around I was able to hide the shock that had taken over my body. Lauren was the fiancée he was mourning. How could I have not connected the dots? I took a steadying breath, savoring each one since it would be my last. Quade's hand was steady; in another world he would have made an amazing surgeon, saving lives instead of taking them.

"Any last words?"

I stared him dead in the eye and lied, "I'm pregnant."

The temperature in the room dropped ten degrees. Quade shrugged at the news and was poised to pull the trigger when his wife placed her head between us. I couldn't see the look she was giving him, but it was enough to have him remove the gun from my chest. A breath I didn't even know I was holding escaped me.

"Quade, I know you aren't going to kill a pregnant woman," she said with a hard shove. She turned to everyone else. "And the rest of you were going to let him? I'm ashamed of all of you right now."

Cash sucked her teeth. "Yara, I know you aren't serious right now?"

"Cash, I know you can't be. You lied to Savion for months about what you were doing for a living, and he was ready to kill you too, but he didn't. He had mercy on you and you can't find it in your heart to have mercy for this misguided woman?"

Cash walked away at that shot of truth serum Yara gave her. I could tell by the fire in her eyes she was just getting started. "Hasani, to be fair, had you not fucked her sister and Zeus didn't kill her, then they wouldn't have tried to shoot Gia, now would they have?"

We killed on the same night. She was the woman he killed, the reason he was able to comfort me. How crazy was that.... I snapped out of my own thoughts long enough to witness Yara starting on Gia, the only person with a valid reason to hate me.

"She went to bat for her sister the same way you would go for yours if the tables were turned. And she said so herself that she tried not to cause any harm. Are you going to be the biggest hypocrite in the room and kill someone for doing exactly what you would do? Any one of you would've done what she did and worse, so don't front like you're any better."

Quade clapped his hands three times, mocking her heartfelt speech. "Any one of us would've done it, but there's a big difference—we wouldn't have got caught. You don't know this bitch from a hole in the wall yet you're up here defending her. What for?"

"Because"—Yara placed a protective hand on her stomach—"as a pregnant woman, I would hope to God someone would have mercy on me and my child."

The Glock hit the floor with a clatter. "You're pregnant?"

"I went to the doctor earlier and she confirmed it with a blood test.

I was going to tell you over dinner, something romantic, but after being married to you for four years I guess this is as romantic as it gets."

Quade embraced his wife. I heard the words "was it the wedding?" to which Yara replied, "Yeah." Now I was feeling guilty as fuck for lying on my womb knowing it was empty. There was a change in Quade when he laid eyes on me. It was slight, but it was enough to know that he might not kill me. Yet.

"I'm not taking her word on it. Make her pee on stick," he said resolutely. "Yara, you got any tests?"

"I used all of them," Yara admitted. "Maybe someone can run to the store and grab one? Savion?"

Savion shrugged. "I could…or we could use the doctor in the room. Gia?"

"I'm going to need for all of you to understand something called specialties. I am not a podiatrist, pediatrician, cardiologist. I am a diagnostician."

"Well then *diagnose* her as pregnant," Savion replied motioning to me with a lazy wave of his hand.

Gia set her eyes on me. She motioned for me to lay down on the table and asked for salad tongs, a pair of latex gloves, and lubricant. Yara returned a couple minutes later with a brand new pair of salad tongs wrapped in a paper towel and a bottle of Sliquid lube. I laid back on the table and spread my legs like I was at the gyno. Although her glares were hard, Gia gently pulled my underwear down and started the examination, slipping the tongs in and stretching my vagina. Yara stood to the left of her, holding the flashlight of her phone over Gia's shoulder so she could see. I closed my eyes, bracing myself for Gia to blow up my spot.

"When was the last time you had your period?" Gia asked after a moment of silence.

I drew a blank. "I…I don't remember."

"When does it usually come?"

"The third of the month."

"Huh."

I wanted to ask what that meant, but I didn't want to blow my spot up. Gia completed the examination without another word. She slipped off her gloves, placed the tongs on the paper towel, and announced, "She's pregnant. I can't tell you how far along without the proper equipment but there's a baby in there. Just like she said. Wanna grab the guys and Cash?"

I was pregnant? Zeus and I weren't always safe, but I changed my birth control patch religiously. Gia caught sight of it as I pulled my dress down and didn't hesitate to rip if off like a Band-Aid.

"You got real fucking lucky today," she said, tossing the patch into the garbage. "However, your luck will run out. The second you drop that baby, it's over for you. You better pray they don't ask me to deliver it either. Birth complications are a bitch. I would hate for you to die before you can see your child."

I placed a protective hand over my stomach, praying for my child and the protection it brought me during one of the hardest times of my life. I was going to give them the gift of life and in return they would give me the gift of nine months to escape the mess Ivy left me in.

HASANI

"I can't believe this shit," Quade said, guzzling down the rest of his Corona and tossing it into the neighboring trashcan. "Yara wants to keep her here in our house. I have to come home every night knowing she's in my basement growing her kid and shit. It's like a weird version of watching Jiffy Pop cook on the microwave."

Savion took his glass of scotch on the rocks to the head. "Sounds about right. I can't believe we have one of the people responsible for Lauren's death and we can't touch her. What do we tell Zeus?"

"Nothing," I replied, rising up from the kitchen island I was posted up against. "We don't tell him shit. He can't even keep it together long enough to get rid of her clothes. Can you imagine what it would do to him knowing we can't find Ivy? He'd tear this city apart until there was nothing left."

Quade scoffed. "Why am I not surprised that your solution to the problem is lying? You lied to us about having another brother, of course you'd keep this shit a secret with a straight face. Fucking liar!"

"So you gon' bring this up every time we get together?" I asked, approaching Quade, who jumped up from his seat with the quickness. Savion jumped between us, telling both of us to take a step back before we did something we might regret. "Savion, move the fuck out of my way. If this nigga wanna shoot the fair one we can take this shit outside right now, but I'm not about to keep listening to the slick shit coming out of his mouth and taking it."

"We ain't gotta step no fucking where, nigga!" Quade barked, reaching over Savion and clocking me in the face.

All of the pent up anger and aggression I felt at being snubbed by my brothers came out in a rush of aggression. I started swinging, uncaring of who the fuck ate my punches. One hit Quade right in the jaw while another knocked Savion in the head. Once he saw I wasn't taking it easy on him, Quade hit me with a few low blows of his own, one landing on my side. Savion, who was stuck in the middle and getting half the blows meant for each of us, tackled me, sending us flying straight into the cabinets. Glasses, plates, and cups hit the floor, the sounds of shattered glass reverberating throughout the house. Cash and Gia came running first, with Yara bringing up the rear. You would think with the arrival of our wives that we would cool it down, but no, I was angrier than I anticipated and nearly hit Yara, who ducked at the last minute. Quade took that as a sign of disrespect and pulled his piece on me. Gia, who stayed equally ready, pulled hers on him.

"Do it, motherfucker. I'd rather be dead than have to deal with any of you ungrateful motherfuckers! Everything I've done for this family and all you can think of is the time I had our father's back when the rest of you didn't! Go ahead, Quade, pull the trigger!"

Gia pressed her gun into Quade's temple. "Both you and I know you don't want to do that. Put the gun down, Quade. I love you like a brother, but I love my husband like a husband. I'll do whatever I have to do."

"Quade, put the gun down!" Yara barked.

Quade's finger stayed on the trigger, and I knew he was going to pull it, when a voice said from the doorway, "What's going on?"

Little Quade stood in the doorway watching the scene in horror. He was dressed in the racecar pajamas I bought him for Christmas and in his hand was the Lightening McQueen plush toy Gia bought him for his birthday. Gia lowered her gun the same time as Quade.

Yara rushed over to her son and comforted him, hugging him tight while telling him that the adults were just playing. Quade took a couple steps towards the pair and was stopped by the look of fear on his son's face.

He turned back to me and said in a cold whisper, "Get the fuck out of my house and don't ever come back."

I left out through the backyard, too ashamed to look Little Quade in the eye. Gia was right behind me, walking with her head down. I didn't know she was crying until I heard the sniffles. I pressed her against the side of the house and tilted her head up to face mine.

"I didn't mean to put you in an awkward position back there," I said, wiping away her tears with the pads of my thumbs. "Quade and I started slinging words...you know I would never do anything to hurt Yara—"

"Did you mean what you said back there? About wishing you were dead?" My silence acted as an answer. "Hasani, I don't ever want to hear you talk like that ever again, you hear me? Our relationship might not be perfect, but you are right where you're supposed to be."

Somehow it went from me comforting Gia to her being my rock. I wiped her tears and took her home where we had passionate make up sex. We allowed our frustrations and worries to fall to the background as we came together as one. I missed being with her like this, feeling her soft skin, smelling the jasmine vanilla perfume she wore, and the warmth that came from our bodies connecting. For all the bad that happened tonight, the only good to come of this situation was that I had my wife back. Or at least I thought I did until I saw the message on her phone:

I'm still thinking about that kiss.

I stared at the message, which didn't have a name attached to it, and tried to figure out what my next move was. There was no denying the fact that I had put Gia through more than she deserved, so it should be no surprise to me that she stepped out on our marriage. But what had me tripping was the "still." *Still?* How long has this relationship been going on for? Had Gia spent our entire relationship playing the victim only to be out here doing as much dirt? I placed the phone back on the nightstand the way she left it and slid back into bed.

Gia laid her head on my chest and wrapped one of her long legs around my waist. "What's wrong, baby? Everything okay?"

If Gia could stay with me after everything I put her through, then I should be able to do the same. Kissing her consolingly on the lips, I replied, "Nothing, babe. Go back to sleep."

~

My other brothers didn't agree with the idea of keeping Zeus from knowing there was a target on his back, but when I popped up at his place with Grayson in tow he was still ignorant to the fact. However, he was well aware that Quade wasn't fucking with me anymore.

"You know how Quade is. Just give him some time to get over it," Zeus said, pouring us each a glass of orange juice. He was looking more like his usual self aside from the bags underneath his eyes. "Knowing that your father wasn't the man you thought he was is a lot to process. He'll come back around, Hasani. Just wait on it."

"Had I known my appearance would cause a rift like this I would've stayed away," Grayson admitted, reaching for one of the polished apples sitting in a bowl and taking a bite of it. "All I wanted was family, but not at the expense of tearing another one apart. Maybe I should talk to—"

"Quade isn't going to let you talk; he's going to pop on sight. You need to give him some space as well. Savion has always been the one to talk some sense into him. We'll come together for a meeting when time is right. Speaking of...what was yesterday's meeting about? I didn't get an invite."

"I thought you were busy?"

"My plans fell through. It would've been nice to be included though. I stepped down as head, but that doesn't mean I relinquished all my rights to being included in family discussions. What happened?"

I gave Zeus the rundown on everything, excluding Quincy and

Ivy's ties to Lauren. Quade already had me feeling guilty for keeping the identity of Lauren's murderer from him, but I wasn't going to keep him out of the rest of our family business. He sipped on his coffee as he listened, nodding his head. Every so often, his eyes went out of focus, proving my point that he didn't need any extra stress on him at the moment.

"With Gia's people and our people on it, we should have her soon," I said with two slaps on the table. "As soon as we have something concrete, you'll be the first one to know. You good? I see those bags underneath your eyes."

"I didn't get much sleep last night." He could see the concern in my eyes and followed up with, "I was cleaning…packing…Lauren's sister is coming by to get her clothes and stuff. They want to donate it to the Salvation Army."

I noticed the suitcases sitting in the foyer. My brother was hurting, but I was relieved to hear that he wasn't sleeping with her clothes anymore. "I know you must be lonely in this house. Have you thought about taking Emma up on her offer to temporarily come out of retirement?"

"You know that's not the first time she offered. She was the first person I showed Lauren's engagement ring to. She offered to come out of retirement whenever we had children." There was that loss of focus again. Zeus slipped into another world. "I'm fine here on my own. I've found a few ways to keep…busy."

"Still, wouldn't it be good to have someone in the house to keep you company? I don't doubt that you're good alone, but I think you need another person here to help you get back into a routine."

Zeus eyed me over his mug. "Gia kicked you out? If you wanted to move in all you had to do was ask."

"Not me." Zeus' eyes slid from me over to Grayson. I could see the "no" in his eyes and pled my case before he could object. "Zeus, what happened to helping him with a place to stay?"

"The place to stay didn't include my place."

"Zeus…"

"He's a doctor; I'm sure there are plenty of hospitals he can apply to that would be happy to have him. I'll cut him a check to get him set up, but I don't want a stranger in my house. Can you honestly say we know everything about him? For all we know he could be working with this Ivy person."

Grayson rose from the island. "Are you really reducing me to being a villain? You know what? Maybe I should've left after my first unwarm welcome. Hasani, I'll be waiting in the car..."

Zeus was unmoved by the outburst. His eyes followed Grayson out of the kitchen and he waited for the slamming of the front door to speak up. "I didn't want to hurt his feelings, but you should have sent him off with a check, Hasani. Quade will never accept him, and at the end of the day I'm not betraying my blood brother I raised for someone else. Savion feels the same way, he just hasn't had the courage to tell you. He may carry our last name but he'll never be a real Townsend."

"Zeus, he went home and found his mother dead from a heart attack. He doesn't have anyone. Can you imagine how much pride he had to put aside to come here knowing he would be belittled and treated like shit? But he did." I rose from my chair, exhausted from fighting this battle. "If you can't do it for me, and you won't do it for him, do it for Pops, because if he was still here you know he would want us to look out for Grayson, official Townsend or not."

I was halfway to the kitchen door when Zeus said, "He can stay for a couple weeks. He can go anywhere he wants in the house except for on my level, understood?"

"Most definitely." I bum rushed him with a hug, laughing at the grimace on his face hiding the smile he was fighting to hold back.

"I don't understand why you won't let him stay with you."

"Gia and I are still fixing up the house. The only furnished rooms we have are our bedroom, her office, and the kitchen. Also...I think it would help you to be around someone who's suffered a recent loss as well. He might be the rock you need."

Zeus replied with a shrug. I stood there, looking at the shell of what had become my brother. He had spent the better part of his life sacrificing to make sure we were good, and in the end, when he was supposed to have his happily every after, it was stolen from him. I honestly don't think he'll ever recover from this without answers to Lauren's death. Everyone was waiting for PI's and foot soldiers to find Ivy. I had a feeling this was one of those situations where I needed to get out into the streets and handle business myself.

"He's agreed to let you stay," I told Grayson, who was sitting in the passenger's seat staring into space. "I know this hasn't been the easiest transition, but the worst is over."

"My college best friend, he lives out in Jersey. He's a dentist. He was the one who pushed me to find you all because he believed that despite our upbringings we could find a common ground. He also told me that if shit went sour I could crash with him and his wife, but they're newly married, trying for a baby...maybe I'll luck out and find a decent job. Basketball teams are always looking. The only thing holding me here is...never mind."

"You've been helping out Giada." I squeezed his shoulder. "She needs you, Grayson. I need you too. I haven't told anyone, not even Gia, but I'm going looking for Ivy myself. He doesn't know it, but Zeus is her target. I need you to keep an eye on him. If any random bitches pop up or he starts acting weird, call Gia. You have her number."

Everything in Grayson's body language was a big middle finger to the entire situation, but he relented. "I'm only doing this because you asked me to. Can you at least keep me in the loop?"

"Of course."

After helping Grayson place his luggage into my bedroom and wishing Zeus a goodnight, I took off into the silent night with no idea of where I was going or even if I would return. All I knew was that no one would care anyway. My wife had another man, my brother and best friend hated me, I was known to everyone as the eternal fuck up. As far as I was concerned, they were better off without me.

GIANNA

I sat on the examination table, legs dangling, as I stared at the text message responsible for ruining my life. Three months had passed since my heart left my body in search of Hasani's, searching for him to explain that the break it experienced was for all the wrong reasons. *I'm still thinking about that kiss.* Carmelo spent our entire relationship manipulating me to the point where I lost my sense of self. I lied to Giada about the confident resolve I put on when it came to leaving my boyfriend. The truth was, I did agree to go under the knife to please Carmelo. I was going to get a Brazilian butt lift using the small stomach pudge I gained over my few years of college. From the consultation to being put under by the anesthesiologist, I felt like I was doing the wrong thing, but I went through with it anyway. Since I didn't have the backbone to back out, God made sure I did with complications early on into the procedure. I woke up confused and in an excruciating amount of pain. Carmelo comforted me, but when he suggested that we try the procedure again later on in the year, I knew I had to walk away before this man killed me in an effort to shape me into who he wanted me to be.

"I have called all the hospitals in the city. They checked the emergency room and morgues. He's not there. One of the nurses had recommended a missing person's report..." Cash trailed off, her expression softening. She was the only person able to keep a cool head over the past few months. "Gia, he's going to come home. I know it has to be hard right now not knowing where he is, but him not showing up in any hospitals proves that he's good."

I placed my phone in my lab coat. "It only proves that he hasn't been found. Yet. The night before he disappeared he wished that he was dead. What am I supposed to do? Hasani isn't tough like Quade—he could end up seriously hurt." Cash embraced me and smoothed my hair. "Cash, something else happened the night of the fight."

I showed Cash the text message from Carmelo. Her eyes flickered from the message back to me. "Gia...you were fucking around on him?"

"My ex sent me this message, and he made sure to send it at night being extra messy. I would never do Hasani like that. Carmelo got what he wanted.... He ruined my marriage."

"Nah, you ruined your marriage by not being real about yours." I shrugged out of Cash's embrace and looked at her like she was crazy. She was sure to return the look. "Yeah, I said it. If one of my exes left a message on my phone like this and there was even the slightest possibility of Savion seeing it I wouldn't wait until I saw him later that night. You should have addressed the message the second you saw it."

"He had already left the house."

"Then find him. You're supposed to do what it takes to make sure your marriage remains an impenetrable fortress. Carmelo shouldn't even have access to you. This should've been nipped in the bud a long time ago."

I cut my eyes at her. "I pointed a gun at him on my wedding day. How much more should it take to keep him away?"

"Telling your husband and letting him handle it."

"It's too late for that now," I said, sliding off of the table. "Hasani's done with me, he's done with all of us. Now tell me where this girl is so I can administer this checkup and get home."

Cash shook her head. "You're not about to do a damn thing in this condition. Go home and get some rest, you hear? She can wait another day."

I bit back the truth, that I hadn't spent a night at home since Hasani disappeared. My mother welcomed me back home with open arms, setting up my bedroom for an extended stay. Giada had returned home as well, spending the better part of her day in physical therapy with Grayson and the team of physical therapists Daddy hired to help her walk again. They were finishing up a session in the gymnasium turned physical therapy center when I arrived home. Giada was dressed in sweats and a loose tee, but her makeup was flawless as usual as was her hair, which was blown out and placed into a ponytail with loose tendrils framing her face. She lit up at the sight of me and rolled over to the entrance of the gym. Every time I saw her in this wheelchair, my heart broke. According to her doctors, the odds of her walking again were slim to none, however, Grayson encouraged her to continue trying regardless of what they had to say.

"Gia, you're home early," Giada chirped, holding her arms out for a hug. I gave her a gentle squeeze like she was fine china and laughed when she squeezed me tight in return. "There's no need to be gentle with me, Gia. I'm not a baby so you can stop treating me like one."

I kissed her on the forehead. "I can't help it. The doctor in me says to stop going easy on you, but the other part of me that's put Band-Aids on your scraped knees can't help it. How was therapy today?"

"The same," Giada shrugged with an air of nonchalance, but I could see the resignation in her eyes. "Grayson's putting together a new set of exercises for me to work on this week. He feels like these aren't challenging enough anymore."

"Because you're mastering them quickly," Grayson cut in, grinning down at my sister. He kept his eyes on her the entire conversation. "The most important part of making progress is staying positive, Giada. You'd be surprised at how far a positive attitude takes you in the recovery process, right Gia?"

"He's absolutely right," I cosigned.

Giada ran a self-conscious hand over her hair. "It's hard to keep positive when I feel like everything I'm doing is in vain. I am twenty-eight years old. My career was just starting. Any hopes of having kids is nonexistent. It's hard to stay positive knowing there's a good chance I might end up alone."

"Giada, you're not going to end up alone. You're smart, funny, you have a beautiful heart, and I can't think of a more deserving person of love than you. Don't let this chair fool you into thinking you're not worthy of happiness."

"Would you date a woman in a wheelchair, Grayson?" Giada asked, locking eyes with her admirer.

"Of course I would date a woman in a wheelchair."

"I find that hard to believe," Giada harrumphed and took off, nearly running me over to get out of the gymnasium.

Grayson's smile fell. I motioned between her and him. "Is there something I'm missing?"

"Giada seems to believe my reason for not asking her out has to do with the fact that she still hasn't walked when that couldn't be farther from the truth. The truth is there's only two things keeping me here, one of which is Giada. If we get together and things go south it'll be harder to stay here."

"What's your other reason?" When he didn't answer after another minute, I took a step closer. "Grayson…what's the other reason you're staying here? And don't lie to me—I'll know."

Grayson nudged his head for me to follow him. We started walking the span of the gym. The floor was redone to accommodate Giada's equipment, but the track remained. "I was the last person to speak to Hasani before he left. He made me promise to stay here and look out for Zeus, which has been a struggle since he's went out of his way to make sure we never bump into each other. I feel like I'm living with a ghost. Working with Giada is the only time I ever feel normal."

This was my first time hearing of Hasani's last words. "Was he angry? Sad? Did you fear for his life?"

"No, he looked…determined. Something changed in him after the conversation he had with Zeus. I have a feeling he went looking for Ivy. That's her name, right? Giada told me one day."

I nodded. "Yeah, her name's Ivy."

"Gia, I don't know what happened between you and my brother, but I know he loves you. He gave me a number to call him in case of emergencies…"

I saved the number in my phone. We made small talk as we approached the entrance to the gym and went our separate ways after. Dinner wasn't for another hour, which meant my mother was in the kitchen prepping whatever extravagant meal she planned on cooking. Ever since I was a kid, my earliest memories of my mother were helping her in the kitchen. Italians were big on food and being a mocha colored sister from one of the roughest parts of Brooklyn, Mom always felt like she had something to prove to the Luchesi family when it came to Italian cuisine. Instead of letting the subtle hints of racism that came from some of my father's family beat her down, she spent her time making recipes from scratch, practicing for years until one day my nonna tasted her steak pizzaiola and gave it her seal of approval. Before she passed away, she left my mother her recipe book, one of the Luchesi Family's most prized possessions. It was sitting on the kitchen counter open to risotto when I entered the kitchen. My mother was stealing peeks at the page as she shredded cheese.

"Something smells good," I announced, washing my hands and jumping in to help with whatever leftover prep needed to be done. I saw the ingredients used to make Nonna's cookies sitting on the opposite side of the counter and decided to start there. "Lasagna?"

"That and a few of Giada's favorites. Baked macaroni and cheese, cabbage, collards, ribs, and I might fry some chicken if I have enough time," Mom replied, looking up from the recipe book and laying eyes on me. "When was the last time you got some sleep, Gianna? There are bags under your eyes."

I shook off her worries. "I slept last night. A full eight hours."

"Laying in bed tossing and turning does not equate to sleeping. Honey, have you considered taking some time off from work? Maybe a few vacation days?" she asked, tucking a strand of kinky curly hair behind her ear as she started checking the pots in front of her.

"I don't need a few days off to stay home and worry. Working is keeping me busy, and if I'm busy—"

"You're not thinking about that trifling husband of yours."

"Ma..."

"Gianna, it's not too late for an annulment. He abandoned you!" she exclaimed, slamming her hand on the island. In a calmer voice she said, "I know you love Hasani, but you can't tell me this man hasn't put you through more than some people see in 50 years of marriage. The cheating, the breaking up, then he walks out on you? I knew I should've said my peace before you walked down the aisle."

I had already made my dough for the ricotta cheese cookies and was pounding it with more force than intended. "What is your peace, Ma? That you're upset I didn't end up with Carmelo? Had some good haired babies and lived happily ever after being a surgeon's wife? Say it: you never thought Hasani was good enough and you're happy he left me."

"I'm happy he didn't waste more of your time than necessary!" She came over to where I was and placed a hand over mine. "Carmelo has grown so much since the last time you dated. He's focused on his career and very marriage minded. He's willing to do whatever it takes to make you happy. You're his heart, Gia."

"What did you just say?"

Mom blanched. "Gia—"

"Those were the exact words Carmelo said to me the night of the bachelorette party before he kissed me. I have spent months trying to figure out how he was able to find me that night and get into my dressing room the night of my wedding." I snatched my hand out of my mother's. "You sent him to change my mind, didn't you? To convince me that I was making a mistake!"

"Where is your husband, Gia? This looks like a mistake to me!"

I slammed my phone on the table. "My husband left because Carmelo texted me about that same kiss you put him up to. You are the reason my husband left me! They say it be your own blood but imagine how I must feel knowing my mother has been plotting on my marriage before I could even make it down the aisle."

"Gia, I was only trying to help!"

I pulled up my shirt and down the waistband of my pants, revealing the faded scar on my stomach. "You were trying to help by sending me back to the man who almost killed me trying to turn me into something I wasn't while shunning the man who has always accepted me as I am. Thanks a lot."

My mother gasped at the scars; I spent the better part of my young adulthood hiding them behind makeup. She reached out to touch it and I slapped her hand away, uncaring of the hurt that flashed across her face. She hit me below the belt and had no right to concern herself with what went on below mine. I snatched my phone off the counter and stormed out of the kitchen before she saw the tears spilling down my cheeks. I thought I heard someone calling me but I was too distraught to answer. My car was warmed up and ready to go as I slid into the driver's seat. I wasn't the least bit surprised to see the house's number blinking on my screen. Anger swelled in my chest and next thing I know, I'm banging my phone against the dashboard, cussing everyone including Hasani, whose leaving took away the option of us working our issues out. I scrolled through my contacts and found the number Grayson had given. It went straight to voicemail.

"Why didn't you say goodbye to me?" I screamed into my phone, breaking down in tears. "Hasani, we have been through too much together for you to just walk away without saying goodbye! Instead of running away from the problem you should have came to me so we could talk about it! I have called hospitals, the city morgue, anywhere I can think of looking for you and I'm tired of it. I want you to come home so we can fix us! Please come home."

I hung up the phone and curled up in a ball, thinking if he didn't call back after listening to me pour my heart out to him our relationship was worse than I thought.

QUINCY

I sat in the bedroom nook, watching as Yara played with Little Quade in the backyard. They went out back everyday, either swinging on the swings or playing catch. Every once in a blue Quade would join them, but he spent most of his days coming in and out the house, talking on his phone in hushed tones. I listened through the bedroom door, hoping one day I would hear that Ivy was caught. She never came up in a conversation, but Hasani did. He disappeared and no one could find him, not even the infamous tracker, Quade. Sometimes he would disappear for a few days at a time, searching for his brother, which allowed Yara to give me a little more space. While Little Quade was off at Cash's house, she would let me sit in the backyard and sip on a virgin sangria. Those were the moments I held on to tight because if I didn't I was likely to lose my mind. Like today, the day Zeus showed up.

It was one of those rare days in the Townsend household where everyone was busy. Quade was flying out to meet a supplier and Little Quade was spending the day with one of his uncles. I wish I would've asked which one so I could prepare myself for him. Yara and I were in the kitchen making dinner when the front door opened, followed by the sounds of Little Quade's laughter. Yara panicked and shoved me into the pantry as her little boy was flown into the kitchen by him. I watched through the slits of the pantry door as he set Little Quade down on the floor. Yara bent to embrace her baby boy. He kissed her on the cheek and gave her protruding belly a rub. My eyes started stinging from unshed tears. I couldn't imagine receiving that kind of unconditional love from someone.

"Did you have fun with Uncle Zeus?" Yara asked, ruffling his sandy curls.

Little Quade nodded his head vigorously. "We played basketball, watched a movie, and went to the arcade. He let me eat as much ice cream as I wanted! Now I gotta poop."

"Go poop, baby," Yara said, holding in her giggles the best she could. "Make sure you wash your hands real good for dinner." She waited for those tiny footsteps to fade on Little Quade's ascent upstairs. "Thanks for taking him out, Zeus. Lately, Quade has been working overtime to find Hasani and keep the company running. He's spreading himself extremely thin."

Zeus took a seat at the kitchen island. He motioned to the extra glass of juice on the island. "You have company?"

"No, I was cooking and in the mood for grape and apple juice. These pregnancy hormones got me changing my mind at the last minute. Yesterday I was eating snickers one minute and peanut butter cups the next," Yara lied with ease, taking my glass of apple juice and placing it into the sink. "Can I get you something to drink?"

Zeus accepted her offer. The tears in my eyes were short lived as I noticed the way Zeus studied Yara as she busied herself with pouring him a glass of juice. He admired her profile, his eyes tracing her jawline and landing on her stomach. Yara caught him looking and laughed this tinkling laugh I never heard before. I could tell this was a normal occurrence between the two.

"Whatchu over there looking at? How fat I've gotten?"

"Yara, stop playing. You look beautiful. Pregnancy suits you well," Zeus said with a warm smile. His eyes lowered to her stomach again, and I saw him go off somewhere far away for a minute. "Do you know what you're having yet?"

"I won't know until my next doctor's appointment. Quade wants a little girl, but I don't care. All I want is a healthy baby with ten fingers and toes." Yara set the glass of juice in front of him. Her smile faltered for a second and was back bright as ever, but it didn't reach her eyes. "Zeus…have you ever spoken to anyone about Lauren and Zoelle?"

Zeus shook his head. "Like a professional? It wouldn't do me any good, Yara. I've come to accept the fact that love isn't in the cards for me. Every time I get close to someone they're snatched away from me. Lauren…Zoelle…gone."

"I used to think the same thing before I met Quade. My mother was killed and I honestly believed that anyone who knew my story would never be able to love me. Amir came along accepted me the way I was, but it wasn't really acceptance, more like tolerance. I learned the difference when Quade came into my life." Yara gave his shoulder a squeeze. "You are going to find someone that loves you the way you deserve to be loved and they won't be taken away, snatched, none of that."

"You know what hurts the most? I never get to say goodbye." Zeus spoke as if he didn't hear her entire speech, and something told me he hadn't. "I never got to say goodbye to Lauren, I never even got to meet Zoelle, and now someone else I cared about is gone."

Yara's already large eyes widened. "You met someone?"

"Shortly after Lauren died, which was why I didn't expect anything serious to come of it. She was mourning the loss of someone the same way I was. Over time, I found myself opening up to her, connecting on a level I wasn't able to with even Lauren." Yara hid her gaping mouth behind her glass. "I hadn't known her long, but I think I was falling in love with her."

I took a seat on the open step ladder in the pantry and placed my face in my hands, taking deep calculated breaths to keep the growing sob in my throat at bay. Zeus was falling in love with me? Other than my mother, I never imagined another person ever loving me. Love was something other people experienced, and I always looked on wishing for even a tiny piece. Hearing from Zeus that our small amount of time spent together meant something to him warmed me in places I was convinced would remain eternally cold. I listened with my eyes closed, remembering each syllable and inflection that passed his lips.

"We were supposed to go on a date. For the first time since Lauren's death I was excited about something. After the first hour, I thought maybe she was running behind. By ten, I was growing worried. I called her around midnight and got her voicemail. Nothing." Zeus finished off his glass of juice like a shot of whiskey. "I spent the rest of the night packing Lauren's belongings, talking to her, deciding if this was the right time for me to move on. Everything in my heart told me this woman was it."

"Have you contacted the police?"

"Nah, she never came out and said it, but she was involved in some funny business. The last time we saw each other she was all messed up. I'm sure it had something to do with that sister of hers. She sounded like bad news."

I lifted my head at the same time Yara's eyes focused on the pantry. "Why don't you leave her name with me and I can have Quade do some digging. He's already out with his team looking for Hasani. They might be able to find out where she is."

"I appreciate the offer, but I have someone on it. One of the best in the business. If she left a paper trail, he'll find it."

Too bad there was no paper trail to find because I was snatched out of my apartment. Zeus rose to his feet and stretched, giving Yara enough time to shoot me a scathing look. The pair exited the kitchen with talks of having dinner sometime over the weekend when Quade returned home. I jumped at the sound of the front door slamming shut followed by the stomping of feet. Yara returned to the kitchen in a ball of fury. She yanked the pantry door open, ready to cuss me out, with the tears running down my face stopping her.

"Why didn't you say something?" she asked.

"I didn't want everyone to think I was with him because of Ivy. You have to believe me when I say I had no idea who Ivy was going after. By the time I found out I was in way too deep with Zeus. The night you took me was the night I planned to come clean," I sobbed, holding my belly to keep the shaking from knocking me over. "I love him, Yara. I had no intention of letting Ivy harm him. You have to believe me."

Yara stared at me for a full minute before replying, "Come on, lets get you into bed. I'll bring dinner upstairs..."

I allowed Yara to lead me upstairs to the bedroom she set up for me. Quade wanted to keep me in the basement, but she reminded him that I would need sunlight to keep from becoming depressed. I slept in Little Quade's room while he bunked with his parents, and the next morning I woke to a bedroom with a twin bed, bookshelf filled with books, and a desk. I spent most of my time at that desk writing in the notebooks left by Quade. One in particular was filled with different apologies I planned to read to Zeus if I was ever given the opportunity. I picked it up from the desk and cradled it against my chest as Yara tucked me in.

"Get some rest tonight. We'll discuss this in depth tomorrow morning," she said before creeping from the room.

God blessed me when he brought Yara into my life. I could see why Zeus was so in awe of her. She had a pure heart, something a lot of people, myself included, lacked. I couldn't think of a single person who would still treat me as good as she had knowing the true circumstances of my situation. The idea of a solution was enough to lull me to sleep, but it was the reality of it that woke me. I was choking, gasping for air as something wrapped tightly around my throat. My hands clawed at the fingers holding me hostage. The first thought that popped into my mind was that Yara betrayed me, thinking it was better to see me dead than have Zeus hurt again. Then common sense kicked in. Yara would never hurt me, but her husband might.

"Please," I mouthed to Quade, who loomed over me like a creature of the night. "Please don't do this."

I expected Quade to sound angry, but when he spoke, there was pain in his voice. "My brother. You're pregnant by my brother? I've kept your phone for the past three months, watching as someone named Marcus called you everyday leaving messages and voicemails. Today I felt this wave of compassion for the man calling looking for his pregnant woman, so I decided to listen to one of the voicemails and you know who I heard? My—fucking—brother," Quade hissed.

He loosened his grip around my throat. Fresh air inflated my lungs, scratching at my dry throat as I gasped for air. "I couldn't tell you the truth because—"

"Because I would have to kill you," Quade finished grimly. "I bet you had this planned with your sister, didn't you? Fuck Zeus, get him to let his guard down, and then…kill him…"

"No, I would never do anything to hurt Zeus. I love him."

"Love?" Quade shook with silent laughter. "You expect me to believe that you love him after everything you and that fucked up family did to him? You killed the real love of his life and you are going to pay with yours."

The cool metal of Quade's gun pressed into my temple. I cried like a baby, blubbering and begging Quade not to pull the trigger. He promised me my baby would be safe. I told him as much, urged him to think of his niece or nephew in my stomach before making any drastic decisions. Much to my horror, he broke down and cried along with me. No matter how much he sobbed, his hand remained rigid, killing any thoughts of overpowering him.

"If you kill me Zeus will never forgive you," I cried, begging him with my eyes to reconsider. "I'm holding a piece of him inside of me. A piece of the love I have for him."

Quade tapped the gun against my temple, shaking his head ever so slightly. "If I let you live, and Zeus finds out who you are, he'll kill himself. I won't let you kill my brother."

The tip of the gun rested against my temple. I watched the tendons in Quade's arm flex as his finger readied itself to pull the trigger. My lips parted to deliver one last request. "Let Zeus do it."

"What?" Quade breathed.

"Let Zeus hear the truth from me. Then he can pull the trigger. It's the least I could do for him," I said, thinking if there was one person in the world who deserved to hear the entire truth it was Zeus. I owed him that much. "I won't fight, I won't argue. I'll tell my story and let him do whatever he wants."

Quade removed the gun from my temple and disappeared from the bedroom like a shadow. I sagged into my pillow, trembling from head to foot. A sharp cramp shot through my uterus and traveled up my spine. Why did this have to happen right now? I rolled onto my side and rocked from side to side, saying a prayer for my baby. Growing up, I wasn't blessed with maternal instincts thanks to my mother forbidding me to play with Barbie dolls out of fear that I would only want to be a mother when I became older. I counted it as a blessing in disguise the older I grew, to the point where I religiously took my birth control meds at the same exact time everyday, but the second I found out I was pregnant, life changed for me. My sole purpose changed to protecting this tiny human being inside of me. Seconds molded with minutes and it felt as if hours passed when the bedroom door opened with a creak.

"Quincy."

His voice was a temporary fix, instantly relieving the cramps. I untangled myself from the sheets sticky with my sweat and sat up, resting my aching back against the headboard. Zeus entered the room with hesitant footsteps, approaching me as if I were a mirage. He took a seat beside me and leaned forward, bathing his face in moonlight. Dark circles lined his eyes and his lips, those same lips I once sucked on in the throes of ecstasy, were turned down in confusion. The door closed with a whoosh, leaving the two of us alone.

"Quincy…what are you doing here?"

There goes the tears, falling against my will. My dry mouth flooded with the saliva that accompanied crying. "I have something to tell you, Zeus." He reached out to hold my hand. I removed it from his reach, using it to play with my other hand as I tried to figure out how to speak my peace.

"After my mother passed away, I got in contact with my sister and she brought me to New York to help her gain back the territory our father lost during a drug war." I closed my eyes, finding it easier to continue on without looking him in the eye. "She made us do a lot of things, most of which involved killing. It was Ivy who took out the lieutenants in Red Hook. Sean is alive because I let him FaceTime his daughter."

Zeus wiped away my tears with the pads of his fingers. I wish he would stop being so good to me. "Quincy, we all got family that makes us do some fucked up shit. You're safe from her now. Stop crying."

"Zeus, I need you to stop talking so I can finish telling you the entire truth," I begged him, refusing to even peek at him and see the hurt mixed with confusion in his eyes. "I shot Giada. Ivy wanted revenge for you killing Kaia."

"She was blackmailing—."

"Zeus." He quieted. "Giada and Sean aren't the only people we caused harm to." I felt the temperature in the room drop ten degrees. He knew. All he was waiting for was the words to come out of my mouth. This was it. I was coming clean and ruining the single chance I had at happiness.

"Quincy..."

"Lauren did what she thought was best for you. She didn't want you to find out about Zoelle from Ivy, so she agreed to pay the million dollars Ivy wanted. Too bad she didn't know Ivy never intended on letting her walk away alive." I lifted my trembling hand and pretended I was holding an imaginary gun. "She wanted me to do it. I was sick to my stomach at the thought of hurting Lauren, who had always been so nice to me, but I knew it was either me or her. Ivy placed a gun in my hand, this silver Beretta, and told me to shoot her. Sadan objected and Ivy killed him. Lauren tried to shoot Ivy and she took my hand... then put her finger over my finger...and she shot Lauren...I told Lauren I was sorry. I was sorry. I never wanted to hurt her. Zeus, I swear I—"

I felt a flash of wind beside me. My eyes snapped open in time to see Zeus' fist fly past me and collide with the wooden headboard. Angry tears spilled down his face, collecting in the parts where it dipped in agony and curled with contempt. That hit was meant for me. I felt the air leave my body as if I was struck. Zeus followed up with a left hook, barely missing my face. I remained still, begging for his forgiveness as he beat the headboard until his knuckles bled. He used his same hands to wipe away the tears, leaving streaks of blood on his face.

"I made love to you, I brought you into my home, I confided in you, and you were the very demon I was fighting. I prayed with the murderer of the only woman I've ever loved," Zeus said, eyeing me with disgust. His hand dipped into his pants pocket and out came the same gun Quade held to my temple earlier. "When my brother handed me this gun I didn't understand why. What would I need a gun for in order to talk to you? Now I know and I'm grateful for the opportunity to do right by Lauren."

A cramp shot through my womb again. I instinctively grabbed at my stomach, wincing in pain. It was slight, but Zeus was able to make out the swell of my stomach. The gun he held tightly was now limp and dangling from his fingers.

"Is that...is that my child?" he said through barely parted lips. My lids picked that moment to droop. I felt my body heat up like a furnace. The moonlit room grew steadily darker with each passing second, and the answer to his question got stuck on my tongue like peanut butter. My last thought before I passed out was that the truth had set me free. Now I was tasked with figuring out where it was taking me.

~

MY BABY. Where was my baby?

The thought was enough to jolt me awake. My eyes snapped open for a second and fluttered shut at the blinding fluorescent lights. There was an intake of breath beside me, loud over the clicking and whirring of machines. More whispering ensued, forcing me to pop my eyes open again to figure out where I was. Yara sat in a hospital chair beside me, watching me with bated breath. She held out a cup of water to my parched lips, which parted at the introduction of the cool drink. I downed the entire paper cup in three gulps, still thirsty as I sipped the last drop.

"My baby," I said, patting the small mountain of blankets covering my stomach. "Please don't tell me I lost my baby..."

Yara moved the blankets enough for me to see my stomach, which remained unharmed. "Your baby is fine, but the stress you were placed under caused some bleeding. I was asleep when Quade came home. You know I would've never allowed him to—"

"It's okay," I assured her. "I deserved it."

"No one deserves what was done to you. I plan on making Quade pay for this..." Yara's threats died at the entrance of my attending physician flanked by two nurses. They went through the process of checking my vitals, which were strong considering the circumstances. The doctor mentioned that not only was I stressed, I was dehydrated. I tuned in and out of my diagnosis, nodding along although my mind was elsewhere. I wanted to know where Zeus was.

"Who is your obstetrician?" the doctor asked. I felt my cheeks redden. Gia did what she could inside of the makeshift doctor's office she made in Yara's basement, but I wouldn't call her an obstetrician.

I was saved from having to tell the truth by a voice saying from the doorway, "We don't have a set doctor as of yet. Our last obstetrician went on maternity leave herself, forcing us to remain on a waiting list for Dr. Rhonda Robinson."

"She's one of the best obstetricians in the city. She's also a friend of mine. I'll see if I can get you bumped up on that list," the doctor said, smiling kindly at Zeus. "Are you ready to hear your baby's heartbeat?"

I perked up, the fatigue and weariness disappearing at the mention of officially meeting my baby. Gia wasn't able to do sonograms from the small setup in the basement, which left me picturing how my unborn child looked. I knew I was going on five months, and according to the print outs she provided me every month, my baby was the size of a large banana, roughly 11 ounces, and curled up in a ball. My imagination didn't hold a candle to the image that popped up on the ultrasound machine. Everything—my kidnapping, imprisonment, and the last three months—faded to the background at the sound of the beating heart filling the room.

"That's...that's my baby," I choked out, reaching out towards the screen. "I can't believe I'm seeing you."

The doctor's brows furrowed. I could tell she wanted to pry, but doing so would ruin the moment, and I needed this moment after so many months of pain. Yara handed me two tissues. I didn't understand why until I felt my cheeks grow tight from fallen tears.

"Would you like to know what you're having?"

"Yes," Zeus and I said at the same time.

The doctor moved the probe around for a few minutes, claiming that the baby was playing possum. "Ah...there we go. Congratulations. It looks like you're going to be welcoming a beautiful baby girl into the world."

"A girl? I'm having a girl!"

"Congratulations!" Yara squealed, maneuvering around to give me a hug. "A little girl to play with my girl! I'm so excited! We have got to start planning a shower...or maybe a push party...what's wrong, Quincy?"

Somewhere in the midst of celebrating I almost forgot about Zeus, who was staring at the machine without saying a word. This was a lot for him to take in. Standing here, looking at his unborn child, humanized me in his eyes. Killing me would be like killing part of him and I think that was starting to set in. The doctor printed out the sonograms for me all while giving me prescriptions for prenatal vitamins and for iron, which I wasn't getting enough of. Yara followed her out of the room, giving us some time to figure out where we go from here.

"If you were to walk out of that door and never come back I would completely understand," I told him as I wiped away the rest of the tears. "But I cannot go back to living in a tiny room like bait for Ivy. I've started over before, it's nothing for me to leave New York with nothing but the clothes on my back and start a new life for myself and my child. Just please don't let them hurt us."

Zeus leaned against the bed and said in a cold tone, "I hate you. The sight of you turns my stomach because all I can think of is..." He took a controlled breath. "I don't like the situation we're in, but I won't have my child raised without me. You won't have to worry about going back to Quade's house. You can stay with me. I have a basement apartment that you're more than welcome to move into."

"I'll take the apartment. I know you're not doing this for me, but thank you, Zeus," I said, hanging my head to keep him from seeing how hard his words pierced me. "You won't hear a peep out of me. I'll stay out of your way and make sure I'm financially able to take care of our child when she's born."

Zeus opened his mouth to reply, whether it was with a harsh diatribe or words of assurance concerning the future of our child, I'll never know. He closed it and walked from the room, leaving me clutching pictures of our daughter. For the first time in three months, I was alone, completely alone with my thoughts. There was no fearing for my life, no stress, a set of four different walls with new surroundings outside of them. A small smile crept up my face as I rubbed my belly. The father of my child hated me, I was left penniless by my treacherous sister, and there were numerous targets on my head, but none of that mattered right now. I was having a little girl. She was the friend I needed while I was at my lowest, and I planned to make sure that our troubled start would set the path for a future filled with love.

ZEUS

Quade stood in front of his car puffing on a cigarette, his eyes fixated on the full moon shining above us. This was the first time we had spoken since the argument we had in my bedroom four months ago. It was crazy how fast time flew. I spent my time mourning Lauren and searching for Quincy while he held everything down. My brother wasn't built for the spotlight—he basked in the shadows—but when Savion was unable to step up because Cash needed help distributing, Quade took on the burden without a flicker of hesitation. He came a long way from the troubled kid I always had to keep an eye on. My brother was a man. I could see it in the way he stood, the focus in his eyes, even his aura was calm.

"It was Hasani's idea to hide the truth from you," Quade said without removing his eyes from the sight above him. "He thought you wouldn't be able to handle the truth. Bullshit. You don't measure the gauge of a person's strength by how they react in their lowest moment, it's measured by how quick they bounce back."

"Is that why the two of you fought?"

He shrugged. "That was part of it."

"Quade…he was right." Quade's head snapped to me, his eyes lighting up in surprise. "Has it ever crossed your mind that Hasani's decisions are never personal? The Assan Brothers fought with their hearts and look at where they ended up. As strong as you think I am, if Pops came to me with that same request I wouldn't have been able to do it. You wouldn't have either. Neither would Savion. We place all this value on being able to lead with an iron fist, but it takes a well-rounded person to be able to rule with equal parts logic and emotion."

"So you have no problem with being lied to!"

"Not if it's for my protection! Lauren's death broke me and knowing that her killer was in the same city as me would have driven me insane. Then, to top it all off, Quincy goes missing. Hasani made the right call."

"I guess he made the right call by having his brother move in with you too, huh?"

I nodded. "He did. I never talk to him, but Grayson being at the house helps. He doesn't do much, just enough to remind me that I'm not alone and that's all I need some days," I said with a small smile. "Hasani made me believe I was doing this for Grayson, but he was really doing it for me. Damn, I miss him."

"Me too."

"Quade, is that what this is about? You're looking for reasons to be right so you don't have to feel guilty over Hasani's disappearance?"

"I wanted to be the one to fix you," Quade admitted, tossing his cigarette on the ground and crushing it with the sole of his boots. "You've spent the better part of our lives fixing me, making sure I'm good, putting me ahead of yourself. I wanted to do the same for you just once. I wanted to have your best interest at heart and I couldn't even get that shit right."

I bit back a laugh. "Are you serious right now?"

"Yes, I'm fucking serious!" This was a side I never saw of Quade. He was an emotional rock that was crumbling right in front of my eyes. "You think I like running the cartel? I hate it. I have more money than I'll ever be able to spend, I never get to see my family, and there's a target on the back of my head. Right now, I have three sets of security watching us right now. Even more at my house. I didn't take this job for the perks, I did it to take some of the burden off of your shoulders, to be there the way you were for me so you wouldn't think I was some emotional leech. I wanted to show you that I can give as much as I take."

You never know how much your words can affect someone until faced with their manifestation. "Quade, you aren't an emotional burden, and I'm sorry for having you walk around for four months thinking I resented you for being as much. You haven't taken anything from me, but you've given me something I never thought I would experience: fatherhood. Without you, I think I would be freaking out right now at the thought of having a child in less than a year. You've humbled me when I was riding high and being your conscience has taught me how to maintain control over mine."

"You didn't have to apologize," Quade said, his cheeks reddening. He was able to handle himself in a gunfight, but heaven forbid you try to have a mushy moment with him.

"A real man is able to apologize when he's wrong," I reminded him with a squeeze on the shoulder. "I'm not without fault, and I think it's important to show you that side of me from now on. I spent so long building up this image of perfection, I forgot to show you how painfully human I am."

Quade pounced, and for a split second I thought he was going to knock me to the floor, when instead he pulled me into a hug, squeezing me so hard I thought I would break in half. For most, such a show of affection might be deemed strange, but I had to remember that I was the closest thing he had to a father. Hell, I was his father, and whenever Pops was mad at me I was consumed with guilt along with a desire to show him how sorry I was. The gestures were small—sometimes a drawing or some craft my mother helped me with—but my father accepted each one with enthusiasm and never used his anger as leverage. I squeezed my brother tight, hoping this would feel as warm as the words I struggled to find.

"It's time for you to go back to living your best life, Quade. I'm ready to take over again," I choked out. "You've done a good job. I'm proud of you, you hear? That weight you're feeling, give it all to me."

A transfer of monumental power happened in that instant. The months I spent wallowing in self pity felt like the blink of an eye, a dark memory I wouldn't be able to recall in a year's time. It was nothing short of disrespectful to Lauren's memory to stop living my life because she lost hers. I had brothers to protect, a throne to take back, and one last Assan to put in the grave.

~

QUINCY SPUN AROUND IN A CIRCLE, taking in her new quarters for the foreseeable future. We stood in the middle of the unfurnished apartment. Lauren and I were in the middle of redecorating it around the time she passed. I was all for making it a man cave since I was forfeiting mine on the top level of the house while she wanted to make it an apartment for Grammy. She hoped that once her grandmother saw an apartment made just for her she would consider moving from Canarsie and letting us take care of her. I had to remind her that there was no way in hell that her fiercely independent grandmother was going to uproot from her paid off house to live in Harlem. The look on Grammy's face when Lauren casually brought it up in conversation let me know I could look forward to my man cave. A chuckle escaped my lips as Quincy finished her revolution. Her eyes lit up, thinking I was smiling at her, and dimmed the second it died on my lips.

"You'll stay in one of the guest bedrooms until this place is finished. I trust with the right resources you can have everything completed?" I crossed my arms, watching those honey colored orbs of hers roll upward and focus on me.

She nodded. "A week is more than generous. What's the budget?"

"No budget. You can use the computer in my office to order whatever you want or need. Groceries, clothing, services. The only rule for living here is that you don't leave. I have men watching this place from ten different angles. You risking your life risks theirs."

A flicker of annoyance crossed her face. "A new prison, just with better amenities. Why am I not surprised..."

"Would you prefer taking your chances on your own? As far as Ivy is concerned, you're dead to her. She won't hesitate to lay you out on sight. Walk out the door, go ahead. I won't stop you."

"You're right. I brought this all on myself. I should be grateful for mercy and not turning my nose up at it," Quincy replied, turning her back to me and wiping at her eyes. It wasn't my intention to make her cry, but I remembered she was carrying a child, our child. "I'll make myself scarce around the house. You won't even know I'm here."

Yes, I would. I would always know where Quincy was because she was part of me with a piece of me inside of her. The bond we shared took a short time to form, but it would take much longer to break. Her disappearance heightened these feelings. I would find myself zoning off, thinking of something she said or did. The kissable birthmark on her collarbone. Her calming words that could soothe the roughest storm. How perfectly our bodies fit. I gave my head a little shake and found myself standing there with the real Quincy, who looked like she wanted to ask me if I was good but feared my reaction.

"You ate?" She shook her head. "What would you like to eat? I'll have someone pick it up for you."

Quincy closed her eyes, and it was her turn to venture off to a faraway land. "I told myself the second I was able to, I would eat a huge cheeseburger with everything on it, some loaded fries, and a pizza pie. Yara is cool as fuck and I owe her my life, but all she has in her house is fish and leaves."

I got out a silent chuckle before her eyes opened. Leave it to Quincy to make me laugh when all I wanted to do was strangle her. Fuck her senseless to put her through the pain her truth made me feel. I had to tame those thoughts; she was the mother of my child and we were tied for the rest of eternity. A million emotions coursed through my body at the sight of her passing out during my confrontation. I couldn't let anything happen to her if wanted to. The hatred in my heart for Quincy didn't come from an organic place. I hated her because I loved her more than I should have. Seeing her face reminded me of the loss of my first love, and the new one that could never be.

~

DINNER AT HOTEL ELYSÉE felt like a work of dark humor. I returned back to where it all began with the same feelings of loneliness. Right now, home didn't feel like home because Quincy was there—simply being in the same space as Quincy was likely to drive me insane. I received hourly text message updates on her and was waiting for the one that let me know she was asleep, so I could go home. My phone buzzed with another update, this one letting me know that Grayson was home. I felt better knowing Quincy was no longer home alone. Who knows, maybe the two of them could bond over my shared indifference of them. I tossed back my scotch at the thought and motioned for the bartender to bring me another one.

"Thank you," I said, inhaling the smell of the single malt drink.

It had slight oak notes that were overpowered by the smell of a woman's perfume. I opened my eyes and locked with the dazzling dark brown ones laid on mine. Her ebony skin was smooth, almost poreless, her lips tantalizing, and her body...I wouldn't start on her body because the only place I wanted to see it was in a pine box. A coffin was too good for Ivy Assan. I glanced around the room at my security, who were seated at tables and either ends of the bar, each of them alert. They were willing to end everything—both this war and Ivy's life—on my command. I should've given them the okay to do so but I wanted to end her life with my own two hands.

"Aren't you going to buy me a drink?" she asked in a thick southern accent. I don't know why, but I expected her to sound like she smoked three packs of Newports a day or something.

I motioned to the bartender to take Ivy's order. She requested what I was having as a show of equality, but nothing would ever put us on the same level. My brothers and I worked for everything we had after it was snatched away by her father, whereas the Assan kids only knew how to steal.

"You didn't come here to kill me," I noted. "You came to talk. So speak your peace."

Ivy thanked the bartender for her drink and took a dainty sip. "I know you think I'm a monster. That everything I've done is to destroy you and your brothers, and you're absolutely right. Boyd might've been a villain to you, but he was a father to me and my siblings. As the oldest girl I have the fondest memories of my father. I was more than his baby girl—I was his confidante. He was always telling me of his plans to become the biggest drug dealer New York had ever seen.

"I met your father once. He came down to Miami to handle some business with my father. A woman that wasn't your mother was with him. They were smiling at each other, acting all playful, and I would've never guessed they weren't together until I heard my parents talking about it long after they were gone. Her exact words to me were 'Ivy, never be so in love with a man that you spend years kissing his mask. You'll only end up hurt when he takes it off.'"

She took another sip, this time making sure to keep me on the edge of my seat. I was gripping my tumbler so hard my knuckles were nearly white.

"What is the point of this story?"

"You have spent your entire life looking down on my father like he was a demon when your father was no better. My father may have fucked around, but I can say that I know all of my siblings, well *knew* since there's only one left. Your father didn't give you that courtesy. I bet if one of the three extra siblings you have came to see you your entire world would fall apart. You would have to accept that maybe your father isn't the saint you made him out to be. It would also force you to accept that you stole from us, and what we're doing is what you would do if the tables were turned."

"In order for us to do that you would have to accept the fact that your father wasn't perfect either. Boyd gave my forty-five-year-old mother a death sentence. He took everything we had and left us to fend for ourselves. We did what we had to do in order to survive. In regard to his death, I have no regrets."

Ivy took the rest of her drink to the head. "Good, then I don't have to feel bad for what you and your brothers got coming to you. I'm waging a war, Zeus. I'm taking everything: your territory, your product, and your soldiers. I already took your wife, can't be too hard to take the rest."

She was baiting me, and I would bait her right the fuck back. "Tell me something: how long were you fucking your father before he died?"

"None of your fucking business," Ivy snapped, slamming the tumbler onto the bar with more force than she intended.

"You got the virus too, don't you? Is that what the money you took from Lauren was for? To buy more medication? Hmmm?"

Ivy rose from the bar with the appearance of someone unbothered, but I could see the cloaked anger all on her face. She placed a hand on my shoulder and dug her talons into my expensive Armani suit jacket. "Don't concern yourself with my pussy because I wouldn't give you any with your last breath. What you need to be worried about is the havoc I'm going to wreak. I won't tell you where, when, or how, but, motherfucker, I am going to take out each and every last one of you bitch made niggas."

With a whip of her hair she was off, sashaying madly from the bar, her boyfriend rising from a table close by. Judging by the frantic look on his face, he had no idea how deep Ivy's madness ran. I spent the rest of my time at the bar plotting on Ivy, replaying our conversation over in my head. On the third revolution something she said stuck out like a sore thumb. There was one person who might be able to save us at the end of the day, but only with the right amount of preparation. I found him sitting in the living room eating a bowl of ice cream, watching Luke Cage. He sat up and pressed pause on the television show at the sight of my standing there watching him.

"I didn't know you were coming home so soon," Grayson said, scratching the back of his neck. "I can take this upstairs to my bedroom—"

"You said you wanted to be one of us, right?"

Grayson nodded. "I am one of you."

"Good, because you're about to prove it. Get dressed, we're on our way to Quade's house. He's going to teach you everything there is to know about guns and mixed martial arts. Savion will give you a rundown of our distribution network—"

"Quade? Guns? What are you getting me wrapped up in?" Grayson asked, standing up and walking over to me. "Y'all have treated me like nothing but a stepchild—"

"You are a stepchild," I interjected.

"And now you want me to learn all this shit all of a sudden, so I can what? Become a drug dealer?"

I shook my head. "She doesn't know about you. Somehow, you've slipped right through her fingers, and you are going to be her downfall. I don't want you to become a drug dealer: you're going to become the weapon we use to kill Ivy Assan."

HASANI

I never left.

Unlike Quade, I'm not a savage, or *la bestia*, able to cut through small towns killing people with no conscience. I quickly learned that as I sat at the Chinese Bus Station, plotting my next move. After my fallout with Quade, I didn't expect any phone calls from my brothers for a couple days, and by then I planned to be long gone on my glorious mission. Standing in front of a bus headed to Atlanta, to the unknown, I had a change of heart. I would stay in New York, keeping an ear close to the street in ways my brothers never could. Shrugging my duffle bag high on my shoulder, I went one place I knew no one would ever look for me.

"Hasani, you want any more bacon?" Sade called from the kitchen. "Speak now before I turn the frying pan off."

I stared down at my half-finished plate of eggs, three slices of bacon, and corned beef hash. "I'm good on bacon. You think you can bring me a glass of orange juice?"

"I got you."

Sade appeared from the kitchen dressed in a pair of sweatpants and a white tank top that accentuated her pregnant belly. No, it was not my child, which made staying with my former mistress so easy—

she needed cash and I need somewhere to lay low. It wasn't my first choice, but on the ride back to Brooklyn I weighed my options. Who could I call on to let me stay in their house long term with little to no questions asked? Plus, was this a person with access to local gossip. My workers' loyalty was to the organization, and I wasn't trying to get any of them killed over tainted loyalty, which was why when I landed on Sade's number in my phone I knew she was the one. Three months later, I didn't regret my choice.

"What's on the agenda for today?" Sade asked with her hands on her hips, peering down at me over her stomach. "You want to me invite my girl, Sharday over? She texted me last night letting me know she had some major tea. You know she be fucking with them niggas over on Park Ave. Their loyalty is to no one, so I wouldn't be surprised if they plotting some shit."

"What about your brother? He heard anything?"

"From what I heard, Savion put some new niggas over in Red Hook. Got rid of Jason's niggas in one swoop. One day they were there and the next, gone. I told Jeremy you're going to look out for him when you come out of hiding."

"I'm not in hiding," I reminded her.

Sade scoffed. "So, then what do you call living in my son's bedroom for three months straight, hiding from visitors, shutting off your phone, and not telling anyone where you are?"

I refused to give her the satisfaction. "Can you call your friend and tell her to get the fuck over here? Last I checked, I pay you to do what I say not have a fucking opinion."

"That's what you think, nigga..." Sade muttered under her breath as she waddled to her bedroom, leaving me alone with my thoughts.

I picked up my cellphone from the table, staring at it. The night I left I didn't even bother to call Gia with a goodbye. Some nights I contemplated calling her just to hear her voice or to let her know I was okay, while other nights part of me felt happy knowing she was hurting the way I hurt. I was always honest with my shit, and her pretending to be a saint when she was out fucking as much as I was, hurt me. My thumb stroked the power button, and in a moment of clarity, I placed my phone back on the table. Sade appeared with her phone in hand, giving it a triumphant shake.

"Sharday's on her way and she said this tea is going to blow my mind. This might be the break you've been sitting around waiting on," she said, disappearing into the kitchen and reemerging with a plate. She took a seat on the sofa, placed her thick legs up on the coffee table, and proceeded to tear up her food. "You should give your wife a call. Three months without hearing from you? For all you know she might've divorced your trifling ass. I sure know I would've."

"Where did you get all this mouth from? I don't recall you speaking half as much while we were fucking," I said, mentally counting on my fingers the amount of conversations we had four years ago.

Sade popped a piece of bacon in her mouth. "I grew the fuck up. Back then I was nothing but a scared little girl honored at being chosen by a Townsend Brother. Intimidated by a name and scared out of my ass at the thought of being caught by your woman. When you kicked me to the curb I was a little hurt, which was how I ended up meeting my ex and getting pregnant by him not once, but twice. No offense, but I have no time to be scared or in awe of anyone who hasn't given the gift of life."

Her statement was enough to have me lean in ever so slightly. For the first time since I showed up at Sade's apartment, I was really seeing her. Gone was the innocent glint in her eyes replaced by a quiet strength. Her slim modelesque body was thick from kids, and she carried it with pride. It was good to know everyone was growing while I remained the same. I was saved from having to continue the awkward conversation by a knock at the door. Sade and I already knew the drill. I cleaned up any indication of me being there as she waddled to the door. I comfortably set up in my bedroom when Sharday's loud voice bounced throughout the two-bedroom apartment.

"Hey, bitch!" she said at the top of her lungs as she entered the bedroom next door. "Damn, something smells good as fuck. What you eating? Why your ass ain't make me a plate? You know I ain't have shit at my house to eat because of my sister's greedy ass kids. Little bastards eat up everything in sight like their no-good daddy!"

"Sharday, I made you something to eat, but you know how this baby is. She gets to moving in my stomach and it's a wrap. I'm making lunch in a few though. Your favorite: tacos. But first I need all this tea, bitch. Being at home cooped up with a baby has me so far out the loop."

Sharday took a dramatic breath and said, "So, last night I'm spending time with Draco, my new little boo that lives over in Sumner Houses. He's telling me how his cousin put him on to this nigga looking for free agents. You already know that nigga stays down to ride for whoever got the biggest pockets. His cousin starts telling him about this rich bitch getting ready for a hostile takeover."

I perked up at the piece of information. Sade played her role well, asking the right questions without seeming too interested. "What the fuck is this bitch taking over?"

"Everything."

"Everything?" Sade echoed. "I don't give a fuck how many soldiers she has, she can't take over an entire borough. Tell your nigga to stay the fuck away from that shit or else he'll end up dead."

There was a pregnant pause. "No, Sade. She's taking over the entire city. All five boroughs."

"Ain't no fucking way—"

"Sade, I sat there and listened to the entire conversation he had with his brother on the phone! How are you telling me what came out of this nigga's mouth is a lie? I'm telling you: this bitch has big plans. They didn't get into too many details, but it's being called Bloody Sunday."

"Did they mention which Sunday?"

"That's the crazy part," Sharday said, her voice lowering to a whisper. "She hasn't told any of them what Sunday. They're going to get a message telling them where they're riding out and they'll go. It doesn't give anyone a chance to prepare."

"Whoever she is, she must be the second coming of Pablo Escobar. Where does she plan on getting enough product to supply all of these territories? Where is she getting the corner boys to sell it if she's taking out entire neighborhoods?"

"My best guess is out of state. It's a lot of hungry niggas elsewhere looking for their next big break. As for the supply, ain't it obvious? She's going for the Townsend Brothers' product. Raid their stash houses and take every bit they have." There was a pregnant pause between the two. "I know you and Hasani didn't end on that good of a note. You could make a couple stacks dropping info on how their network works. I heard she's paying money for anyone who knows anything about the brothers. If that ain't some payback for that nigga breaking your heart then I don't know what is."

"Girl, I'm not getting in the middle of no drug war. I have children to think about," Sade said, shooting the idea down almost immediately.

So that was her plan? Raid our stash houses, causing a shortage in product. When the streets were dry she'd come through with this attack and take us out, decimating our numbers. It was genius, and also the exact plan we used to take over Boyd's territory, except on a smaller scale. However, what Ivy had planned was going to rob a lot of mothers of their sons. I couldn't let this happen. As I listened to the rest of the conversation, I started formulating a plan. By the time Sharday was gone I knew how we would beat her at her own game.

"That shit is crazy," Sade said, taking a seat on the opposite side of the twin sized bed, her hands grabbing fistfuls of the Spiderman sheets that dressed her son's bed. "You know I would never rat on you, right? I was mad as fuck at you, but I wouldn't gain anything from being bitter over a nigga I knew wasn't mine to begin with."

"I need you to."

Sade's eyes widened. "What? Hasani, what are you up to? You know what? I don't even know why I'm asking because I'm not getting in the middle of it. I have kids to think of!"

"And if you want them to grow up with their father and uncles you need to do me this one favor. It's the last one I'll need from you. The payout will be large enough to the point you won't ever have to want for anything again. You can help me stop this before it ever begins."

"How?" I told Sade the makings of my plan, and her eyes nearly bulged out of their sockets. "You want me to lie, Hasani? What if she catches on that I'm not telling the truth?"

I shook my head. "She won't, because I'm going to make sure everything you tell her is the truth by the time you reach her."

I could tell Sade still wasn't sold on the idea of meeting up with Ivy, but she went along anyway. I repeated to her the focal points of our business, leaving out enough details that she would have to fill in the rest. If she walked in there with a whole script Ivy would see right through her. When I felt confident that she knew everything, I told her to forget it all. We hadn't fucked in years, so the information couldn't seem too fresh either. Ivy was smart, almost too smart, and if I was going to win I had to think smarter not harder. Once I was done with Sade, I had to make a few tough phone calls, the first one being to Gia. I powered on my emergency phone to make sure I didn't have any messages from Grayson. To my surprise there was one.

It was from my wife.

Gia was strong-willed, independent, and I never imagined my leaving affecting her to this level. To hear the pain in my wife's voice and know it was because of me fucked me up on the inside. I blinked my eyes a few times to hold back the tears.

"I want you to come home so we can fix us! Please come home," she begged at the end of the voicemail.

I placed my phone against my lips. "No need to cry, baby. I'm coming home."

~

HER SOFT SNORES filled our bedroom, music to my ears after months of sleeping in silence. The moonlight hit her sleeping figure perfectly, illuminating her curves, which accentuated from the last time we saw each other. I tip toed across the bedroom, not wanting to scare her awake, and leaned in to smell her hair. The scent of lavender and honey filled my nostrils the same time as a Glock 27 was pressed into my throat.

"This gun has a hair trigger. If I even feel like you're lying to me, motherfucker, I'mma give you a new hairdo," Gia said calmly.

I didn't expect any other welcome from my wife. "I got your message."

The gun disappeared and next thing I know, I'm being tugged into Gia's arms. She ran her hands through my hair, giving it a gentle tug as she peppered my face with kisses, the last one landing on my lips. I wasn't expecting this kind of greeting, but I wasn't mad at it either.

"I can't believe you're here," she said through a mouthful of tears. "Hasani, why would you leave without talking to me? Do you know how worried I've been about you? The way you were talking the night before leaving I thought you were…I thought I was going to find you in a morgue. I don't care what you're going through, please never leave me like that again."

Gia sat up and turned on the lamp, giving me a better look at her. Although she put on a fair amount of weight since the last time we saw each other, her face told a different story. Stress acne dotted her forehead, her nose was red from being blown too much, and her puffy eyes had to be the byproduct of the voicemail I received. My wife was broken and I had to fix her. I knew the only way we would be able to get past it was with honesty.

"I ain't think you would care about me leaving because you had someone else on the side. I wasn't gon' check you on it because I felt like it was only a matter of time before you did me how I did you. Then I started wondering if this had been going on long before I found out. Overall, I didn't have the heart to confront you and I didn't like the way you cheating made me feel."

Gia nodded her head the entire time, and a "ain't this 'bout a bitch" laugh passed her lips. "You mean to tell me that all I had to do to make you act right was having someone send me a text message about a kiss? The thought of some man's hands running all over my body, tasting my juicy ass pussy, fucking me like a roughneck and spoiling me like a king, was enough to humble you? I'm pissed as hell at my momma, but I might have to thank her for this one." She shook with silent laughter. "That text came from my ex boyfriend, Hasani, and the kiss was an ambush thought up by my mother thinking she could prevent us from getting married."

"So you never..."

"Cheated? No, unlike you, I'm loyal as fuck even when I shouldn't be," Gia shot back, shaking her head in mild disgust. "You really think that little of me, Hasani? To think that I would marry a man I didn't love and cheat on him? I have spent months sitting here, wracking my brain, worried sick about you, and never took the time to think of how I would react when you finally came home."

"You can't get mad at me for how I felt, Gia!"

"Yes, I can! You promised to be here until death do us part and ran over a text message. I handled Carmelo tonight, and trust me when I say we don't ever have to worry about him coming between the two of us ever again."

"Damn, Gia, you murked him?"

"Of course not—he's part of the family. I broke his left hand and promised to come back for the right if he ever contacted me again." Gia did that little head shake when she was feeling especially triumphant. "I never ran, Hasani. I'm not mad for you not being able to handle infidelity even though it makes you look hypocritical as fuck. You didn't give me the benefit of the doubt I have given you. It hurt to know you didn't even trust me enough to make things right between us."

I hung my head in shame. "You're right. I'm sorry for leaving you without an explanation."

"I'm sorry for hiding that kiss from you. Carmelo means nothing to me, and hiding it gave him more power and relevancy than he needed," Gia apologized, taking my hands into hers. "How about we lay everything out on the table once and for all? No secrets between us. A true do-over?"

"Let's do it," I said, kissing her hands.

"Okay, let's start with you. Where have you been? Miami, looking for Ivy's family? Baltimore? I heard she has people there, but we haven't found anything yet."

I scratched the back of my head. "Eh...Sade's house."

"'Sade' the bitch you were cheating on me with?" Gia's eyes widened and turned to slits. I caught the right hook as she threw it but missed the left one. My head snapped to the side, a little bit of drool flew from my mouth, and I had barely straightened my head back out when Gia placed that Glock back on me. "You better tell me something good, Hasani. That the bitch held you hostage and you escaped her house and came straight here."

"I can tell you something better: she's going to help us get Ivy."

Gia lowered her gun, placing it on her lap. "Start from the beginning."

I came clean to Gia, telling her the entire story from the second I left to the point I returned. The smile on her face when I divulged my plan was one reserved for Christmas. Just by the glimmer in her eyes I could tell she had some shit up her sleeve as well, and when she mentioned having the backing of her family, I knew we had this in the bag. We lay in bed making plans, our fingers intertwining every now and again. My lids started to droop and I was slipping into a light slumber when I felt Gia's soft lips press against mine.

"Three months," she said against them. "Three months without my husband. You can imagine how I'm feeling right now with you by my side. Show me how much you've missed me, Hasani."

Whatever reservations Gia had concerning my fidelity while I was away disappeared the second I made love to every inch of her body, licking, sucking, and stroking her on the inside and out. As I watched her sleep with the mid-morning sunlight warming her skin, I felt bad for her. Bloody Sunday was coming and she would probably spend it with morning sickness because I'm positive I got her pregnant. Kissing her on her cheek, I pulled her close, and whispered the names of our future children in her ear, hoping one might stick.

I STARED up at the house with a heavy heart, mulling over whether I should go against my brother's wishes and step back into his life. Quade was more than my brother—he was my best friend—and I hated how we left each other. When I died, Quade took it the hardest, deciding that he would rather chase leads to avenge my death than be with Yara. Somehow he even managed to be mad at the fact that I was alive. Ever since then, we were tight with each other and when he hurt, I hurt, like right now while sitting here looking at his house, the one place I wasn't welcomed. If Gia could forgive me for running out on her, then I believe that—

"Fuck, Quade!" I shouted, holding my chest, clutching at my rapidly beating heart. I rolled down the window with a shaky finger. "Didn't I tell you that if you keep sneaking up on me like that I'mma put some taps on your shoes? You scared the shit out of me."

Quade, who was standing at my window watching me, didn't even flinch at my fright. "You're the one parked in front of my property. You lucky I came to see who it was instead of giving my security permission to murk you with no questions asked."

"I came by to talk to you," I said when I finally got my breathing under check. "Hop in."

I expected an argument or some type of pushback, but Quade did none of the above. He crossed over the car and climbed into the passenger's seat without another word. We sat in silence for a few minutes, unable to find the right words to start off the conversation. I opened my mouth to apologize but was pleasantly surprised when Quade beat me to the punch.

"Zeus found out about Quincy. He said you were right, that he wasn't in the correct mental space to process the entire situation," Quade said, staring straight ahead. "He also told me any decisions you make are never personal. I never thought about it like that because I've spent my entire life making decisions based on my emotions, which was how we ended up in my kitchen with guns drawn."

"Gia was gon' turn you into a fucking Fruit Loop," I said, shaking my head and laughing at a situation that wasn't so humorous three months ago.

Quade cut his eyes at me, but that didn't stop him from laughing at the scene too. "I missed your annoying ass, man. The reason why is because I wanted to say that I'm sorry. Like you said, you were obeying our father's last wish and I should've respected that. You know what really hurt though? You hid this secret from me. I don't give a fuck who you hide stuff from, but we tell each other everything down to where all the bodies are hidden."

"I never really thought about it like that," I said, which was true; I was so busy focusing on hiding everything I forgot to include Quade, who held on to all of my secrets the same way I did his. "I'm sorry for hiding Grayson from you. From here on out it's nothing but honesty between the two of us. We good?"

"We been good," Quade replied, holding out his hand for me to dap.

I leaned in for the dap and was knocked into my window with a bone crunching hug. *At least I know this nigga's still eating his Wheaties,* I thought as I patted him gently on the back. My eyes misted with unshed tears. I felt the love and yearning with Gia, but here with Quade, I felt brotherhood. I remembered the days where we would fight over toys and girls, over whoever could have the last ice from the freezer, and my mother's solution was for us to hug it out. A breath I was holding in expelled and I was filled with peace. I could feel her right now, in this car, in Quade, and it was good to know she was still here, keeping us together in a world where enemies were looking to tear us apart.

QUINCY

I had no intentions of leaving my apartment today. Living with Zeus was the equivalent of coasting through a dream; you were well aware of what was going on but you had no real power. I could have anything delivered to me at any time, day or night, but it would never feel like the real thing. My pizzas were hot but would've tasted better sitting in a pizza shop. The flowers I had smelled beautiful, however, they would never compare to a visit to the Botanical Gardens. And Zeus? He was a beautiful man—smart, caring, and kind—to everyone except me. I swear some days I would spot him just staring at me, and not in a loving way. More like he wanted to kill me. I took it in stride, and kept out of his way like I promised, but I had a feeling if Zeus laid eyes on me today, it would lead to nothing but a premature grave.

"Quin?" Grayson called from the other side of the door. "You up?"

I rolled myself out of bed the best I could, heaving as I trudged over to the door and swung it open. Grayson stood there holding a big, greasy bag of lunch, my favorite kind. I followed him down the hall and into my fully remodeled kitchen. It was Clipper Ship Blue, a bright bold color that matched the white table and accents perfectly. I chose the bright color because if I was going to be confined somewhere for months at a time, I wanted it to at least feel like home. However, after a few days of loneliness, I knew no amount of paint would bring me solace. That was where Grayson came in, becoming something of my best friend even if he didn't know it. We were the black sheep of the Townsend family and it bonded us in a way I never imagined.

"You've been quiet all day," Grayson said as he popped open the plastic containers and placed them on spotless white plates. "I called Zeus to see if he at least came and checked on you, which was pointless. He didn't answer his phone. As of right now, I'm not even here for Hasani since he's been back for a minute. I'm here for you. Months of no moral support can't be easy for you, Quincy."

"I deserve it."

"You had no idea!"

"I had the gun in my hand...I saw the life leave her body," I took a sip of juice to calm my nerves.

Grayson placed a comforting hand over mine. "You may have had the gun, but you didn't pull the trigger. It wasn't in your heart to hurt Lauren, and you didn't. Quincy, I know it's easy to place the blame on yourself, and everyone places it on you as well, but the only person responsible for this entire situation is Ivy."

"I know, it's hard not to take the blame because maybe if I do—"

"He'll forgive you? He has no choice but to because this little one is coming any day now," Grayson said, giving my stomach a playful rub. "The two of you can't raise this child together if he's going to have hate in his heart towards you. I won't allow it."

I laughed. "What are you going to do about it?"

"Run away. With you."

My baby girl and her safety were the only things holding me here. I didn't have any money, a safe place to stay, or an idea of where I could go without having to look over my shoulder for Zeus or Ivy. Grayson was my rock, and I appreciated him looking out for me, but I think he missed one big hole in this plan.

"Giada. Did your girlfriend slip your mind while making this plan?"

Grayson shook his head. "She wants to run away too. According to her, life at home isn't too good with Gia and her parents beefing. She feels torn between the two. We're all looking for a reason to escape."

"I'll sleep on it," I said, although there wasn't much to consider.

Every time I made those plans to run away, it wasn't money or Ivy that kept me put—I believed in my heart that one day Zeus would forgive me. I felt it whenever we went to doctor's appointments together. He collected sonograms and beamed whenever the doctor called him "Dad." It was the only time he addressed me, whether to ask if I needed something to drink or to make sure I was comfortable. I looked forward to those now weekly visits, where I got to escape my prison and be normal even if only for a few hours. Leaving would ruin any chances we had of being together again.

"What do you have planned for the rest of your day?" Grayson asked as we finished our meal. "I would stay, but I promised Giada I would take her on a walk outside with the weather being nice today."

"Hiding out. Today is Lauren's birthday."

Grayson let out a low whistle. "Damn, I completely forgot her birthday was today. That's where the cake and flowers came from." I blanched at the mention of cake. "Quin, don't even sweat today—"

"I won't, I promise. I plan to stay in my bedroom and mind my business. I bought myself a few good books, I'm set for the rest of the day. Zeus won't see me unless he comes looking for me, which we both know won't happen."

Grayson helped me clean up the small mess and was off to spend time with his soul mate. Yes, I called Giada his soul mate because there was no better way to describe what they had. Anyone could see the love he had for her just by the smile that tugged his lips at the mention of her name. They met at a point in time where they needed each other the most and everything fell in place. My thoughts were still on the couple when I heard it. A crash from upstairs.

"Nope, not going to look," I said, getting comfortable on the queen sized bed I spent most of my time in.

A moan from the kitchen traveled through the air vents. I tossed my book aside, slipped into my house shoes, and headed through the door I swore to only use during emergencies. I came out from underneath the stairs with a view of the kitchen. A small puddle of dark red liquid was slowly making its way across the sparkling white floor, sparkling with the help of scattered shards of glass. I lifted the maxi dress I wore as I stepped into the kitchen. Zeus was sitting on the floor drinking a glass of Johnny Walker Black Label, his hand wrapped in a dish towel. His head rolled to the side at the sound of my appearance.

"What the fuck are you doing up here?" he slurred.

"I heard you from downstairs." I motioned to his hand. The towel was soaked with blood and showed no sign of stopping. "You need to get that looked at. I'll call Grayson to patch you—"

"Fuck Grayson. I don't need him and don't need you helping me. I got everything under control," Zeus said over me, taking another sip of his drink.

"No, you don't." The words came tumbling out of my mouth before I could stop them. "Look at you. You're going to end up passing out from blood loss if you don't get your hand looked at. If you don't want me to call Grayson, at least let me patch it up."

I thought Zeus was going to give me some more lip, but to my surprise, the drunk got off his ass and sat at the kitchen table. I grabbed the first aid kit kept in the bathroom and returned to find him staring at a large white box sitting on the table. Her cake. I studiously ignored the box and focused on cleaning the cut, which turned out to be a large gash across his palm. The kitchen remained silent save for Zeus hissing every now and then as I cleaned the cut.

"You need stitches," I said, looking him in the eye for his approval. "It's going to hurt."

He raised his glass to me. "Do what you gotta do. As long as I got a full glass I'm fine."

I threaded the needle and thread with slightly trembling fingers. Being this close to Zeus, smelling his cologne, feeling his eyes staring a hole into the side of my face—had a flurry of nerves erupting in my stomach. So much my little girl jumped. Zeus noticed. He put down his glass and placed his good hand on my stomach.

"Don't touch me," I choked out.

He moved his hand. "I can't touch my own child? Wow..."

"As long as she's inside of my body, no you cannot," I countered, blinking back tears. I wasn't going to let him have me all in my emotions today but riding an emotional roller coaster came with the pregnancy territory. To be honest, I didn't want him touching me because all it would do is serve as a reminder of what I wouldn't have —the love of the man I loved.

Zeus resumed drinking his drink, grimacing every now and again as I stitched his hand up. Long before she grew ill, my mother was a nurse and versed me in advanced first aid techniques. I could hear her in my ear and feel her over my shoulder, reminding me to make my stitching even and to keep my hand steady. When I finished, I let out a breath I had no idea I was holding and was ready to remove myself from Zeus' presence. He had me so mentally fucked up my stomach was in knots, panging every few minutes or so.

"Thank you," he said, staring at his newly bandaged hand. "I...uh... was trying to pour myself a drink and the glass, the *fucking* glass—"

"You don't have to explain anything to me," I said, washing my hands, keeping focused on the red bubbles falling off of my hands instead of the father of my child, who was climbing to his feet with the help of the wall. "I'm going to go back downstairs and stay out of your way—"

"Take a slice of cake with you."

I cut the sink off. "Zeus, you can't be serious right now."

Oh, but he was. I watched as Zeus staggered over to the island, picked up a stray knife, and made a beeline for the cake box sitting on the table. He pulled at the intricate cardboard flaps keeping the box closed, and there it was, one of the most beautiful cakes I had ever seen. It was white, with pearls and delicate lilies covering the entire cake.

"I found this baker in the city that specialized in making fondant flowers. They look real, don't they?" I nodded even though he wasn't paying me any attention. "The waiting list was crazy long. I ordered this cake long before her ring was picked out. I remembered to cancel everything except this. I guess on some level I wanted it to celebrate her even though I knew seeing this would make me feel..."

Zeus stabbed the cake hard, hitting the bottom of the box with a thud. He cut an uneven chunk from it and ate the oblong slice of cake, forgetting I was there until he saw me out the corner of his eye. The knife sliced through the cake again, coming up with another oddly shaped slice, this time more rectangular than triangle.

"Here," he said, approaching me with the slice held out as he chewed on his own. "Have some. It's vanilla. She liked vanilla."

"I don't want any of that cake, Zeus."

He placed the cake right underneath my nose, filling it with the cloying smell of vanilla. "Here, take the cake, Quincy."

"I said I don't want it!"

Zeus inched the cake closer to my face until it was pressed against my lips, and in true drunk bastard from, mushed the cake into my mouth. "I said eat the fucking cake. You helped kill her, I shouldn't have expected you to help celebrate her life."

I snatched his slice of cake from his hand and threw it right in his face, sending bits of cake and pearls flying. "You're not celebrating her life either! You think walking around moping while pissy drunk is a fucking celebration? How about living with dignity after she's gone? How about living in general? It has been nine months since she died and you're still walking around like some broken victim with no intention of fixing himself!"

"You've never loved, have you?" Zeus asked, his voice barely above a whisper. "No one's ever loved you either? This is how people mourn!"

"This isn't mourning! It's an obsession! An unhealthy obsession, Zeus. You keep using Lauren as a reason to act out and do whatever you please! Drinking, being a fucking asshole, shirking your responsibilities. This man, this mean, angry, *bitter* man isn't the man Lauren fell in love with. And it's not the man my stupid ass fell in love with either."

I turned around and came face to face with Hasani, Gia, Cash, and Savion, each looking equally uncomfortable at catching us in the middle of such a nasty argument. I shoved through the couples, too embarrassed to stay around and see Zeus' reaction to my proclamation of love. My tears were kind enough to wait for the door to my apartment to close before falling, and when they did it was a rainstorm. I held on to the bannister and took baby steps down the stairs, crying the whole way down. Two pairs of gentle hands guided me down, not letting go until I was seated at the kitchen table. A piece of tissue dabbed at my lids while a warm washcloth wiped off the cake on my face. My eyes fluttered open and there was Gia, staring back at me with this unreadable look in her eyes.

"I don't give a fuck how mad Zeus is at you, you didn't deserve cake in your face," she said, tossing the washcloth into the sink and pressing the tissue into my hand. "Hasani and Savion will fix his ass right up. You deserve an apology, right, Cash?"

Cash was setting up three mugs for the kettle of tea she had on. "No doubt. Zeus was never this...unraveled. He's always been the perfect gentleman. Disrespecting a woman? Never."

I motioned to my face. "Never say never."

"I've watched him closely ever since Lauren died, and the only time he seemed to be getting back to his normal self was with you," Gia admitted, her eyes locking with mine. "You were keeping him grounded, and I wish I would've known this before we took you away from him. We were all operating on anger and hurt, thinking more of ourselves than him. Seeing you like this, pregnant with my niece and going through it with Zeus, I feel like I failed her. Especially since I spoke with Sean and found out that the night we took you was the night you planned to come clean."

For Gia to sit down woman-to-woman with me and apologize meant a lot to me. Cash apologized for fighting me as well, admitting that she once lived a double life in the beginning of her relationship with Savion.

"I know what it's like to have the man you've prayed for all your life right in your grasp and one tiny truth can fuck it up. I was once on the end of those punches but I didn't have a baby to save me," Cash said, placing mugs in front of us and taking a seat. "Savion's love for me did, and deep down on the inside, Zeus loves you too. He can't start a chapter with you until the one he has with Lauren is closed."

"That will never happen," I promised them. "Even if we were to end up together I'd always live in her shadow. I'm over it. I'm ready to move on with my—ahhh!"

Gia's eyes widened. "How long have you been in pain?"

"Not too long. This only started while I was arguing with Zeus. It could be Braxton Hicks contractions. I'm not due for another week."

Cash cocked her head to the side. "You think babies care about a due date? Chenille came three weeks early. My water broke in the middle of an important meeting which ended with my lieutenant and Lauren carrying me to my car and driving me to the hospital. Joel has more bodies on his guns than I do and he nearly fainted at having to look at Chenille crowning."

For women who hated me for months, Gia and Cash did a complete 180 as they helped me get myself together to head to the hospital. I was dressed, with my go bag ready, when the men came downstairs. Zeus trailed behind his brothers, a bottle of water in his hand instead of scotch. The cake was gone from his face as well, replaced with a somber expression. He stepped past his brothers and approached me humbly. For a second, I could see the Zeus I first met.

"I apologize for the way I treated you earlier, Quincy. I know I haven't been the most present father-to-be since I found out you were pregnant, but I plan on being better from here on out regardless of what happened in the past. I hope you can forgive me," Zeus said, his voice thick with sincerity.

I nodded my head, blinking back tears. This was all I wanted from the beginning. The real Zeus. "I accept."

Gia shoved my Yves Saint Laurent duffle into his chest. "Now that we've got that handled, it's time to get Quincy to the hospital before she pops out Baby Townsend on the kitchen floor. Which gives you… twenty minutes to sober up until we get to New York Presbyterian."

Zeus didn't need the twenty minutes. At the mention of me being in labor he got it together quick, and no one would've guessed that thirty minutes ago he was sprawled out on the floor in a drunken stupor. Everything I wanted from him since the night we reunited was given to me. Zeus placed aside whatever grudge he was harboring and remained my rock for the next thirty-six hours. He kept me hydrated during the hardest contractions, grounded when I was ready to give up, and held my hand as I gave birth to our daughter, helping to pull her out on the final push. I cried watching him cut the umbilical cord. A tiny cry filled the room. It was official.

I was a mom.

"Grace Vanessa Townsend," I announced, smiling down at Grace, who returned to me wrapped in a hospital blanket, her tiny eyes closed as she sucked hungrily on her finger. "I made her middle name my mother's name. I hope you don't mind."

"It's beautiful," Zeus said, pulling up a chair beside me, his eyes never leaving Grace. "Quincy, I know I haven't been the best father or roommate, but I want us to start over. You're right; I can't keep living my life stuck in one place. I need to be there for both of you. Friends?"

I smiled at him. "I'd like that."

Zeus was full of energy—he barely slept the entire time I was in labor—and I was wiped out from giving birth. Somewhere around Grace's second feeding, I dozed off against my own will. When I opened my eyes my first instinct was to check my arms for Grace. I found her sleeping in the crib beside me. Zeus was knocked out as well, snoring in a chair parked next to her. So if he was sitting right there then who was sitting in this seat next to…

"Ivy?"

It came out as a question but I knew my sister from anywhere, even with her completely dressed down sans makeup. She was dressed in hospital scrub and wore a short curly wig. Brown contacts finished the look, making her a complete plain jane. For a second, I thought she was going to kill me in cold blood the way she did Saidya. My betrayal was worse than plotting on her legacy—I fucked and got pregnant by the enemy.

"I didn't come here to fight," she said, raising her hands to show me she was unarmed. That meant nothing; Ivy was notorious for having something up her sleeve. "You're my sister, Quincy. I wouldn't kill you without cause."

I motioned to my new family, peacefully sleeping beside me. "I think this is cause enough."

"No, it's not." Ivy shook her head, the tight curls in her wig shaking. "You had no idea you were betraying me until it was too late. I should have let you in on the plan sooner. That was my fault."

I shook my head. "No, it wasn't. We were all expendable to you, Ivy. Each one of us had a purpose until we didn't. You knew I was fucking Zeus, didn't you? You planned on using me to get to him, but Gia caught on so you decided to cut your losses and let them have me? It would be one less body on your hands. This wasn't about us having our father's legacy: it was all about you."

"You damn right it's about me," Ivy confirmed, the kind smile she wore transforming into a grimace. "I have given everything I have to become the woman I am today. My body, my power, my innocence. Even if I wanted to, I can't let this fight go."

"Why did you come here?"

"I came to see my niece."

"You don't like children."

Ivy sighed. "I also came to offer you a spot on my team. A quarter of the net profits."

"I don't want anything from you, Ivy."

Ivy rose from her chair, and for a minute, I thought she was going to stall off and kill the three of us. Instead, she took my rejection in stride. "I extended this offer for my niece because I thought she should have at least one of her parents being that her father is going to die pretty soon. I'm taking down the entire Townsend family and New York will be mine. You better make some plans for your baby girl because the second I walk out of that door, you're the enemy. Blood won't mean anything."

"You see, that's your problem, Ivy," I said with a sad laugh. "You think you're invincible. The one small thing you overlook will be your downfall. I'll see you on the other side."

I kept my eyes on her as she made her way to the door, waiting for the slightest movement so I could scream at the top of my lungs. Ivy turned as she reached the door and said, "I knew you would chose him over me. All you weak ass bitches are the same."

Her words were laced with anger and…hurt? I didn't even have enough time to figure out which one because Zeus woke up minutes after she left. He was all smiles until he saw the look on my face.

"What's wrong? Is it the baby?"

I opened my mouth to tell him when one of the attending nurses entered with a bouquet of roses in her hand. They were all red except for one. A black rose sat in the middle of the bouquet with a note attached to it.

"Someone must've been in a rush making this arrangement," the nurse said, setting the roses on the table beside my bed. "Would you like the card?"

I accepted the card with a trembling hand. The nurse made light conversation with us as she checked on Grace but figured after a few tries it was best to keep her mouth shut. I opened the envelope and pulled out a card with a hand painted red dot on it. I held it out to Zeus, who stared at it for five minutes before admitting that he had no idea what it meant.

"It's a circle. A bloody circle. Everything's going to come full circle. This is the day she's coming," I said, placing the card in Zeus' hand. "She's going to strike on the day we completed our first job together."

"You mean—"

"Yeah," I confirmed. "The war starts the day she killed Lauren."

IVY

I used to come from a close-knit family. I had more brothers than I could ask for, and even more sister than I ever needed. My fondest family memories came when my father would bring nine of his ten kids together for field day. As the oldest boy and girl, Ahmad and I were made team captains. Samiel's little sick ass would sit out, which evened us out. For the next eight hours, we would play tug of war, basketball, and race the large racetrack in the sports arena he would rent out. Even at the age of ten I was getting my sisters together, coaching them to play harder, smarter than the boys. Despite my efforts, we lost each year. My father would high five Ahmad and the rest of the boys with this look of pride in his eyes that he never used for us. I spent my entire life trying to get him to look at me that way, hoping for it even after he took my body so many times I began giving it to him willingly, but I never received it. However, today was the day I would win my father's favor, whether he was alive to see it or not.

"Ivy." Rome knocked on the bathroom door three times. "Ivy, you've been in there for a minute. You good?"

I popped the last of my meds and swallowed them with a large glass of water. "Don't worry about how the fuck I'm doing. Is the team good?"

Pause. "Yeah, we set out here. We're waiting on you."

X "If I come out there and everyone isn't ready, prepare to get my foot up your ass, Rome," I barked as another wave of nausea hit me. This new cocktail wasn't supposed to turn my stomach, but these HIV cocktails have always hurt more than they helped. I finished off another glass of faucet water, wiped my mouth on the back of the black hoodie I wore, and swung the bathroom door open, happy to see my team of soldiers jump at my appearance. "For the first time in your life, you managed to do as I say," I said to Rome, who stood in front of the group of fifty men. "Let's roll out. We got a lot of ground to cover."

Tonight was the first part of my plan. I was unable to find a connect willing to step on the toes of the Townsend Brothers, which left me with no choice but to take deading a nigga on his pack to a whole new level. I got word from Hasani's ex side chick that they received their product twice a month at a shipping yard in Brooklyn. They rotated the days by moving them forward three days, which was a decent enough system. The product was then transferred over to stash houses all over the city, ready for distribution. Not only did we plan on intercepting the drop, we were hitting each of the stash houses, stealing the remainder of product they had. They would come searching for me and I would lower the boom, hitting their organization with a loss they couldn't bounce back from.

"I spoke to Draco. He's got his boys by the stash house over in the East, waiting for the go. Same for Keith and Monty," Rome said, as we pulled up to the shipping yard.

I spotted tail lights in the distance. They were already here. "Tell them to go in five. Don't leave anyone alive."

Three work vans were perfectly parked next to a car carrier trailer filled to the max with both brand new and used cars. Six men worked in unison to pry off the cars' interior parts, seats included, to pull out brick after brick of coke. Our team of ten crept up on them, only splitting at the last minute to make sure no one was lurking. I gave the signal to strike as they finished taking apart the last car.

"Put your hands in the fucking air," I commanded, coming around the corner with my AK in the air, zoning in on the nigga standing to the side watching instead of participating. I used the rifle to point to the phone in his hand. "Drop it on the ground. Now."

The iPhone clattered to the floor as a man came from the front of the car with a rifle of his own. Rome planted two in his chest before he could squeeze the trigger. One of his buddies used the temporary distraction to pop off from the other side of the van. The soldier to the left of me handled him, which kept me focused on the leader, who stood in the middle of the gunfire unflinching. Like the rest of his men, he dropped to his knees and placed his hands behind his head. Our van pulled up right in time. Three soldiers formed a line and passed off the 100 keys to each other, filling the back of the van in three minutes. I aimed at the tires of the van, flattening the front ones to keep them from pursuing us.

"Lay down and stay the fuck down," were my last words to the men as I climbed into the back of the van.

The doors shut behind me and we were off, racing through rows of shipping containers. I took a seat on the mountain of drugs, satisfied with how smooth the entire job went. Rome pulled his phone from his pocket and started connecting with the lieutenants. Everything went smooth with the first two; according to Draco and Monty, there wasn't much product at both locations, which made security lax. However, his entire demeanor changed as he spoke to Keith.

"You did the right thing. Bring him back to the warehouse. We'll be there in half an hour."

"Who are they bringing back to the warehouse?" I asked the second he ended the call.

Rome smiled wide. "You won't believe who was at the stash house out in the Stuy, preparing himself to receive a shipment. One of the Townsend Brothers."

"Which one?"

"That's the thing; it ain't one of the four. It's some other nigga named Grayson."

One of Big Zeus' illegitimate kids. I spent a lot of time trying to find them, thinking I could use them to turn on their brothers. One son was doing a bid for attempted murder; his daughter was raised by another man, rendering her useless; and then there was Grayson. There was a chance the other two kids didn't belong to Big Zeus, but Grayson? He couldn't deny the child of his true love if he wanted to. Imagine growing up in the shadows without your father while your brothers took him for granted. It was the recipe for revenge.

"Get him up off the floor," I said as we entered the warehouse.

Grayson sat in the middle of a tarp with his hands tied behind his back, gagged by a black bandanna. His eyes zoned in on me as I took a seat on the table where my soldiers started laying out the bricks. Keith helped Grayson up off the floor and stared at me, waiting for my next command.

"Uncuff him."

Keith did as he was told, digging through his pockets for the keys, and freed Grayson, who kept his eyes trained on me. Grayson rubbed his wrists for a few seconds before snatching the bandanna from his mouth and replying, "It took you long enough. Where we at with the plan?"

I motioned to the table next to me, now filled with $3,000,000 in coke. "Right on time. You ready for Bloody Sunday?"

Grayson cracked a smile. "By the end of today, Jesus won't be the only one who wept."

~

IF I HAD to fuck a Townsend, it would be Grayson. He was the right kind of dirty. To spend the better part of a year up under his brothers' asses, groveling so they would accept him, and never slip in character was something I would've never been able to achieve. We met at a bar one night while he was mourning the loss of his mother. I patted his back, whispered all the right words in his ear, and after some encouragement, I told him he should seek out family to be with during this rough time. He insisted that he had no family, but I kept prodding and poking him in the direction of his brothers. With some assurance from me, he relented, packing up his life and meeting up with his brothers. Their first interaction went better than I thought, with him moving into Zeus' house on the very first night. From there, Grayson was my spy, slowly gaining the trust of his brothers and feeding me information on their whereabouts. Paired with the information I received from Sade, without Grayson, tonight would have been impossible.

"How much were you able to get from the stash houses?" Grayson asked, leaning over to look through the window of the private office we sat in. "I know mine was running extremely low, we had ten bricks sitting around, which is low considering this time of year."

"The one Keith hit was running low too, but there was plenty of money to be had," I replied, staring at Grayson's profile. He was Big Zeus reincarnated with that strong jawline, deep brown skin, and juicy lips. I had wanted to go there with Grayson plenty of times, but his excuse was that he was done having casual sex. With my condition, casual sex was all I could offer. That didn't stop me from occasionally lusting though.

Grayson turned back to me, a large smile playing on his face. "I can't believe we did it. Got them niggas for everything. Ain't no bouncing back from something like this. They gotta be sick as fuck right now."

"You going missing doesn't help either. That ransom video should be hitting them right about now," I said, snapping my finger as the office clock hit 3 a.m.

"I can't wait to see the look on their faces when they're staring down the barrel of my nine." He shrugged his shoulder. "Looking as stupid as I felt going to them thinking we could be family. Do you have any idea how much pride I put aside to seek out those motherfuckers? They swore I was living some amazing lifestyle when I was suffering too. All I know is one thing: I want Quade. I want to look that smug motherfucker in the eye and take the light out of it. *Poof*," he said, mimicking the pulling of a trigger.

The motion brought a smile to my face because Grayson would never be afforded that opportunity. Yeah, I said I would fuck him, I never mentioned us being lifelong partners. His goal was to get revenge and my goal was to run an empire, and as far as I was concerned, there was no room at the top for two. Not to mention, Grayson was disloyal as fuck. If he could turn on his brothers, there was no question that he could turn on me. Like my sisters, he served a purpose, and his time was slowly coming to an end. However, I would give him a courtesy I never extended to any of them. A last drink.

"Oh, you bringing out the bubbly," Grayson said at the sight of Cristal I pulled out from a drawer.

I popped the champagne open and poured a fair amount into two red solo cups. "I thought we should celebrate. To the come up from a downfall."

Grayson knocked his cup against mine. "To the come up."

ZEUS

Today was the beginning of the end. Since the day my father went to jail due to Boyd's treachery, life for us has proven to be difficult. We had everything snatched from us—our mother wasted away, our father died slow, and the stability we had was gone in a short span of time—yet we had each other and that was all we needed to make it here today. I didn't care what the result was today, as long as I left this world with my brothers, then I would be alright.

"Heavenly father, we come to you humbly today not with a laundry list of results, but the tools necessary to get there. Strength to overcome what we imagine will be difficult obstacles that threaten to snatch us at every turn, courage to face the enemy with nothing more than your favor shielding us, protecting for every young man willing to risk his life for us today, and deliverance into your kingdom for those who will fall today on either side of the line. In Jesus name we pray, Amen."

"Amen," everyone repeated, ending the prayer.

We remained in a circle, memorizing each other's faces in the event that the next time they were seen was in a casket. Cash and Gia were stoic; after all, they knew what they were getting into when they signed up for a spot in the game. It was Yara who took this the worst.

She kept talking about this feeling in the pit of her stomach that she couldn't shake. We kept telling her there was nothing to worry about, that if we did things right there wouldn't be a war to begin with, but she wasn't listening. The one person who could ease those fears refused to. Quade never once quelled her fears and I was starting to feel like we were on the outside of some sick joke.

"Quade, don't go," Yara said, holding on to his arm so tight her fingers turned white. "You can sit this out and no one will think any less of you. We have children. Our kids can't grow up without their father."

"Yara, I can't sit at home while my brothers go walking into a war zone looking for Grayson. Do you know how that would make me look?"

"I don't care about how it would make you look because you would be alive!" she screamed, punching him hard in the chest. "It isn't all about you now. I didn't sign up to be a single mother, Quade! I thought you learned how to pick your battles, but I guess I was wrong!"

The punch didn't move Quade in the slightest, but it didn't stop him from holding the spot as if he was injured. "Yara, what's gotten into you?"

"Do you know how old you turn at the end of this year?"

"Yara…"

"Thirty." Yara tried calming herself down with a few breaths, but her emotions were getting the better of her. "Remember the day we met? You told me that you didn't expect to live past thirty. If you go out there today, I don't think you will."

Quade hugged Yara, he held her tight as she broke down and cried. The reality of what we were stepping into hit everyone at once, with Cash being the first one to break down. Savion escorted her from the living room as the silent tears fell. She was staying behind as well. The only woman coming along was Gia, who felt like she had nothing to lose in this fight. However, she motioned with her head for Hasani to follow her outside to the car, leaving me standing there with my hands in my pockets. Quincy's appearance saved me from the intimate moment. Grace was in her arms, staring around the foyer with those curious eyes of hers.

"Grace wanted to see Daddy before he left," Quincy said, taking Grace's hand and using it to wave at me. She snuck a furtive glance in my direction. "I hope I wasn't interrupting anything. Are they going to be okay?"

I closed the living room door behind me. "I'll give them a few more minutes to say...goodbye."

Grace perked up at the sound of my voice. For a three-month-old she was an alert little one, spending most of her time listening in on conversations she couldn't participate in. I traded off with Quincy, keeping her for the better part of the day while Quincy took nights. We met up in the evening for dinner, better known as family time. It wasn't perfect, but we made it work. Holding Grace in my arms and feeling the loving oozing from her was proof enough.

"Daddy will see you tonight, tater tot," I said, nuzzling with her and melting with the way she grabbed my nose, squeezing it like she did everything else she could get those chubby little hands on. "I love you more than anything.... You came along when I was going through a world of pain and made everything better. You'll always have my heart, you hear me?"

Somewhere in the midst of my conversation with Grace my eyes found Quincy's. I can't lie; a month after she came home I caught her walking around in a nightgown and got an eyeful of her post baby body. The slight curves she had when we met were enhanced by motherhood. She even had this glow about her that lit up the entire room. This morning was no different. Her hair was pulled up into a high ponytail and she was barefaced except for a hint of pink lip gloss, making her lips look extra pouty. I had to taste them. Quincy's eyes widened as I leaned in, but her surprise didn't stop her from meeting me halfway. Our lips brushed when the living room door opened.

"Let's get the fuck outta here," Quade said, making a beeline for the front door.

Yara was sitting on the couch crying into her hands. Quincy took Grace from me and went to comfort Yara. They had grown close since our daughters were only a month apart. Yara and Quade's baby girl, Lovey, was upstairs sleeping with Little Quade. She was broken to pieces right now, but Yara would have it together in time to greet her children when they woke. Scary part was, as they opened their eyes, some of our soldiers might be closing theirs.

"We could give her the territory," I said as we tucked ourselves into the car. "Pack our shit, grab our families, and go far away from here. Money ain't a problem; Hasani hid it all offshore anyway. Why go out there and kill ourselves over a legacy both of our fathers died for? Let young men walk out of their houses today and get gunned down for us! For our bottom line! Can one of you give me one good reason why we're doing this right now?"

Quade spoke up, from his spot next to me in the passenger seat. "You answered the question. This ain't about us—it has everything to do with our legacy. We sit at the head of it, but everyone willing to go to bat for us is the foundation. You think they give a fuck about dying? Niggas knew what the game was the second they signed up. They don't fear death; unlike the mothers who ain't want them and the fathers who abandoned them, death has got to be the only motherfucker on this planet that won't let them down. As long as they leave with pride it ain't a thing. That's why we're going."

I stared up at my home. Quincy stood at the window, watching us as she bounced Grace up and down. "You're right. We out."

HASANI

I spent the entire ride staring at Gia's profile, memorizing the curve of her lips and the way her button nose that turned red whenever she was angry. This might be the last time we see each other. None of us had any idea what Ivy had planned. According to our lieutenants, there were unknown soldiers driving through everyone's territory. The Haitians were close to attacking and the Puerto Ricans weren't going to stand for this disrespectful shit for much longer. Every hood—from the Bronx way out to Staten Island—was waiting on the word. We didn't want this to end in violence, but it felt inevitable at this point. I hadn't said it out loud, but I knew the odds of all of us making it out of this situation alive were slim, and I kept praying in my head that this fight would take me before it touched a hair on Gia's head. I tried everything from putting my foot down to having her father get involved—nothing could keep Gianna Karaleah Luchesi-Townsend from getting her hands on Ivy.

"Gia, I want you to promise me something," I said as we pulled up to the rendezvous point. "If something happens to me, you get the fuck out of here. Fuck Ivy, fuck this war, fuck everyone. Make me that promise."

Gia gave a curt nod of her head, and I imagined the curls she tamed into a bun for today shaking. "I'll run. I promise. But I want you to make the same promise to me. I know what I'm risking by going with you guys today. I don't want you fighting for me and you, Hasani. I'm responsible for myself. If I go down, you better get Ivy so I can whip her ass in the afterlife."

There was no way in hell I was going to leave my wife behind if something happened to her, but I knew Gia wouldn't budge until I made the promise. I suspected she did the same for me. "I promise."

"Y'all really want your last words to each other to be a lie? 'Cause I would toss Cash over my shoulder and still get down with these niggas," Savion cut in, giving us a *why the fuck you lying* look.

Quade laughed from the front seat, except there was nothing warm about it. "When you love someone, you'll tell them whatever you have to in order to keep them happy."

Yara was halfway through a conniption when we left the room. I can't even imagine what Quade had to tell her in order for him to walk out the door without her attached to him. Whatever it was, he certainly didn't regret it. Our eyes met through the rearview mirror and I knew this was his way of having my back. It was much appreciated. All that mushy shit was pushed to the side the second we stepped out of the car and walked through the field of Stadium Park where at least fifty men stood. In the center was Joel, Cash's newly promoted partner, and his brother Ben, who was due to take over the Red Hook territory if he handled his business today.

"Joel, how many you got in windows?"

"I got my best on windows and roofs of every building, which allows us to focus on the ground. Everyone here is ready to go on your word," Joel replied, motioning to the men of all ages standing vigilant, ready to go.

Zeus' phone interrupted the conversation, the ringtone a soft melodic piano playing, which was the opposite song my heart played. He picked up with a curt, "Yo." His jaw set at the sound of Ivy's voice seeping through the phone. "We'll be there in ten."

"Where she at?" Savion asked before he could properly hang up the phone.

Zeus shot him a self-satisfied smile. "Two minutes away."

While he might have bought us three extra minutes, five tops, there was no being ungrateful for Zeus' white lie. Everyone was split into teams of two, with more than half coming with us while the other half hung behind. When Gia suggested that twenty people stay behind everyone looked at her like she was crazy, but I let them know if my woman said that we make an uneven split then we would. Thirty-five of us approached the block where Ivy was supposed to be waiting with Grayson. Soldiers surrounded us, with the center of the grouping containing Gia, who was outfitted with a bulletproof vest and bulletproof jacket. We purchased them by the dozen and while they wouldn't be able to survive this possible hail of gunfire, they would give us an advantage.

We were halfway up the walkway when Quade spotted the little kid first. He was no older than eight, sitting in the park by himself, watching our approach. My initial thought was that he was running out of fear, but when a group of men came running in our direction I understood—he was the lookout. Ivy planned to ambush us, and we walked straight into her trap. Too bad she didn't know we had one as well. Shots fired from windows, taking out the first row, leaving the second row surprised yet unfazed by the loss of life right before their eyes. We collided in a mess of fists and bullets, creating one of the bloodiest battles I would ever live through.

The concrete was painted with blood, the essence of fallen soldiers spilling into cracks and crevices where roses would never grow. I watched with my own eyes as a boy no older than twelve wielded an AR-15 like it was an extension of his small yet strong arms. He sent a spray of bullets into his approaching enemy, filling their vests with a hail of bullets. I closed my eyes for a millisecond, which was all it took for the experienced men to fill him with hollow tips. He dropped to the floor like a rag doll, hid body crushed by a sudden stampede of young warriors engaging in hand-to-hand combat. Their deadly dance was mesmerizing, with each slice of a knife, strike of a fist, the rippling of skin from the impact bouncing off the early morning sun.

"Gia, where's the next set?" I shouted over the hail of gunfire.

Gia, who was skilled in mixed martial arts, played it close to me, using her face to lure niggas in while I took them out. We were doing a good job of it, but in the distance, I could see more soldiers headed this way. At the rate we were going, they would wipe us out. Gia noticed at the same time and pressed a button on her Apple Watch. Not even a full minute later, the sound of a roaring truck filled the air. A bus stopped in front of the walkway and out jumped men dressed like soldiers, each carrying AK 47's.

Quade spotted the reinforcements and shouted, "DROP!"

Our team dropped as bullets tore through the air, hitting those too slow to react to the command. The same soldiers we saw were stopped mid-run, tumbling over their fallen brothers, who hit the bloodied cement with a resounding thud. I laid on top of Gia, protecting her from the hail of gunfire that was returned from the roof. A couple of the Italian soldiers were hit before they took out the threats, sending the men from up above toppling over the railing and landing in the bushes.

"You good?" I whispered to Gia, who opened her eyes after the gunfight ended.

She nodded. "I'm fine, but we need to get to Ivy. I'm sure she wasn't expecting to be taken down. She's going to run."

Quade had the same thought. He was the first one to jump into action, climbing to his feet and helping up Zeus, one hand still on his piece. Savion and Joel were helping others to their feet. Gia and I were amongst the last to get up, the main reason being that I wasn't ready to risk losing her again.

"We need to get everyone out of here before the police show, which is in another five minutes," Joel said, checking a message from our own lookout on his phone. "You know where she is?"

I looked around at the addresses on the buildings, with my eyes landing on one in particular. "I know exactly where she is."

My brothers exchanged looks with each other, but that didn't stop them from following me into the corner building. The second we stepped into the lobby we were greeted with gunshots from the second landing. I caught the culprit with two shots to the chest. He flipped over the railing and landed on the stairs.

"Let me take lead," Quade said, stepping in front of me. "Where are we going?"

"You don't remember this building? We're going to Boyd's apartment."

The last time we set foot in this building, Quade was meeting with one of Boyd's countless women, convincing her to help us set him up. My jostling of his memory was all he needed to help lead us up the stairs. Savion stepped in front of me on the next landing, and Zeus on the landing after that until I was in the back with Gia. For a second, I was offended, thinking they thought I couldn't handle myself, but I knew what they were doing: trying to protect me from dying in front of my wife. I changed spots with Gia and protected us from behind. We reached the seventh floor and were greeted by two more of Ivy's soldiers. If she was throwing them out to get killed this quick, she must've been desperate. What I wanted to know was, what had her staying in place?

The answer was Grayson holding a gun to her head.

"You got this one," Ivy said, cracking a wide smile as we entered the apartment. "This slick motherfucker has spent months plotting with me, talking shit about all of you, and whining that he didn't want to help me anymore. How did you get him, Zeus? Hmmm? What the fuck did you have that I didn't?"

Zeus stepped over the body of Rome, the boyfriend who helped Ivy almost kill my Gia. I wished I would've pumped him full of bullets myself. He approached Ivy with a Kool Aid smile on his face. "I had him all along. Grayson knew from the jump that his mother's death was suspicious, and upon further inspection, he discovered a needle mark behind her ear. The second you stepped into the picture, too good to be true with your shoulder to cry on, he knew you had something to do with it, which was the real reason he came looking for us."

"It was the hardest year of my life, but this moment makes it so worth it," Grayson said, digging the barrel of his gun so deep into Ivy's throat it was a wonder she could still breathe. "I want you to admit it! Tell me what you did to my mother!"

"That crazy bitch let me right in, thinking I was one of those hallucinations she was having. She fought the best she could, but after missing a few meals because she was off of her medication, there was no way she was winning against me. I shot her up with some potassium chloride. She was dead and I got the broken Townsend Brother I needed."

Zeus turned around, and for a second, I thought he was going to take the high road, but he surprised us all by turning around and hitting Ivy with a punch so hard he nearly knocked Grayson off his feet. Ivy spit out her two front teeth and laughed at the anger on his face. He cocked his hand back, ready to hit her with another one, when Savion interjected with, "You can fuck this bitch up all you want when we get her to the warehouse, but right now it's hot as fuck outside."

Savion was right; I could hear police sirens in the distance. Gia and Savion stepped out first, keeping an eye out for anyone approaching. Grayson led Ivy to the front door, making sure to keep a tight grip on her. He had her halfway to the door when Rome rose up on his side, pointed his gun at Quade, and shouted, "I'LL ALWAYS LOVE YOU IVY!!!" Quade could've taken him out had he not shoved me behind him and fired at Rome as two shots were sent in our direction. One landed in the wall where I was standing, and the other sliced through Quade's neck, sending blood spurting everywhere. Zeus was the one to finish him off, shooting him so many times his dead body bucked. Ivy used that second of chaos to kick Gia in the stomach, knocking her into Savion and elbowing Grayson in the diaphragm, knocking the wind out of him. She was gone in a flash. Gia jumped up like a panther, ducking out the door with Zeus hot on her heels.

"Quade," I said, placing my hand over his neck to stop the bleeding as I set him on the living room floor. "Quade, I need you to stay with me. We're going to get you some help. Just stay calm."

Grayson's loss of breath was only a minor setback. His chest heaved as he stripped from his shirt and started to administer first aid to Quade, whose blood ran in rivulets through my fingers. He was trying to speak but I kept telling him to keep quiet. I didn't want him telling me something I didn't want to hear, like how there's no point in trying to save him.

"You're not dying today, Quade," I told him as Grayson worked overtime to stabilize him as Savion assisted. "Stop looking at me like that. We just got back on good terms, I'm not losing my brother. Fuck that!"

Quade's eyes locked with mine and when he spoke it was raspy. His oxygen was getting cut off. "It's okay," he rasped. "I'm gon' be okay. It doesn't hurt…I'm not in pain…"

I remembered speaking those exact words as I felt myself leaving this world. "Quade…you gotta live for Yara. Yara and your kids."

Quade smiled at the mention of Yara's name. The smile was short lived. His body sagged and the light in his eyes dimmed. Savion reacted first, pounding Quade in the chest and screaming as I broke down, rocking his body back and forth. We had been through a hellish year behind this bullshit, but tonight it caught up to us. We lost a brother. Nothing was bound to be the same.

GIANNA

I busted through the staircase door and stopped, listening to see where Ivy went. She would want me to go downstairs looking for her. This building was only ten stories with one staircase, not leaving her with too many options. She could be hiding on the other two levels or the roof. I could search all three but that would give her the opportunity to make a run. The exit door opened and there was Zeus, his gun raised and his eyes dangerous.

"You take the next two floors and I'll take the roof," I said, starting up the stairs, taking them two at a time.

A gust of wind whipped around me. She was on the roof. The sound of Zeus exiting on the next landing faded to the background as my adrenaline started pumping through my veins. I kicked the roof door open and was punched in the face, the blow nearly knocking me down the stairs. Ivy ran like the bitch she was, making a beeline for the staircase door on the other side of the building. Imagine the look of shock on her face when the door wouldn't budge. I barreled straight into her, sending us both to the ground. Rocks and granules of concrete scratched my cheek, the stinging feeling almost blinding me. I frantically felt around for my gun and spotted it a few feet away.

Ivy's eyes traveled to the last weapon that gave her a fair shot of making it out of here.

"No, bitch!" I screamed, grabbing a chunk of her hair with one hand and using the other to land a mean right hook.

Ivy fought as dirty as she was. She picked up a handful of gravel and threw it at my face. My hands instinctively went to my eyes, protecting them from the tiny granules and rocks that threatened to blind me. A swift kick landed in my stomach, winding me. Ivy was the type to take pride in kicking someone while they were down, which was why when I felt the air of that second kick I grabbed her foot and twisted it, knocking her back to the ground. I wiped the remaining dust from my eyes and opened them in time to see Ivy lunge at me. Her hands wrapped around my throat, squeezing with the little bit of strength she had left. I grabbed her neck as well and took it one step further by head butting her. She keeled back, screaming as she held her bloody nose. I rose to my feet and staggered over to the gun. It was within an arm's reach when Ivy came barreling into me. We hit the rickety fence, which creaked at the introduction of not one, but two bodies.

"What now, Gia?" Ivy said, grabbing me by the neck and leaning me over the fence. "You was talking all that shit, now you ain't got nothing to say? Say something, bitch, say something!"

I cracked a smile that turned into full on laughter. "Ha. Ha. Ha."

"What?"

"I just wanted you to know what the last laugh sounded like before you went to meet your daddy."

Bullets tore into the air, ripping through her chest and exiting out inches from my face. Ivy stared down at me in disbelief, as if after everything she put everyone through she believed she was untouchable. For a second, I saw what I thought was fear in her eyes. She better be scared considering where she's going. I locked my hands on the railing and using all my lower body strength, threw her over the railing. Zeus stood there, gun in hand, wearing an expression between triumph and disdain. I didn't understand why until I felt the railing start to give. He grabbed me as a piece of it broke, swinging in the air from side to side. We shared a shaky laugh and looked down below. There was Ivy, sprawled out in the grass, her legs bent at an awkward angle that let us know she wasn't going anywhere. Ever.

"It's over," I said, staring down at her body, my heart nearly leaping from my chest at the thought of her getting up and running off to wreak more havoc. "She's really…gone."

The sound that came from Zeus was a mixture of happiness and… relief. Ivy had taken so much from us over the span of a year, and every time I saw my sister struggling to stand up and walk on her own, I feared I would never find the person responsible. Killing Ivy meant more than ending a war. It was closure for everyone her entire family terrorized. No more innocent people would be harmed in the name of her father. I could get a good night's sleep. I could have children with my husband. My peace of mind was restored.

It was a good feeling.

ZEUS

We stood around the unmarked grave, staring into the hole that held more secrets than we could keep separately, so it was best they spent eternity together. The beginning, middle, and the end as I liked to think of it. Boyd represented a time in our lives where we hit rock bottom with no idea whether or not we were going to make it to the end of the month, let alone a year. It took a lot of hustling and planning, but after his death we came out on top. Ghetto was a reincarnation of the very demon we thought we slayed, and a reminder that it was better to remain ready than have to get ready. Without him and his brothers, I don't think I would cherish mine as much as I did. And Ivy? Ivy was the last reckoning, proof that even when we're underestimated we can still come out on top.

"I appreciate you waiting for me to get better before burying her," Quade said, staring down at Ivy's body. "Fucking Assans. Did everything in their power to bring us down and look at where they end up: right underneath these roses. Boyd always said he was a family man. He got two of his favorites with him."

"I don't consider it a coincidence that the ones he loved the most were sick," I said, referring to Ivy's HIV status. "Can you imagine spending your whole life idolizing a monster? Boyd brainwashed his kids to the point where they actually thought they were doing more good than harm. They really thought he was a good father."

"He was a good father." All eyes zoned in on Quincy, who was standing next to me with her arms hugging her tight. "To whoever he thought he could use. He was a good boyfriend to get whatever he wanted. Boyd was a good man for all the wrong reasons. Don't pity my siblings because they grew up thinking he was a good father; pity them because they died believing he was."

Quade blinked twice in agreement. We turned our attention to Savion and Hasani, who picked up Ivy's body, which was wrapped in a black sheet, and tossed it into the hole right on top of Ghetto's crispy corpse and Boyd's skeleton. They picked up shovels and began filling the hole with dirt as Grayson poured in brand new bags to help with displacement. Cash walked over to the hole and mustered up a big ass glob of spit, sending it shooting into the grave. She returned to Gia, who stared at the burial with a small grin. Yara decided to sit tonight out. Quade avoided the topic of his wife, but we all knew she was taking his near death experience hard. Shit, we all did.

Gia and I came downstairs brimming with triumph to find blood. A lot of it. Savion was pacing the living room floor with tears running down his cheeks. I asked him what was wrong and spaced the second I heard "Quade" and "dead." Quade couldn't be dead. I refused to hear any of that noise until I saw him. We found him thirty minutes later at Methodist Hospital where he was rushed into surgery. Those were the longest six hours of my life. According to the doctors, if it wasn't for Grayson stabilizing Quade on the ride to the hospital he wouldn't have made it. Now on his first night back home he was spending it helping us close this chapter of our lives once and for all.

"We done here," Savion said, plucking off the gardening gloves he wore and pulling a $20 bottle of Hennessy from the back pocket of his jeans. "Everybody's gon' take a sip and speak their peace once and for all. After we walk out of here, that's it; we're back to the grind. Who wants to go first?"

Hasani extended his hand for the bottle. He held it in the air and said, "It's been a fucked up year for all of us. I just want to apologize to the three of you for keeping Grayson a secret. I should've spoken up a long time ago. And to Gia, I love you and thank you for putting up with me and my shit when you didn't have to."

"I love you too," Gia said, pecking him on the lips. After he took a swig, she accepted the bottle and said, "I always wanted a brother growing up, and now I'm blessed to say I have four. Yes, I'm including you too, Grayson, because my little sister can't stop talking about you. Last month we were all faced with an almost certain fate, and I can't think of a better team to go out with."

Cash was up next, taking two gulps. "I ain't got much to say but that I love all of you. I wish we all would've made it through this, but in the end, we got more than revenge—we got closure."

"That's right," Savion cosigned, pulling a shot glass from his pocket and pouring himself a shot. He waved away our protests at not having a glass of our own. "Quiet that noise. A nigga stays ready. Anyway, I just wanna say that it feels like nothing less than a blessing to be standing here with my brothers. This shot ain't for me; it's for all the fallen soldiers we lost last month. God bless."

Savion poured the shot onto the grass and took the bottle to the head for himself before passing it off to Quade, who motioned to his neck. "You wouldn't happen to have a straw in your pocket, Inspector Negro? I didn't think so. All I got to say is I feel blessed to be alive and um…thank you, Grayson. You saved my life." Quade held his hand out to Grayson, who grinned and slapped it, coming in for a brotherly hug. "Your ability to get that close to Ivy and not be killed by her is nothing short of impressive. Not to mention you put your life on the line. I doubted your intentions, but it's obvious you're down for us, which does make you a Townsend…a real one."

Grayson accepted the bottle with a smile on his face. "Damn, I don't think any of you will understand how much that means to me. I know the last thing any of you wanted was another brother under these circumstances, and my reception wasn't warm, but I just want to thank all of you for giving me a chance to prove myself. Especially Zeus, who took a big chance on me knowing things could take a sharp turn. I love all of you."

He was right; when I took Grayson under my wing to learn the game, my goal was to have him take over in the event that Ivy was watching us too hard. But when Grayson admitted that he met Ivy, and that she encouraged him to meet us, I figured out her plan and let him play right into it. Grayson spent months playing both sides and carefully collecting intel for us, which was how Hasani's idea of setting up a fake delivery came into play. They got 100 kilos of corn-starch mixed with baby powder and Grayson, who had Ivy's loyalty enough that she would let him roam free with no restraints. With the training Quade gave him, he was able to take out every soldier in the room and grab Ivy. To be honest, I wasn't sure what we were going to walk into that day—Grayson could've flipped on us at any time or played us from the beginning—but I was both proud and relieved to see it was one of our own holding it down for the team.

"Welcome to the family," I said, accepting the bottle and taking a swig, frowning at the cognac punching me in the back of the throat. "Savion, remind me to expand your palate. I love everyone here, including Yara, who wasn't able to join us. Last year was a rough one for me, and I wasn't the best person to be around, but none of you gave up on me, even when you had every right to at times. Thank you."

Quincy accepted the bottle and took a sip. "When my mother died, I called my sisters because I was searching for family, like Grayson. I didn't go along with Ivy because I believed in her goal, I did it because I didn't want to be alone. Luckily, I met someone who didn't want to be alone either, and I know it wasn't ideal, but I fell for him. She's not here, but I want to thank Yara for speaking out on my behalf. She saved my life."

"She was right; none of us are perfect and that's why we all get along so well," Cash said, waving off Quincy's worries. "We don't think of Boyd whenever we look at you. At least, not anymore. Plus, whenever one of these crazy bastards tries to kill you and you survive, that automatically makes you family."

Gia nodded her head in agreement. "I actually became family the opposite way, but it still counts."

"Funny you should say that because Quade almost killed me the first time we met," someone said from behind us.

Everyone turned to find Yara standing there, hands in her hoodie pocket, watching us with a smile on her face. She moseyed up to the group and wrapped her arms around Quade's waist. He bent the best he could and kissed her on the cheek, eliciting kissing noises and wolf whistles from the group.

"Are we drinking?" she asked, her eyes resting on the bottle. Quincy handed her the bottle, which was nearly done, and she took a dainty sip. "Speaking of the day I first met Quade, he told me that he didn't plan to live past 30 and I told him that I planned on living a full and happy life only for his bitch ass to tell me that was boring."

"It still is," he cut in with a smirk.

She rolled her eyes. "I thank God everyday that I wasn't given what I imagined went with those words because I wouldn't be as happy and fulfilled as I am right now. Some days are hard, and scary, and I get scared, but I wouldn't trade my husband and family for the world. I love all of you. Welcome to the family, Quincy and Grayson."

Yara tossed the bottle to Savion, who did us all a favor and chugged it, much to Cash's disdain. He placed the cap on it and put it back in his pocket. "Aight, so what are we getting into tonight? I'm starving..."

"Emma's fine with watching the kids all night," Yara piped up. "Her only rule was that we don't make any more while we're out."

"No arguments there," Gia said, scratching the back of her neck.

"Dinner sounds good."

"I would love to go dancing," Cash said wistfully.

None of us were going to argue with the ladies, who all lit up at the mention of dancing. It was nice to see them filled with this much joy. We all went home, got dressed, and decided to meet up at Tavern, this nightclub we opened up earlier last year. I arrived first in a pearl white Rolls Royce Phantom, opting for a driver tonight. It gave me plenty of time to admire Quincy, who was wearing a slinky Versace dress. Despite nearly kissing last month, Quincy and I pushed any mentions of us dating aside. With most of my time spent looking out for Quade at the hospital, I wasn't ready to focus on a relationship. But now, looking at those toned legs and thighs thick from pregnancy, I was ready to focus on myself again.

"You look beautiful," I said as I helped her out of the car.

Quincy tried to play it cool, but a blush snuck up her neck and settled on her cheeks. She fingered the lapel of the cream Armani jacket I wore. "You're looking handsome as well."

We were standing there like two awkward teenagers when the rest of my brothers pulled up. Hasani was first, showing up in a royal blue Wraith. Grayson followed behind him, arriving in a black Lamborghini Aventador with Giada by his side. Savion the speed demon came next in a red Ferrari 488 GTB that had the valets fighting to park it. But it was Quade who stole the show.

"Did this lil' nigga just pull up in an Aston Martin Valkyrie?" Savion said, his mouth opening and closing in shock.

The fight between the valets was long lived as Quade stepped out of the car dressed in a black Zenga suit with Gucci loafers. The entire outfit, including the single gold chain hanging around his newly healed neck, had Cash written all over it. He came around the car and helped Yara, who glanced back at the car and laughed.

"I find it hard to believe that someone who still tucks their shirts in khaki shorts could pick out this bad boy," Savion said in disbelief, his eyes following the car down the street to the parking garage.

Quade shrugged. "My car finally gave out on me and I told Little Quade he could pick out the next one. I still need an everyday one but this'll do for now. I was thinking maybe one of those old school Cadillacs."

The conversation continued on upon our entrance into the club. All eyes remained on us as we trekked upstairs to the standing VIP section we had for celebrations like tonight. I helped Quincy upstairs like a gentleman, trying to ignore the sparks flying between us. It didn't help when she looked over her shoulder and grinned, her eyes narrowing mischievously. Bottles of Dom Pérignon greeted us, along with a fine dining menu. I was starving on the entire ride, but now sitting next to Quincy, my stomach was in knots. My brothers noticed

I was acting different and called me on it the second the women disappeared to the bathroom.

"What's going on between you and Quincy?" Savion asked, nudging his head towards the group as they left the section. "The vibes I'm getting are that you aren't dating but you wanna date—"

"She's definitely down to fuck if you are," Hasani observed.

"—She loves you, wants to be with you, but she's scared to divulge those feelings because she fears Lauren will always have more of your heart than she will. So either you gotta tell her that you've forgiven her or leave her the fuck alone," Quade said, sipping his drink as he watched the crowd.

Grayson cosigned, adding on, "The choice is yours. Don't wait too long though, or else she'll make the choice for you."

I knew what my choice was the second I laid eyes on her returning from the bathroom. She was laughing at something Yara said. Her laughter was infectious, causing the rest of the women to laugh. I don't think Quincy knew how special she was. I underestimated her worth once and I promised myself that I would never do it again. She was the one I wanted. Forever.

"I see you made your choice," Quade said, evidently impressed. "Any woman to hold your attention while standing next to Yara is the one." I shot him an incredulous look. "I'm just saying..."

Quade was right. To be honest, I was never in love with Yara, but with the idea of having a woman like her. Everything from her beauty to the way she carried herself were qualities that I sought in a woman equally yoked for me. Lauren contained those qualities yet she always felt like she was engaged in a silent competition with Yara, feeling the need to love me harder when she was the one for me. However, as I stood here looking at Quincy, I felt that need for a Yara ebb and fade away because here was the woman I wanted to be with.

"Quincy, can I talk to you alone for a minute?" I asked, meeting the small entourage of women before they reached the section.

The foursome shot slick looks at each other and returned to their significant others. I led Quincy over to the balcony overlooking the club. Down below, everyone was partying and having a good time, popping bottles, dancing on one another, and living life as if they didn't have a care in the world. Once upon a time I would have envied them for being so happy, except right now I felt the scales tipping in my favor. I had no worries and a beautiful woman by my side.

"We haven't discussed where we stand," I said, turning my attention to her.

There was that blush again, setting Quincy's cheeks aflame. She focused on the crowd down below, her eyes never straying. I took her chin between my fingers and brought her face to mine until our eyes met.

"If I stood here and told you that I didn't love you it would be a lie, Quincy," I admitted. "I'm months too late, but my feelings for you have left me feeling like they were a betrayal to what I had with Lauren, but I'm slowly learning that Lauren would want me to live my life even though she's gone. A piece of my heart was taken when she died, and while I don't think that hole will ever close, that doesn't mean it can't heal. You and Grace have given me the second chance I didn't think I would have. I love you and I'm ready to start over. Fresh. With Ivy out the way, I think we can move forward."

Quincy closed the space between us, her perfume invading my senses. She fingered my lapel on her ascent to my check, which she stroked as she stared at me through those long lashes of hers. I felt numb underneath her touch. Her face tilted upward and I met her the rest of the way, pressing her against me as I kissed her with my entire being. The night we first met, made love, and the way her body felt against mine came rushing back, and it felt like only minutes passed instead of months. Quincy was made to be mine and I would never let her go. With no secrets between us the only place we had to go from here was up. But for right now, I would settle for taking her home and showing her exactly how much I had missed her. We had a lot of making up to do.

QUINCY

I woke up in Zeus' arms, my skin flushed from the heat emanating from his body. We spent a few more minutes at the club with everyone, tossing back drinks and dancing to a few songs before Zeus announced that it was time for us to leave. I didn't argue; I handed out hugs and kisses like candy and followed my man out the door. Our lips met as our bodies collided in the backseat of the Phantom. A year had passed since I last had sex and a bitch was fiending for some loving. Zeus delivered everything I wanted and more, leaving me spent as the Sunday morning sun rose. Despite only going to sleep a few hours ago, I was wide awake and excited to spend a morning with Zeus and Grace as a family. Turns out, he had the same thing in mind. Kissing me on the cheek, he asked me to get dressed and meet him downstairs in an hour. I wasn't sure where we were going so I kept it simple, donning a simple Carolina Herrera wrap dress and placing my hair in a chignon. Zeus was dressed in a suit as usual—a nice navy blue Burberry one with a pink shirt—which didn't give me a hint in the least bit. When we picked up Grace from Yara's place I assumed brunch was on the menu, but when we arrived at the cemetery, I knew who we were going to visit.

"I should've asked you first," Zeus admitted as he parked in front of a tree. "If you don't feel comfortable we can leave. I…um…the last time I came here was for her funeral. I couldn't stomach the thought of coming here alone."

"I get it." I felt the same way when it came to my mother.

Lauren's headstone was made of black marble with her name etched in snow white. Her epitaph mentioned her being loved and gone too soon, both statements I could agree with. I met Lauren once, years ago, before I left for college. She was kind to me, kinder than my own sisters were. We didn't spend much time together, but what I learned from observing her interactions with my brother Steez was that he didn't appreciate her and no one checked him on the way he mistreated her. On my first night back home I prayed to God that she would find someone who loved and cared for her. Seeing her back in that hotel room, dying to keep her secret, that she carried another man's child while with Steez, tore me up inside. A wave of grief hit me, so strong that I had to hand Grace to Zeus. I fell to my knees in front of her headstone, sobbing uncontrollably.

"I should've killed Ivy," I said between sobs. "I should have killed her the second she told me to kill Lauren and none of this would've ever happened. It's all my fault. I should have sacrificed myself."

Zeus dropped to his knees beside me, pulling me close and planting a soothing kiss on my forehead. "Your sacrifice wouldn't have changed Lauren's fate. Ivy would have still murdered the both of you. That entire situation was out of your control, Quincy. I've forgiven you—now it's time for you to forgive yourself."

"Zeus…I know what happened to Zoelle." The words passed my lips like a whisper, but when I felt Zeus tense I knew he heard me. "I've waited for the right time to tell you what happened, but there never was one. I wasn't present, but just knowing makes me feel equally guilty."

"Tell me," Zeus choked out. "I…I can handle the truth."

"Lauren was pregnant and Steez was overjoyed. They had pregnancies but none stuck because he couldn't keep his hands off of her or stress would cause her to miscarry. But this time…the baby was perfectly healthy. I have no idea how she sold the timeline to Steez—

according to Ivy, she knew early on that she was pregnant and slept with Steez to make him believe the baby was his—but I know he was just as happy to have a baby coming. They went shopping, decorated a room for their baby girl, and Steez threw her a lavish baby shower. It was all a front for what he was going to do next.

"Lauren gave birth to Zoelle two weeks earlier than expected, which made her two weeks late in reality. Zoelle was happy, healthy, beautiful. She went home as expected and two nights later…two nights later Lauren woke up on top of Zoelle. She tried everything she could but it was too late. Zoelle had been dead for hours. There was an investigation which ruled that Zoelle's death was an accidental death and no charges were pressed. Imagine going months thinking you killed your child, suffocated your baby, and having to live with that pain. Now imagine the man who was supposed to love and protect her telling you the day after the investigation that he looked at you asleep with your baby and knew it wasn't his. So he took a pillow and…"

"You don't have to finish," Zeus said, rocking me back and forth as I broke down dissolving into another fit of tears. "Crazy part is, Lauren kept in contact with me for a year after we met in Vegas. I kept telling her to leave him and come with me. She kept promising to when the time was right and then…nothing. She disappeared without a trace."

"I would imagine that she felt like she failed Zoelle, and in turn, failed you. Too bad no one was around to tell her that nothing was her fault. Steez was the monster. To kill an innocent child…."

We remained that way for a long time, with Grace's coos keeping us grounded at a time where all we wanted to do was break down. Zeus held me tight, murmuring in my hair that it was okay, everything was going to be okay, and I then I felt it. A breeze in the otherwise still cemetery ruffling my hair and rubbing across my back. She was here. She had forgiven me. I was allowed to forgive myself. As I kneeled with Zeus, clutching our daughter as he faced his own fiancée and daughter, I started to think that it wasn't a coincidence that Zeus and I met. That somehow, in a twisted turn of events, Lauren gave him the family she wasn't able to. My fingertips brushed the edges of her headstone, and I made a silent promise to her that I would take care of Zeus, love him the way he deserved to be loved, give him the life he dreamed of, and make sure that her memory was never forgotten.

EPILOGUE

One year later...
Gianna

Giada grabbed handfuls of her wedding gown and spun around for the cameras, basking in the attention that was specially reserved for her wedding day. I stood on the sidelines, snapping pictures as she did for me on my own wedding day two years ago. My eyes stung from unshed tears wishing to be set free. Giada had defied all of the odds placed against her and was walking without the help of crutches. Who did she have to thank? Her husband, who prayed with her from day one and made it his mission to make sure the impossible became possible. He stood right beside me, taking pictures with his phone, beaming with pride at his wife, his treasure as he had called her in the romantic wedding vows they read at the wedding ceremony.

"You better take care of my sister," I told Grayson, smiling up at him although he knew me well enough to know I was only fronting for the cameras taking pictures of us. "We both know what I'm capable of."

Grayson shook with silent laughter. "Hasani told me there's nothing like marrying into the mob. A coward would be scared, but if I hurt her, or break her heart, I'll deserve whatever you dole out."

"Gia, Grayson, come take a picture with me!" Giada squealed, motioning for us to join her impromptu photoshoot. "I need my two favorite people in this shot!"

We stood on either side of her and posed for enough pictures to qualify as a full spread in a fashion magazine. I was poised to excuse myself so the newlyweds could take some more pictures together when Giada spotted Hasani and called him over. Hasani, who had a plate of both Italian and southern appetizers, placed his plate on a table where he could keep an eye on it and approached us.

"Come on! Don't act like you don't want to take some pictures with the love of your life, who is looking especially beautiful tonight," Giada said, motioning to the nude peach gown she designed for me. The dress filled out the extra curves I started developing over the last couple of months. "Put a hand on that big ol' booty and smile for the camera!"

Hasani didn't need an invitation to place his hands on any part of my body. As of late, he couldn't keep his hands off of me with his favorite place being my stomach. I giggled as he planted light kisses on my neck and whispered in my ear, "I can't wait to get you out of this dress tonight, my little meatball. I got some special sauce to cover you in."

"Hasani!" Giada and Grayson said at the same time.

I kissed him on the lips before his fresh behind could continue. The photographer captured the moment on camera, and next thing we know, we're posing for pictures by ourselves. Hasani got down on one knee and placed a kiss on my stomach, confirming the question I was bombarded with since the start of the reception. We wanted to wait until I was farther along to share the news, but we would keep the other half of our secret to ourselves.

"I can't wait to tell everyone that on our first try, ya boy hit it out the park by making twins," Hasani whispered in my ear, this time much lower as he pulled me close. "Gia, we got company and I want you to behave..."

I knew exactly who he was talking about too. The photographer grew excited at seeing my parents approaching. After all, they were footing the bill for this lavish wedding. He motioned for them to step into the frame so he could take some pictures of us together. My father kissed me on the forehead and placed a hand on my stomach, his smile warm and genuine. I choked up at him having to find out that he was going to be a grandfather along with everyone at the wedding instead of during the private announcement Hasani and I made to immediate family last month. He hugged me and rubbed small circles into my back.

"It's okay, *cara*. I understand. There's no need to cry. Let me wipe away those beautiful tears," he said, pulling a handkerchief from his pocket and dabbing at my face. "I miss you, Gianna. *We* miss you. I was unaware of what your mother and Carmelo conspired to do, but I respected your desire for space. However, my heart can no longer take it. Your mother would like to apologize if you'll allow her to."

I lost a piece of my heart when I found out that my mother sabotaged my wedding. It wasn't even the act itself that hurt; it was her experiencing the same familial distaste and acting upon it like she was above Hasani when she was once in his shoes. That was enough to cut me deep and love her at a distance, which was needed for Hasani and I to rebuild our bond stronger than ever. Nothing—not family, friends, old lovers—could break what we had. We took it one day at a time, falling in love with each other all over again with no distractions, while learning valuable lessons that would pave the way for decades of wedded bliss to come, with the first lesson being to stop running when the going gets tough. These lessons were the reason why I could stand in front of my mother with my husband and allow her to see how wrong she was.

"Honey, I'm sorry for meddling in your marriage. I raised a smart, headstrong, and capable woman who knows what's best for her," my mother said, dabbing at tears that formed in the corners of her eyes.

I shook my head. "I'm not the one who needs an apology, Mom. The love we have for each other is unconditional. You owe one to Hasani."

"Gia..." Hasani started and stopped at the look on my face.

Mom shook her head. "No, she's right. Hasani, I'm sorry for what I did. You've proven more times than I can count how deep your love for my daughter is. I promise to never question it again and embrace you as a son like I should have a long time ago."

"It's all good, Mrs. Luchesi," Hasani said, hugging her and placing a polite kiss on her cheek.

"You can call me 'Mom,'" she said with a smile, the same one she reserved for Giada and me. This was the woman I wanted at my wedding, but I would take her here and now.

Hasani slung his arm around my father. "Do I call you 'Pops'?"

"You can call me 'Pops' and I can call you an ambulance," Papa replied. "Mr. Luchesi will do."

Giada and Grayson returned in time to find us sharing a laugh. She fanned at imaginary tears. "I knew my wedding would be the place to get the family back together. This has been a hard year on all of us. Nothing makes me happier to know that Grayson and I will start our marriage off with everyone starting over. How about some advice for a long lasting marriage?"

My parents came through with the basic bits of advice, including "a happy wife equals a happy life," but it was Hasani who dropped a beautiful gem. He spoke with love and wisdom all while never taking his eyes off of me.

"When you have her eye, keep it. When you have her heart, nurture it. When you have her soul, treasure it," Hasani said, his words eliciting claps from the other couples listening.

There were those stupid tears again. Hasani wiped them away and kissed my cheeks. I knew he was keeping it PG for my parents, but I wasn't having any of that. This time I was the aggressive one, closing the space between us and planting a big one on his lips. I could hear camera shutters and a gasp from my mother, laughs from my sister, and what sounded like my father's knuckles cracking. I broke the kiss and smiled up at Hasani, who looked like he had been knocked in the back of the head and had those little hearts revolving around his head.

"My advice is simple," I said, staring at my husband, the true love of my life. "Never let them go."

Hasani

I was covered in a light sheen of sweat as I exited the dance floor with Gia, who was surprisingly athletic for a woman carrying twins. From the day I met Gia, I always wondered when her black side would come out, and it wasn't until our second date at a nightclub did I find out that it was whenever Cash Money took over for the '99 and the 2000. The DJ played it tonight and we got it in so hard there's a 50/50 chance we might be having triplets. All that dancing caught up to Gia, who returned to the head table to grab something to drink and get some rest before another ratchet anthem came on and she needed my assistance at being the life of the party. I needed some fresh air. The garden was filled with people who had the same thing in mind, including my brothers. They were far away from the group, standing next to a tall bush. I crept up on them to see what they were up to. My plan to scare them was ruined when Quade came around the corner and snatched me behind the bush too. There I found these niggas staring down at a ring box in Zeus' hand.

"It's about time," I said, taking the box from his hand and getting a good look at the five carat diamond ring sparkling underneath the moonlight. "Cushion cut diamond with two half-cart diamonds flanking it set in a platinum band. This is a ring you give to the woman you're ready to spend the rest of your life with. When are you going to give it to her?"

Zeus accepted the ring back and placed it in his pocket. "My confidence is shot when it comes to doing this. The last time I proposed to a woman after a wedding…"

"She died," Quade finished with sad shake of his head.

Savion nudged Quade in the ribs. "There was no need to remind him," he said in a half whisper to Quade, who wasn't the least bit bothered by the truth. To Zeus, he replied, "Do it when the time feels right. For me that was on a Venetian water taxi in the Sienne right underneath the Eiffel tower. Fireworks went off when Cash said yes."

"Damn," we said in unison. I added, "Since when are you a romantic?"

"Since Cash planned the entire thing and told me to have her ring ready. The woman knows what she wants," he said with a chuckle. "How'd you propose, Hasani?"

"In Gia's living room when I came home. I had everything planned out for the following night—dinner, flowers, the whole nine—but I saw her and I couldn't wait. Ask her when the thought of another second without her being your wife feels like too much to bear."

Savion wiped away a fake tear. "That's truly beautiful. I'm moved, I really am."

"Shut up," I said, shoving him. "What about you Quade? How'd you know when the time was right?"

"You were dead, everyone was falling the fuck apart, and tomorrow didn't feel guaranteed. So I thought to myself 'if you have one last day on Earth, what would you want to do with it?' The answer was simple: marry Yara."

"What's the answer now?" Zeus asked.

Quade shrugged. "Wake up next to Yara."

There was a rustling in the bushes. We turned in time to see Grayson appear, wiping at fake tears also. "Who knew some cold niggas like you were soft on the inside?" We started cussing him out for eavesdropping until he pulled out freshly cut cigars. Lighting one up, he said, "I fell in love with Giada the very first day I met her. My mother was gone, none of you wanted anything to do with me, and I felt alone in the world. Giada was struggling with her own fears. We meshed and everything about her felt...perfect. Quincy loves you, Zeus. There were days where she wanted to pack her stuff up and leave, but she didn't. She knew she would have to wait for you."

"What do we have here?" Yara and Cash chimed, their arms clung around each other as they watched us through gimlet eyes. Yara made a mad grab for Quade. "We were sent to get all of you for the last dance of the night."

We all headed back towards the party, which was still in full swing. I had a feeling the ladies were missing us and didn't know how to say so. Yara and Cash pulled their husbands along and Grayson hurried in front of us, leaving Zeus and I to make the trek alone. Through the windows we could see everyone on the dance floor having a good time, including Gia and Quincy, who were dancing with each other.

"They came a long way, didn't they?" Zeus asked as he stopped short, continuing to watch the women through the window.

"When you throw in Giada asking her to be a bridesmaid, you've got a miracle." I paused thoughtfully. "We all got played by them, taken advantage of, and she got the worst end of the stick when you think about it. We've always had each other. Imagine how lonely she had to be to stick with them, blindly putting her faith in motherfuckers who never intended to take care of her. She was just as much of a victim as we were."

Zeus patted his chest where the ring box rested and I thought of the advice I gave to Grayson earlier. Clapping him on the shoulder, I asked him, "Do you have her eye?"

He nodded. "She has mine as well."

"Do you have her heart?"

"I do, and her mine."

I gave the box a pat through his jacket. "Then it's time to have her soul and when you get it, make sure you treasure it for the rest of your life." It was my turn to watch Gia through the window and fall in love with her all over again.

Zeus slung his arm around my shoulder. "Sounds good to me."

Zeus

My brothers' proposal stories stuck with me long after the wedding, and while I knew shared private moments would always be cherished, I realized that Quincy's entire existence was spent hidden, whether it was in a small room at Yara's house, or the basement apartment of my brownstone. Even when we got together most of our time was spent inside as if I was unintentionally hiding her. I couldn't propose to her the same way. It was her turn to be shown off to the world with a grand gesture.

"Do you know this is our first official date?" Quincy said as we cruised down Broadway on our way to what she thought was a romantic dinner for two on a private yacht. "I never took you on the date I promised you, my pregnancy was nothing but drama, and after Grace was born we poured our all into taking care of her. Even after we got back together we never made it out on a well thought out date."

I stole a peek at her through the corner of my eye. She looked beautiful tonight in the black Atsuko Kudo latex dress she wore with a pair of matching Louboutin So Kate pumps. Her hair was a halo of curls with the left side tucked behind her ear, giving me a perfect view of her profile. Her words were spoken lightly, but I could see the way her Ruby Woo painted lips pouted at the thought of us never going out in public. I remember the very first time we went out with Grace, a picture of the three of us was taken and set ablaze to social media, accusing me of having something to do with Lauren's death so I could be with Quincy. The police never bothered me because of the trumped up conspiracy theory, but after that incident Quincy didn't like placing our relationship on display and I never pushed it. I should have.

"My parents used to do date night. Every Thursday night, my father would take my mother somewhere nice. How about we make Friday nights our date night, starting with this one?"

Quincy turned towards me and her frown turned into a toothy smile. "I would love that, Zeus." She looked out of my window, seeing for the first time that we weren't heading for the pier. "Are we at Central Park? What's going on over there? I see a crowd..."

I parked in the spot I had security reserve for our arrival. Quincy stared at me like I was crazy, her eyes following me through the windshield as I crossed over to open her door and continued to bore a hole in the side of my face as we approached the crowd, which parted at our arrival.

"I thought it would be nice for us to see a concert in the park," I said, guiding her up the walkway, which lit up with every step we took thanks to the hundreds of lights I had installed. "You don't mind, do you?"

Quincy's eyes lit up in wonder as we grew deeper into the park.

She shook her head, sending her curls brushing against my face. "No, I don't mind. I have never seen anything done like this for a concert. Who are we going to see?"

"It's a surprise," I said, giving her waist a playful squeeze.

Faint music could be heard playing from the other side of the field. Quincy went from playful and excited to nervous. I was positive she had figured out what was going on, but when we cleared the thick cluster of trees and stepped out onto the field lit by people holding white candles in the air, Quincy couldn't contain her shock.

"Zeus," she said, holding her chest at the sight in front of us. "What have you done?"

A full orchestra filled the large field, serenading us with an instrumental version of "Endless Love." I could see Quincy trying to figure out what the song was as I led her down the white velvet carpet sprinkled with gold and red rose petals leading to a white tent, a white grand piano waiting patiently to begin the show. The closer we grew, Quincy noticed that the front seats weren't filled with members of the orchestra, but our family, who helped me pull this together. Tears were rolling down Quincy's cheeks as everyone smiled up at us.

"I can't believe you're doing this," Quincy said, fanning at her eyes as we approached the piano. I helped her take a seat at the bench and slid in next to her. "I know you're not about to sing..."

I laughed at the shock on her face and eased her worries with a kiss on the lips. Yes, I was about to sing. The orchestra quieted as I took over the piano, playing the song like I practiced all week. Adjusting the microphone, I sung, *"My love, there's only you in my life. The only thing that's right."*

Quincy leaned into the microphone and sung in a rich throaty voice, *"My first love, you're every breath that I take. You're every step I make."*

"You betta sing, girl!" Cash shouted from the audience.

My heart swelled with love as I sung with Quincy, and suddenly I was feeling all of those feelings my brothers told me about at once. Sitting next to Quincy, admiring her beautiful face and listening to a voice given to her by angels, I couldn't take it anymore. The second the song ended I got down on bended knee, took the ring box from my pocket, and popped it open.

"Quincy, I am asking you not only in front of our friends, but the entire world, to be my wife. It took us a long time to make it here, but I couldn't think of another woman worth sharing my life with than you. Will you marry me?"

Quincy rose from her seat and dropped down on her knees in front of me. The entire crowd cheered as she reached inside of her purse and pulled out a ring box of her own.

"That's right, boo! Propose to your man!" Gia shouted as Cash and Yara cheered her on.

My brothers looked at each other and back at the scene in front of us. Quincy cracked her box open, revealing a platinum band covered in diamonds. This was right up my alley and was something I would have picked out myself. Upon further inspection…I did pick this ring out.

"I had Quade take you ring shopping because he was the most inconspicuous," Quincy said with a laugh. "I have loved you for a long time, Zeus Townsend. With all my heart. I knew I wanted to marry you that day in the foyer when we shared our last kiss. So when you came home, I decided it was time for me to work on my proposal. I told Yara and Cash, and they hooked me up with a job. I saved every last penny to buy you this ring because you're worth every diamond. Will you marry me?"

"You first!" Hasani, Grayson, and Savion shouted.

"Yes!!!" Quincy screamed, leaping into my arms and kissing me like she wanted to be wearing a maternity dress to our wedding. I slipped the ring on her shaking fingers and smiled as she did the same.

There was only one person missing from this celebration. She came toddling up the walkway with the help of Emma, who had taken to Quincy and Grace like they were her own daughters. Grace plopped herself down in front of us, more infatuated by the people smiling at us than her parents, who couldn't stop kissing each other. On his wedding day, Quade gazed at Yara like she was the only woman in the room, Savion only had eyes for Cash as he dropped to his knees and put his life on the line for her, Grayson's eyes lit up anytime Giada's name was mentioned, and there would never be enough fingers to count the times per day I saw Hasani stop and study Gia. What made it better was I could count moments where I would catch their wives doing the same. I never knew that feeling, where the love of your life is the only person that matters until I was surrounded by hundreds of shouting people and all I could see was Quincy.

"Are you ready for forever?" I asked over the din, which wasn't as loud as it was minutes ago.

Quincy pressed her lips against mine. "Only with you by my side."

ABOUT THE AUTHOR

Born and raised in Brooklyn, Tya Marie is the author of sixteen novels, including her debut series, A Brooklyn Love Affair: Vixen & Gino's Story, and the Amazon Best Selling series, Grimey: Married to the King of Miami. Her writing style is a mix of urban street lit with contemporary fiction, the product creating a unique writing style that has become her signature. With a B.A. in English and a B.S. in Criminal Justice, Tya plans to infuse her past studies into her upcoming novels, giving them her own personal touch. Tya currently resides in Brooklyn and when she isn't writing she's connecting with fellow authors and fans alike.

Stay Connected

Authoress Tya Marie

Facebook Group: Tea With Tya Marie

ALSO BY TYA MARIE

A Brooklyn Love Affair: Vixen & Gino's Story(4 Book Series)

Never Should've Loved a Thug

The Heart of a King: In Love With a Savage(2 Book Series)

Grimey: Married to the King of Miami(2 Book Series)

I Got a Crush on You: A Bad Boy Romance(2 Book Series)

Ain't Nothing Like a Real One: Faded Off an Inked God(3 Book Series)

Chosen by the King of Miami: A Grimey Love Affair(2 Book Series)

So Obsessed with a Brooklyn Boss (3 Book Series)

His Savage was Her Weakness (3 Book Series)

When a Heartless Thug Holds Me Close: A True Love Story(3 Book Series)

NOTE FROM TYA MARIE

Readers,

I want to thank you from the bottom of my heart for not only taking a chance on this series, but me as an author. When I started writing this series I had no idea how much you would fall in love with the characters, and it has left me humbled and eternally grateful. This isn't where this journey with these brothers ends, but for right now I think I'll let them bask in their happily ever after (lol). While you're here, can I ask you for a tiny favor? Can you leave a review? I love hearing what my readers think of the story and any suggestions they have for stories in the future. Thank you in advance for the continued support.

Love,

Tya Marie

Royalty Publishing House is now accepting manuscripts from aspiring or experienced urban romance authors!

WHAT MAY PLACE YOU ABOVE THE REST:

Heroes who are the ultimate book bae: strong-willed, maybe a little rough around the edges but willing to risk it all for the woman he loves.

Heroines who are the ultimate match: the girl next door type, not perfect - has her faults but is still a decent person. One who is willing to risk it all for the man she loves.

The rest is up to you! Just be creative, think out of the box, keep it sexy and intriguing!

If you'd like to join the Royal family, send us the first 15K words (60 pages) of your completed manuscript to submissions@royaltypublishinghouse.com

LIKE OUR PAGE!

Be sure to LIKE our Royalty Publishing House page on Facebook!

CPSIA information can be obtained
at www.ICGtesting.com
Printed in the USA
LVHW082141030119
602714LV00018B/621/P